WTF MOMENT

WTF MOMENT

BOLAJI TIJANI-QUDUS

Copyright © 2011 by Bolaji Tijani-Qudus.

Library of Congress Control Number: 2011906836
ISBN: Hardcover 978-1-4628-6544-4
      Softcover 978-1-4628-6543-7
      Ebook   978-1-4628-6545-1

Website address
wtfnovel.com
wtfmomentnovel.com
BolajiTijaniqudus.com

Follow me on:

www.facebook.com/wtfmoment

www.twitter.com/bolajiqudus

All rights reserved. No part of this book may be reproduced or transmitted in any form or by any means, electronic or mechanical, including photocopying, recording, or by any information storage and retrieval system, without permission in writing from the copyright owner.

This is a work of fiction. Names, characters, places and incidents either are the product of the author's imagination or are used fictitiously, and any resemblance to any actual persons, living or dead, events, or locales is entirely coincidental.

This book was printed in the United States of America.

To order additional copies of this book, contact:
Xlibris Corporation
1-888-795-4274
www.Xlibris.com
Orders@Xlibris.com
97739

Acknowledgement

With God, all things are possible. I give all praises to him.

To my wonderful boys, Bolaji and Bolade, thank you for being born. I am blessed to have you both.

To my family, my beautiful sister Kemi. Thank you for your unconditional love and support.

Shout out to my Editors Maria Pecot and Anju Hypollite. You rock!

Cheers

CONTENTS

Prologue 9
1. Looking at the Front Door 12
2. The Boys and I 19
3. Mumbo Jumbo 29
4. Curiosity Kills the Cat 36
5. Along Came Amanda, Part 1 53
6. Interlude 63
7. Heat of the Moment 66
8. Introspect 69
9. Along Came Amanda, Part 2 75
10. Many Moods 89
11. Along Came Amanda, Part 3 99
12. Haters 115
13. The Wow! Experience, Part 1 123
14. WTF 132
15. The Wow! Experience, Part 2 140
16. Live and Let Live 153
17. Dip and Move 163
18. After Spring Comes Summer 173
19. Falling In Niagara 183
20. Pieces to Peaces 204
Excerpt from 'Inside Looking Out' 213

Prologue

"I'm too busy for this crap today," I mumbled, checking my caller ID when my office phone started to ring.

I picked it up, and before I even had a chance to say hello, Monica screamed in my ear, "Whose number is 121-201-3344?"

"What are you talking about?"

"You know what I'm talking about. Why are you playing dumb? Why don't you come out and say who it is and how long you've been messing around," she continued, screaming.

"What?"

"The tramp texted, 'Hey you! Are you going to be at the gym tonight?' What woman texts a man, 'Hey you!' if she is not sleeping with him? Tell me!"

I could hear the pitch in her voice, which usually spelled doom for me.

"What woman are you talking about?" I responded.

She started yelling again.

"Come out and say it so we can resolve this situation!"

"What situation are you talking about?"

I had no idea what she was talking about. My other line beeped. I was scheduled to be on a telephone conference call that was supposed to have started a minute earlier.

"Let me call you back. Talk to you later," I said.

I hung up the phone before she could continue her yelling and questioning. I wondered whose number it was Monica was talking about. I had left my other cell phone on the living room table. It was primarily for my workout clients. *What the hell is she doing going through my phone anyhow? Well, it can wait. I have work to do at the moment.*

I completed my conference call and called her back an hour later.

"Hello?"

"What's up?"

"What was the fuss about earlier?" I asked as calmly as I could, disguising my irritation.

"Well, you took too long to respond, so I called her," she said.

"Whom did you call?!" I asked, alarmed.

"The chick Cynthia, who was sending you *Hey you* messages!"

"Oh wow!" I said, bursting out laughing. "And what did she say to you?"

"She said nothing was going on between you two."

"Where did you get the illusion I was sleeping with her?"

"*Hey you!* sounds intimate to me, and that is all I know," she continued.

"Are you serious? Do you know how many women say *hey you* to me? My buddy James's girlfriend says *hey you*, but I'm not sleeping with her!"

She became quiet on the phone.

"I don't know where you're getting all this from, and I don't know what your problem is. Why are you going through my phone and making random calls to people? It isn't new for me to have women's numbers in my phone, and I've never hidden that. Why now? Why today?"

"I don't know. I have just been having this feeling you're messing with someone," she said.

"I would appreciate it if you would call her back and apologize. She is my client! I have never been involved with her, and I never will be. You're sounding off on an innocent *hey you* message. What is it with this soap opera BS? This is so embarrassing!"

"So? I just need to know whether you already started messing around," she added.

"Anyway, I'm about to get off this phone because I still have work to do. I will talk to you later." I sighed and hung up the phone.

I was heated. If I had been messing around with Cynthia, I wouldn't have left my phone lying around the house. I'm not stupid. I leave my phone because there has never been anything to hide. Now I had to call Cynthia and apologize. I hoped she'd allow me to continue to train her. Perhaps she would be put off by the drama that unfolded and stop working with me altogether.

An hour later, I called Cynthia and apologized profusely and promised it would never happen again. I still needed her business, and she had a slew of friends she wanted to introduce me to—they all wanted to get in shape. Cynthia accepted my apology. She didn't seem to be bothered. I was glad she had taken it in stride, and she promised to show up for her training session the upcoming Wednesday.

1. Looking at the Front Door

I was standing there staring at the front door at two o'clock in the morning as though I were in a trance. I saw nothing around me—no walls, no paintings, no windows, no furniture . . . just the front door. It was as though I were in a sandy desert.

I kept looking at the door with my car keys in hand; my suitcases were on the floor next to me. I was thinking about what awaited me outside that door! Freedom and sanity were all I could imagine!

Fast-forward thirty minutes: I was still standing there looking at the front door. I could feel beads of sweat forming on my forehead. I really needed to leave. I couldn't deal with this situation anymore. I was at the point where I was about to lose it, and one more day in the house with Monica was not an option. I was so overwhelmed; I was not even myself anymore. I would have exploded if I stayed there past that very moment.

"God, please help me." I felt myself shake; an angry rage had overtaken my whole being. It seemed as though I had been standing there for an eternity, frozen in time.

I started to gravitate toward the front door. *I want to get out of this house!* I thought. *I have no idea where I'm going or what I'm going to do. I feel confused, very angry, in a daze . . .*

"Daddy! Daddy!" my three-year-old daughter, Emmanuella, called out to me. Her voice was ringing out in the still night, breaking the spell I had been in.

"What are you doing, Daddy? Are you going out?" she asked, as she walked down the stairs to where I stood.

"No, sweetie. Daddy is just standing here thinking." I picked her up and kissed her cheek.

I walked her back to her room and read her a book, which soothed her back to sleep. I pulled the covers over her and kissed her forehead. I turned the lights

WTF MOMENT

off and glanced back at my princess, and my eyes welled with tears as I gently closed the door.

Down the hall, the master bedroom door was shut as it has been for the past year. The guest room was where I had been laying my head at night. I picked up my suitcases and headed out the front door.

As I drove off, the life I shared with Monica began to flash right before my eyes.

I wondered *how we had reached the point of no return.*

We had good times in the beginning but we have had more bad times the last few years. I recalled when she came into our office when I was working in the Marketing department at my then corporate gig. She was part of the auditing team from an accounting firm—Rawlings & Rawlings CPAs. We build a great rapport during the months of audits. We had lunch together almost everyday. I had told her about my impending business venture and she offered to be my personal accountant to help manage my finances. We talked about how we were both frustrated with the dating game and wanted to find the right one and get married as we were approaching our thirties. The parents on both sides were still together and we felt it was time to continue the tradition. We both had our high education degrees and were doing well in our respective jobs. *There wasn't much left to do* we had thought. We were perfect on paper and it seemed we would make a good team.

After a year of dating, we started to plan on getting married. Soon enough we got pregnant and sped things up and had our wedding. It was a small affair with about two hundred people, mostly family and close friends assembled in the beautiful Temecula Valley's Wine Country in Southern California.

*   *   *

I drove past an area which triggered some scary memories. At one point, things were so bad I had contemplated driving off a cliff. The freeway leading to our city passes through a mountainous area with a long, winding road. There is only one thin layer of aluminum railing that separates the opposite lanes. During winter, the fog around the mountain makes driving difficult.

It had been raining one evening. It would have been easy to blame an accident on the weather conditions if I had happened to drive over the cliff. I could not believe I'd had those suicidal thoughts! But I did. I was exhausted and desperately trying to escape the turmoil I was going through then. Usually, going home felt like going to prison to serve a life sentence with no possibility of parole. It was torture, and I couldn't take it anymore.

BOLAJI TIJANI-QUDUS

One other time, I had been in a similar dazed state in the garage. My car had been running, and the garage door had been closed behind me. I didn't know how long I'd been sitting there, but the fumes from the car exhaust had clogged my breathing passages. Those suicidal thoughts told me to sit there and end my life of misery. Only the thoughts of my daughter stopped me from continuing. *Who will take care of her when I'm gone? She will grow up with shame knowing her father left her and went out unceremoniously.* I had too much pride to let that happen.

That long drive from our exclusive residence at the Queensbury Golf Course was a solemn one. I had just left a huge part of my life behind. I kept telling myself *all I needed to do next was to focus on my business and my daughter.*

Being part owner of a specialty sports fitness center that had seen a boom in business recently was a consolation and something to look forward to. We grossed two million dollars at the end of last year. Five Star Gym became a chic and preferred place for gym enthusiasts who detest the meat-market, open-space type of chain fitness centers.

The business had been profitable. It launched right before we got married, soon afterward we had been had been able to move into a five-bedroom, five-thousand-square-feet, million-dollar-plus home with all the trimmings, in one of the most prestigious neighborhoods in Northern California. Blackhawk, another exclusive and pricey city, was just a few miles away.

I was bent on making sure my kids would have the option of never having to struggle as I did, growing up cash-strapped. I also didn't want to grow old and rely on social security. My parents and my wife's parents had been at their respective jobs for twenty years on average. I always felt I should put my energy into my own business rather than someone else's.

My father worked for a major corporation for many years until he retired. He is old school and relished being able to be with one company for a long time. But as a retiree, he doesn't have much to show for his career. Their house isn't paid for, and social security is barely enough to keep them afloat. I help out by paying their mortgage and insurance premiums.

When I worked in the corporate world, I observed how large the CEOs lived. They'd show up every now and then, walk around, smile, make bogus speeches, and you wouldn't see them again for another year. Yet you bust your butt working overtime for the company so it can be successful. Meanwhile they earn a $1.5-million salary and play golf almost every day while their employees are expendable. It didn't make sense to me. I should be busting my behind making a million for my family to enjoy.

WTF MOMENT

Initially, when Five Star Gym opened, my partners and I worked long hours to break even and eventually turn a profit. I still work that way because I personally train and teach boot camp classes. Monica hated I had to work so much. She would make statements such as "Why don't your single partners work more? You should work less since you're married!"

I told her the new business required me to be there, and it was my brainchild. I couldn't just leave it in the hands of my partners. I would never have peace of mind if I did that. The gym was a side investment to them. But for me, it was my life . . . the reason I had gotten my MBA in sports administration. Five Star Gym was always what I wanted to do. I had envisioned the gym would be able to run itself a few years down the road, and we would expand as well. Until then, I had to bust my butt.

I always thought diversifying was a good way of staying ahead when it comes to building wealth. I had dabbled in real estate just like some of my peers did. I invested heavily in a condo project two miles from downtown Brookdale. My buddy Phil and I and four other business associates bought a forty-unit fixer-upper apartment complex. Our plan was to convert to condos and sell after remodeling. We replaced the carpeted floors with hardwood; we equipped each unit with a washer and dryer. We basically gutted it out and gave it a rousing makeover, replacing everything. We would sell a two-bedroom for $400,000, which was a bargain in Northern California. Then the real estate bubble busted, and the economy tanked—2008 was the beginning of a bad dream for most.

Besides the $1.2 million loan we had taken out for the condo project, I had dumped in $250,000 of my own personal funds.

I had saved another $100,000, which I was hoping to invest in another gym in a lush, upcoming city just fifty miles away.

Things were a bit rough after the crash. I wasn't making extra money on the side from buying and selling homes anymore, so my only income was the $150,000 per year from Five Star. I had been making an extra $250,000 easily from real estate when the going was good.

I told Monica she would have to return to work for a while until things picked up. I even suggested we short sell the house and move into my rental condo close to Brookdale.

She wasn't having it. She insisted she didn't want Emmanuella to leave her school and friends. I was upset that I had to beg her to work with me. I was shocked she couldn't see the dilemma we were in. I didn't think I should have had to explain that to her. The writing was on the wall. I didn't receive support from her. She spent a lot of money on a few get-rich and work-from-home

15

schemes that required monetary investments. When I asked her what happened to each business idea, she would tell me it wasn't for her and that she'd found a better one.

My Uncle Fred referred Monica to his friend who was looking for a senior financial analyst. She had gone in for the interview only after we argued about it. She turned down the job offer without conferring with me, and that to me was an act of betrayal. I had paid her tuition when she returned to school to get her master's degree in business two years earlier.

After Emmanuella was born, Monica didn't want to go back to work right away. I had compromised and made it clear she would have to be in school if she wasn't working. We had a mutual understanding that she would get a better job once she earned her degree. By then Emmanuella would be turning three and would be ready for preschool.

When the time came, things didn't go as originally planned. Monica became comfortable with staying at home. I understood she wanted to be a housewife and raise our daughter, but we just couldn't afford to do that at the time.

What if I refused to work and wanted to be a stay-at-home dad while she slaved away? That would leave her scrambling for extra money. I would be the bum, the lazy, selfish husband.

It was only a matter of time before our cushion savings was depleted. With no extra funds, my dream of expanding the business went out the window. It was a serious setback, but she never saw it that way. She felt I was too obsessed with making money and hustling. I think that started the downturn of our relationship because we were never on the same page. I was even more upset when I heard about a copycat gym which had recently opened up near the city we wanted to expand into.

Another big issue we had was Monica wanted us to move down to Southern California where her family and childhood friends were. She had grown up in Los Angeles. Her parents were first generation immigrants from Brazil. They worked hard and did well for themselves. Monica is the only child and definitely spoiled. She had always said she was miserable without her folks, and she wanted us to leave everything because that was how she felt.

I didn't agree with her. I couldn't leave a burgeoning business at the drop of a hat. It didn't sound practical to me. I explained to her that if we were to move, it wouldn't be right away.

"Sell the business and start another one," she said. "We could stay with my family if we have to."

Her father even called me and said "Monica was telling me you guys are moving down here. Good move Devin. Maybe you can help me with some new

WTF MOMENT

ideas for my waste disposal business. We are doing well but I would like to expand. With your business edge we can make a very good team."

Why is everyone already making plans for me? I had thought.

She couldn't understand I had a client base in Brookdale which I built, starting out as a trainer for various sports clubs. I had used that leverage in building Five Star Gym. I didn't want to sell and have to start over in another city I wasn't familiar with. Monica did not understand why I couldn't do it. She hated me for it.

When she didn't get her way, she would hold a grudge forever.

"You are not supportive of me," she said.

I saw our marriage as a partnership, and we had to do what was best. Relocating was not in my short-term plan.

I felt her wrath following that conversation. Anytime I brought up a plan, she would veto it right away, citing I didn't support her plans, so she didn't feel the need to do the same for me. That was the beginning of the end for us because we never agreed on anything.

* * *

Before we separated, sometimes Monica would call me nonstop until I picked up. It was very annoying. She would make requests such as "Could you pick up some remote batteries on your way back from work?" She could have gone to the convenience store down the street. I was getting phone calls every half hour it seemed: "Where are you? What are you doing? When are you coming home? You should be here with me right now; I really need you now! Why do you work so much? What about me and my needs? I need to go do things too. A real man would be home with his family! I need help with this child!"

Those conversations got very annoying. Even when I showed her I detested it, she still continued to call. She would even call my friends if I was playing ball or hanging with them when I happened to miss her calls. She would call the front desk at the gym if I didn't pick up. Usually what she was calling for could have waited. Then she started checking my phones and calling random women clients. I was irritated with her and started to ignore her and would shut down which in turn irritated her more because she wanted to talk and argue.

In so many words, we found ways to blame each other for our demise. The frustration made us hate each other. When two people grow tired of each other, their faults are magnified. Neither could do anything right in the other's eyes. That was how it became with us.

I wish I never went through the motions with Monica. The hustling qualities she told me she liked about me when we first met were the same qualities she detested and loathed. We argued forever it seemed. She would call me degrading names and say she wished she had never met me. She'd say I was the worse thing that had ever happened to her.

One time Emmanuella had to intervene. "Stop it you two! That is not nice!" she said. I felt ashamed she had to see us that way. I promised myself that evening, I would never argue in front of her again. So when Monica started her shenanigans at home, I simply stopped indulging her. She started to withhold sex, which didn't bother me anymore because the sight of her had begun to disgust me altogether. The "good morning" and "good night" exchanges ceased, and then we stopped talking altogether. The only time we communicated about anything was when she wanted me to pay for something or when Emmanuella had needs.

That went on for a while and led to the inevitable—the separation.

2. The Boys and I

The usual suspects were congregated at Kenny's house. It was game night, featuring football, poker, pool, drinks, and plenty of smack talking.

Kenny is a few years older than I am. He had just turned thirty-five a few weeks earlier. We had clicked as workout buddies. I was there through his traumatic breakup with his ex-wife Tracy.

Since his divorce five years earlier, he always dated young, twenty-something-year-old women. Sometimes he called them his assistants. I teased him about the ladies assisting him to undo his pants. "How many assistants can one man have?" I once asked him. He replied that the young women liked his style because he was a seasoned older gentleman.

When Kenny walks into a spot, he's always dressed impeccably and clean cut. He seems younger than he looks. He's only about five seven, but he is muscular and walks around as if he were seven feet tall. I always told him he should have been a martial arts combatant or bodyguard since he has a black belt in tae kwon do.

I was happy he had finally gotten his independent record label off the ground, and he seemed to be doing well for himself. He liked that he could sell products directly to the consumer without the middleman. He made more profit that way.

Kenny played ball with us sporadically. At times he would even stop by our Saturday basketball pickup games and watch. At the end, he would critique our game with intrinsic details of our moves—made shots, missed opportunities, and botched plays. We'd joke and tell him to apply for a coaching or scouting job with local colleges and professional teams.

Kenny is always a gracious host. There is always plenty of food to eat. We almost have to beg him to allow us to bring munchies. That evening was no exception. Since I was the first to get there, I treated myself to an array of dishes. Kenny's barbecued ribs were to die for.

We had spent the last hour arguing about who had more game in pool. Moments later, Phil and his cousin, G. Dave, walked in, and we exchanged hugs and pounds. I was really surprised to see G. Dave. The *G* stands for Geek. He hangs out with us every now and then. Since I've known him, he has always been shacked up with one woman or another. Every year, he seems to find someone new he is in love with. He looks up to Phil. Dave would tell women at the club Phil was "The Rock" because he had a striking resemblance to the popular former wrestler-turned-movie actor. Sometimes he would say Phil and I are twins or brothers as we are built similarly.

Phil and I have been inseparable since college, and I consider him one of my closest friends. He is a little more outgoing than I am, but we rub off each other nicely when we are out. We both work out regularly. He is an inch shorter than I—six one to be exact. He has his way with the ladies, so I see why Dave likes to leach onto him.

Phil can talk up a storm. It was no surprise to me that he became a sports agent. He could have played professional football, but a devastating knee injury quelled his dream. Phil has always been sharp anyway; he put himself through school and earned an MBA. With his connections in college, it wasn't difficult for him to partner up with someone and set up a sports management company.

Phil hadn't even hung up his coat before he started yapping his gums. "You losers are still learning how to play this game after all these years? You all haven't improved one bit. You guys might as well hand over the sticks, sit back, grab some popcorn, and watch the professionals play. Maybe you can learn a thing or two," he said, laughing.

I shook my head in disapproval and said, "There you go again; I was the one who took you by the hand and taught you how to play this game when we were in college. Remember? Now, how are you going to come over here and start disrespecting your mentor?"

Kenny started giggling as he sharpened his stick, "Both of you shut the hell up! Neither of you guys have game. It's my house, and I run the table. If you all doubt me, please put your money where your mouths are."

"There you go, always talking about taking someone's money," I said, as I walked around the table pumping my chest. "I'd whoop your butt in your own house. Tell you what, when I finish knocking you around on this table, you should load it on my truck. It is serving no purpose here. You might own it, but you have no skills!"

WTF MOMENT

Dave suddenly said, "Guys . . . guys! Listen. Turn the TV up! They're talking about Franklin Williams from the New York Tigers. He supposedly called off his wedding just hours before the ceremony yesterday. He was to marry Ginger Price—the gorgeous former lead cheerleader from his team."

Franklin was known to be a Casanova, and most were initially shocked to hear he was getting married. He had dated the biggest, hottest pop and movie stars around. The paparazzi followed him around wherever he went.

"That's crazy," said Dave. "He didn't even bother to show up to let his friends and family know what was going on. He gave his best man his Platinum American Express card for his guests to use and enjoy. One thing I do know—Ginger sure is fine! He must be gay to leave her at the altar!"

"What's wrong with the guy changing his mind?" asked Kenny. "I'm pretty sure he paid for the whole wedding so why is she the victim here? She only got her feelings hurt, nothing more. We can't speculate on why it happened. Give him a break!"

"Canceling a seven-million-dollar wedding means avoiding a seventy-million-dollar divorce settlement," offered Phil. "She was a dancer and cheerleader for Christ's sake! She has always dated athletes and rock star musicians. The good looks and banging body is all she's got going for herself. Have you heard her speak? She's not very bright. I'm sorry."

Dave's sullen look indicated he was not in agreement with Phil. I held my laughter because I didn't want to hurt Dave's feelings further. He has always been a sensitive guy.

"It's funny," continued Phil, "how people say a guy is gay because he dumped some hot chick. Maybe he met a hotter chick! How about that? Even the hot and beautiful can be dumped too. More power to him. I wouldn't be getting married either if I was young and rich. I would be having sex with different women as if it's going out of style. And if I did get married, it would be to a fine, rich woman who would be bringing as much as I am to the table."

Kenny laughed. "She probably thought she hit the jackpot. Franklin just signed a $55-million extension just two months ago. I know she is kicking herself right now. She messed up though. She should have slept with one of Franklin's friends and paid him some money to make sure Franklin was drunk the night before the wedding. By morning time, Franklin would have had a bad hangover and wouldn't be thinking straight. He would have said *I do* before he realized it was too late. But all jokes aside, she may be fine, but for every fine woman out there, I will show you a guy who is tired of her crap!"

Phil chimed in, "I wonder how long he had been thinking about it before he pulled the plug at the last minute. All I know is breaking up is way better than divorce. I'd rather walk out on my wedding and deal with the shame afterward. That's much better than a lifetime of misery with a woman who would make me have regrets. In my opinion, he is better off. She probably wanted him for his money anyway! I have no sympathy for her."

"Amen," offered Kenny.

Phil kept going. "All professional athletes should have prenups before tying the knot. Forget marriage and the inequalities created by the judicial system and its lawyers. I love being single; marriage is overrated anyway."

"I think it's foul," said Dave. "Leaving someone at the altar. Have you all seen Ginger? I'd wife her up immediately if I ever got the chance."

Phil shook his head. "You're missing the point, Dave. For a man not to show up at his own wedding says a lot. There must have been an issue there we don't know about. What if he found out some damaging secrets about her? He might have just realized she was a gold digger."

Kenny laughed again. "Maybe he just found out she slept with the quarterback, the running back, and the coach!"

"I don't care man," said Dave. "She's a keeper! She is so fine. I wouldn't even bother using a condom with that beauty. I'd enjoy all her goodness raw!"

Phil exclaimed, "You're crazy Dave! Did you just say you'd hit it raw because she is fine? I got a news flash for you—AIDS and herpes do not discriminate. I don't see the logic. I've heard quite a few guys say that. I think a good amount of these model-looking women have more sex than the average woman because they always have guys lined up around the corner trying to get a piece of their love. They have more options. For that reason alone, I think they are more susceptible to diseases because guys are either sleeping with them or trying to! As ignorant as I may sound, think about it. If a fine woman with a killer body in a revealing outfit walked in here right now, all four of us would try to talk to her and try to get her home tonight. So my response to you, Dave, is good-looking women are overrated."

"That's how insecure guys get in trouble. Marry a woman because she is cute? Please! There is no correlation between being fine and being a good wife. All that beauty is for show," Kenny chimed in.

"My dad once told me," Kenny continued, "when I was a youngster, to never marry a woman because of her looks alone. Hell, you can give a regular chick a touch-up, and she can come out looking hot. Talk about a diamond in the rough. We always run after all the video and magazine vixens. When we get our hearts broken, we want to be bitter!"

"You can't trust some of these pretty women either!" said Phil. "Most of them have no personalities. They never had to develop one because they were

WTF MOMENT

told they were so pretty at a very young age. They are spoiled and have been handed everything. They've never had to work for anything. They grow up thinking that's how life is supposed to be. I treat all my women the same. You're not getting any special treatment because you're cute!"

"You're right!" said Kenny. "You know what else? I've dated my share of pretty women. They are truly overrated! Most of them don't even know how to make love. I can remember at least ten ultra-fine women I've had sex with, and I can't recall anything exciting about the sex. My top five sexual experiences were with average or slightly below average chicks. Honestly!"

It was Phil's turn to laugh. "Why is this guy trying to be politically correct? Slightly below-average chicks! You meant to say ugly? That's more of your flow anyway."

Kenny chuckled. "Whatever, man! And no, I said average or slightly below-average! I stand by my statement."

"If you say so," said Phil, laughing.

Dave, who had been fiddling with his phone texting someone back and forth, decided to share. "That was my cousin Ron texting me. He wants me to help him move his belongings. His lady just kicked him out. He should have never moved in with her anyway."

"They've been living together for a while now, right?" asked Phil.

"Three years," said Dave.

"Devin knows all about that," said Kenny. "How are you holding up, bro?"

"I'm keeping my head above water," I said. "Monica is trying to take me to the cleaners. I have to pay her mortgage, her car note, food . . . everything. She doesn't even care that I need to live too. And she wants an extra grand for entertainment!"

"Entertainment?" said Dave. "What! That's really messed up. I didn't see Monica as being that kind of woman. I guess things change when people go through divorce."

"She's not the same woman I married," I said. "I know we both realized we were wrong for each other, but she is still a good woman underneath it all. It's not her. I know she is being pressured by some folks to go about things the way she is right now. I spend so much time in court and at the lawyer's office these days. It's sickening."

"You seem to hold it together even though you're dealing with a lot," said Phil.

"What can I do?" I asked. "I still have to live and figure out how to improve the quality of my life. She is not going to break me. I promise you that."

"Seeing and hearing all these stories makes me sympathize with all those guys who just say *F it* and disappear without paying child support or alimony," said Kenny. "Imagine a guy busting his ass working a regular job, then he as to hand over most of his earnings to some vindictive bitch at the end of the month! Of course, I understand when he quits and goes back home to live with his mom and becomes a bum. I used to judge those kinds of guys, but not anymore. I have been through it. My brother just went through it. He almost lost his mind. He lost a lot of weight, lost his job, and he hit rock bottom. He is finally just getting his life together. My Uncle James went through it too."

"Some of these bitter women think the only way to get back at a man is through his wallet," said Phil. "I think it's cruel. How could you sleep at night knowing you're hindering a man's growth and crippling his finances? Marriage is for the birds. I'm fairly rich, good looking, and I'm enjoying my life to the fullest."

"Don't you think that will get old at some point?" asked Dave.

"Different folks, different strokes. It's not just for me. Why deal with all the craziness? Don't get me wrong, some folks are happily married, but they are few and far between, and I commend those who stick it out. But I truly enjoy being single—no headaches. It's what works for me," Phil said.

"Hell will freeze over before this one gets married," I said, laughing and pointing to Phil.

"But you know what?" Phil responded, "if it does ever happen, the woman will have to be near perfect and drama free. And I know that is almost impossible. But can a guy wish a little?"

Kenny laughed. "There is always hope," he said.

Kenny and Dave's game of pool started to get really intense. Phil walked to the balcony to talk on the phone. One of his women must have been calling him, and he didn't want us to hear the conversation. I started to half-heartedly watch a basketball game on TV. My mind was all over the place. I was trying to decide whether I should start to date again. I was still trying to get used to being without a significant other, but being single isn't easy either. I didn't know which was worse—being single and lonely, or married and miserable. I got off the sofa and walked over to the kitchen for another can of beer. I saw Phil through the screen door chatting away on the phone with his mystery person. He walked in a few moments later.

"What's up man?" he asked.

"Nothing much, bro. I'm just chilling. Who was the woman on the phone? You sneaky bastard," I said, laughing.

Phil grinned and shook his head. "That was Candis. She is stressing me out."

"Who is Candis?"

"You got jokes, huh?" he chimed.

"You have so many, I can't keep up anymore."

WTF MOMENT

"You know Candis. We work in the same building," he continued.

"Oh yeah, I remember her! Are you still fooling around with her?"

Phil scratched his head and said, "I think I'm going to leave her alone. She's just too moody for me. Being a lawyer makes her think every conversation is a debate. I appreciate how bright she is, but trying to show off at every opportunity is a turn-off. She's not a bad person, but she has too much going on within herself. Her accomplishments and profession are all she talks about, all she cares about. There is more to people besides what they do for a living."

"You got yourself a rigid woman. I can relate. I dated one before. It could be tough dealing with a woman who may be oblivious to how obnoxious she is."

"Rigid is the right word! She has problems having orgasms too," he said with a sigh.

"Are you serious? That is so sad, to be deprived of the greatest feeling in the world. Maybe it's a psychological issue or maybe even medical, but it happens. How do you deal with that?" I asked.

"Well, I don't have to worry about it anymore; we're no longer on speaking terms as of five minutes ago."

"She really has never had one? How old is she?"

"She's thirty one now and has been having sex since she was fifteen. I think she could have orgasms on a regular basis if she put her mind to it. It's all about knowing your body well. Heck, the last woman I dated climaxed multiple times in a session—seven times in a span of twenty minutes on one occasion. She even has an orgasm just from me nibbling on her nipples. Damn! I miss her. This is the first time I've been with a non-orgasmic woman. She comes up with different excuses, and even says I need to make her cum!"

I started to laugh. "Really?"

"She is a lost cause. I've tried to talk her through it, but she is too bottled up. She never learned how to let go. Yes, a guy should know what he is doing with his magic stick, but climax can be reached with efforts from both parties. All my ex-girlfriends had no problem reaching climax. I led and helped them get to the mountaintop, but they would contribute as well. It takes two to tango. I'll be damned if some lady makes me question myself. I still have some exes banging on my door wanting me to rock their world," he lamented.

"I totally understand what you mean. I haven't dealt with a non-orgasmic woman before. But I know most guys will encounter at least one in his lifetime. I wouldn't even worry about it if I were you. You win some, you lose some. Some women just know what it takes to climax easily. Case in point—your ex who can do it over and over again. She is a sexually mature woman. It's all about getting in tune with one's self," I said.

"Yes, sir!" he concurred.

"By the way, what ever happened to Jasmine? She was cute, nice, and collected."

"Hmm, she is still around, but we don't hang like we used to."

"So what really happened?" I asked, laughing.

"I like her, but I feel she will never be content," he said. "She has never had a boyfriend longer than a year. I won't be surprised if she remains single for a while. She gets bored rather quickly. She was still kind of seeing someone when she started dating me, and we started to have sex before she actually ended the relationship. That was a red flag to me. She has too many guy friends too, and spends too much time with them. I've got female friends, but I don't hang out with them consistently, and I don't spend hours on the phone with a woman I'm not dating. She claims women are too catty for her, so she prefers to have male friends because she is comfortable with them. She introduced me to at least twelve guys who were *good friends*. I've only seen her with one female friend."

"That is a tricky one. It's okay to have male friends, but I bet you some of those guys would jump into bed with her the moment they had the opportunity. That is what we do!" I chirped.

"She had actually slept with a few of these so-called men friends she introduced me to. She claimed it had happened unexpectedly and she'd nipped it in the bud immediately afterward. She also said she felt obligated and sorry for one because he was really nice and had been broken-hearted from a failed relationship. Who knows how many of them she slept with? Every time she introduced me to a male friend, I'd have to wonder whether she had slept with him. It felt awkward, and I know I'm far from being a jealous guy."

"Did she come out and tell you about the guys she messed around with, or did you ask her?"

"Yeah, she told me about a couple of them. I found out about another one through a mutual friend," he replied.

"It sounds as though she puts herself in tricky situations."

"Granted, she used to be a tomboy and played basketball in college," said Phil. "I still don't buy that as the reason she hangs out with men most of the time. I think she just likes to be close to men, period, and has convinced herself otherwise. Basically she likes to have options without coming off as being promiscuous. Maybe I'm being judgmental," he quipped.

"It is hard to be friends with the opposite sex. I'm not saying it isn't possible, but someone always has an agenda. I can understand why you had your reservations," I said.

"My sentiments exactly! As you said, most guys who are friends with women are just waiting for an opportunity to come up when the women are

WTF MOMENT

vulnerable. You know I'm telling the truth! Ninety percent of men want to tap that booty especially if the woman is attractive," Phil continued.

"I agree," I said, laughing.

"Right?" he asked, laughing as well.

"Okay, Mr. Casanova, whatever happened to Maxine?"

"Bro! That was so last year! What's with you asking about my love life?" he asked, laughing.

"You know I like to live vicariously through you."

"Yeah, whatever!" He smirked.

"So what happened to her? I thought she was reserved, beautiful, and had manners."

"To be really honest with you, she wasn't always fresh, so I kind of eased up on her. But we still talk on the phone every now and then."

"What do you mean she wasn't always fresh?" I inquired.

"You know how I feel about cleanliness when it comes to women and their downtown area," he said.

"Uh uh," I nodded, laughing.

"I'm serious. Maxine was a really cool chick, but her stuff was always humming."

With a befuddled look, I asked, "Really?"

"Sometimes during foreplay, I like to play with a woman's kitty and discretely smell my finger. If it's not fresh, then we have a problem! If a woman has been out all day and then comes to my house with the intention of having sex, she'd better take a shower. I think it is rude not to!"

I laughed. "I would drop hints, *Care to join me in the shower?* That way, I would eliminate the chance of a mishap."

"Even after a shower, Maxine would still have an odor."

"Maybe she didn't know she had a problem," I added.

"That is absurd. What woman wouldn't know she isn't fresh? Give me a break! It's all about personal hygiene. Some women take exceptional care of their stuff, and the ones who don't are just nasty! Plain and simple," he bleated.

"True," I said. "Then again, maybe it isn't that she is unsanitary; she might not be taking care of herself properly. A woman has to be in tune with her own body. She has to eat right and watch her intakes. She may be allergic to certain foods or medications and not even know it. Certain underwear could cause a bacterial infection down there. Some women do not wear underwear at times, to allow the Garden of Eden to breathe."

"And how do you know all these things, doctor?" he asked, laughing.

"Remember I lived in a house with women—four older sisters and two female cousins."

BOLAJI TIJANI-QUDUS

Dave ran into the kitchen and grabbed two cans of beer. "What's up, fellas? What are you guys talking about?"

I sighed and pointed to Phil. "I'm listening to Phil's story about a funky kitty kat."

"Happens all the time! I encountered one a while back. She took her panties off, and the whole room stank. When I was about to enter her doggy style, she exhumed so much funk, my eyes watered. I gagged and almost threw up!" Dave said.

I started to laugh uncontrollably, and Phil almost choked when he tried to laugh and drink at the same time.

"Did you kick her out?" I asked.

"No, bro. It was late at night. We had just made it in from the club. We were both tipsy, and her ass looked so freaking good! I had been trying to sleep with her the whole summer, and she wouldn't let me. I felt lucky to get her to come to my apartment that night, and I didn't want to do anything to change my fortune, so I held my breath and pounded it. I never invited her over again," Dave responded.

"What the hell?" I asked, laughing.

"You nasty bastard! Get your nasty butt out of here and get back to your pool game," Phil said, playfully punching Dave.

"Whatever, guys! Both of you should have seen the woman. You would have done the same thing," he said, laughing and half running out of the kitchen.

"Not everyone is as nasty as you, Dave!" I yelled.

"Can you believe that dude?" Phil asked.

"Why are you surprised? He is the same guy who laid a towel down and had sex with a woman during her cycle. Remember?" I said, laughing.

"Oh yeah, I almost forgot he takes nastiness to another level," Phil added.

"You can say that again!" I nodded in agreement.

"Anyway, I'm back to prowling the streets again," Phil said, smiling.

"Amen!" I concurred.

With our beer bottles lifted, we cheered.

3. Mumbo Jumbo

Emmanuella had her mother call me on her behalf. We spoke for a while. She said she had missed me. I missed her so much too. Sometimes I had separation anxiety when she wasn't with me. I smile when I think of how sweet she is. Her wisdom is beyond her years. I went to Queensbury to visit her the next day. We hung out, and I helped her with some of her homework. I gave her a bath, and she asked me to read her a book as she got ready for bed. I asked her to pick a book from the shelf, and she handed me one titled *Time for a Change*. I opened it. The first paragraph read:

> Divorce: Is a legal judgment ending a marriage. After a husband and wife get a divorce, they are both free to marry again whenever they see fit.

- Half brother or sister
- Alimony
- Stepparent

As I read it, I wondered why Monica would be showing and reading such a book to our three-year-old. It had graphics showing two dogs—Daddy Dog and Mummy Dog—yelling at each other, and a puppy running to hide in the closet. There was another image of Daddy Dog drinking with beer bottles all around him. He looked upset, and the puppies were watching him from afar, looking scared. This was not what had happened at our house. Granted we have had our fights, but we didn't have a dysfunctional home like the one depicted in the book. Our daughter is the happiest kid around. Maybe a few times she had seen us argue.

As I glanced through the book, I felt the anger overcome me. It was so graphic I could not even believe my eyes. What three-year-old girl could understand what divorce meant?

I was so annoyed. I tossed the book behind the clothes drawers. My daughter wanted to read it; I guess she was intrigued with the pictures. That was too much information for a little girl.

I read Emmanuella a fun story book instead. She soon fell asleep, and I left for home. I didn't even bother talking to Monica about it that evening because I knew it would turn into an argument. I had promised myself to make sure Emmanuella never heard or saw us argue again.

I called Monica the next day and asked her about the book. Her reply was that our daughter wasn't too young to know. She claimed the book was perfectly okay and that all the people she had spoken to said it was appropriate. That was another problem. Some of the people she talked to had broken marriages, and some of them were single mothers. I didn't understand how they could be experts. When Monica and I were together, she used to say she was happy that I wasn't like some of the men her friends were with. Now that we weren't together anymore, I was being lumped together with those same men.

It was laughable to me. She seemed to have forgotten how I had slaved to send her to school for her MBA. I would leave for work at five in the morning and returned home at eight in the evening, six days a week. I took care of the home, paid all the bills and took care of her and my daughter. It's funny how I'm a deadbeat all of a sudden. I think it's what made me angrier than anything else—that my morals, ethics, and family dedication could be questioned in such a manner. It's unbelievable how some women forget the good things so often but remember all the wrong things all the time. I thought about the times I would come home and be baffled to find the house in the state it was in. She would be home all day, and the house would be dirty—toys everywhere. The sink will be packed with dishes, and to make matters worse, there was usually no food in the house. The least she could have done was to have empathy for a guy who had been working seventy hours all week.

If you're going to be home all day, the house should be somewhat tidy. Anytime I brought it up and asked why the house was always a mess, she would respond by saying, *Why don't you stay home all day with a kid and see what it's like?* I understand the little one running around the house, but that is not an excuse for the place to look as though a hurricane ran through it. I was able to help only on the day I didn't work, which was Sunday.

A few times she had the nerve to call Merry Maids—a house-cleaning service—to help her with the house. I had to protest and nipped it in the bud quickly.

WTF MOMENT

I sat there at my desk having flashbacks about all the drama we used to go through.

I also used to be bothered when she consistently compared me to her father. She would make silly statements such as *my father fixes everything in the house. He goes to the Laundromat with Mom to wash clothes . . . he washes dishes . . .*

I would always tell her I wasn't like her father. I worked long hours and was always tired by the time I got home. I know I didn't fix things around the house immediately, but I still got to it when I could. She had a laundry list of all the chores I didn't do every day; after a while, everything that came out of her mouth sounded like mumbo jumbo.

I was happy I wasn't there in that house going through the motions, but I was sad I wasn't seeing my daughter as regularly as I wanted to. She didn't deserve the mess that had been created by her parents. She is smart and beautiful. I never imagined she would be raised in a broken home, and every time I think about it, I get depressed. I have to do everything in my power to make sure I'm constantly present in her life, no matter what. If she gets unconditional love from both Monica and me, she should be okay, I kept telling myself.

As I was walking up to my place after work the evening following the doggie-divorce book episode, a man appeared from nowhere and startled me.

"Are you Devin?"

"Who is asking?" I replied, as I took a few steps backward and put my hands in my backpack pretending to be reaching for something.

"I didn't mean to startle you, sir. I'm just here to give you some important information," he said, as he handed me an envelope.

I cautiously eyed him as I took the envelope from him.

"You've been served," he said.

The return address read, "The Superior Court of Queensbury."

I opened up the letter when I reached my place. I was dumbfounded for a few seconds at what I had just read. I had been talking to a buddy the previous day about finding a good divorce lawyer. *I guess she beat me to it. It's really happening!* I thought.

I was sad at first, then I was happy that we were moving on. We had been separated for over a year now anyway. It was time to make the next step. I called Phoenix, my lawyer buddy, right away. He referred me to an associate of his who dealt with family law.

A few weeks later, my lawyer passed on some documents for me to read through. There were allegations that I was hardly supporting Monica financially. That was shocking to me. I didn't understand. *Did she just expect me to hand over my paycheck to her every month? What the hell has she been doing with all the money I have been giving to her?*

I had stayed with Phil for six months when I first moved out of the house. I still made sure my paychecks were going to our joint account, and I took out only enough for gas and food. I wanted to make sure there were enough funds and a cushion for her when we finally decided to divorce. Phil was generous and allowed me to stay with him for free. The allegations came about because I decided to get my own place. All I wanted was to have a space for myself and have a comfortable environment for my daughter when she came to visit.

I had notified Monica about the changes and told her I would start paying the mortgage at my place and therefore, I needed to split my income into two. My tenants had vacated my rental condo.

Of course she resisted and sent me texts, and we went back and forth.

> *From: Monica*
> I would still need you to give me six grand a month to take care of our finances.

> *To: Monica*
> That is about 70% of my income. How will I pay my bills if I give you all that? I have a mortgage too! I can only do $4,000, which should cover your mortgage for now. Actually we might need to modify that loan, or better yet, short sell the house. I don't think we can afford it right now. There is 20 grand left in our account now, which should hold you up until you get a job. You should really get that job to supplement us.

> *From: Monica*
> You can go stay with your parents! Your daughter needs money, and we have bills to pay. 4G will not be enough!

I was angry. *Go stay with my parents? What nerve! She thinks I should just toil and work for her!* I started to wonder whether she had lost it and was delusional. She should understand I had to maintain a household too. What grown, thirty-something-year-old man lives with his parents? I was keeping Emmanuella every weekend anyway. She would need to eat when she was with me, and she would need clothes and other things.

> *To: Monica*
> Are you serious? That is just so funny! Anyway, I think 4G will be sufficient.

WTF MOMENT

From: Monica
I hope they kick Emmanuella out of school! You're not handling your responsibilities! How am I supposed to take care of this kid by myself? That is so messed up; you're going to abandon your own kid.

I was so agitated when I read her text. Abandon my kid? What the hell was that supposed to mean. This woman knows that is not who I am. She is the same woman who told me that one of the qualities she admires in me is that I'm a good dad. *Now I'm a piece of crap? Wow!*

To: Monica
What are you talking about? I just explained to you that I'm moving into the condo, don't you understand that? I've got to get my own life started, and I have expenses. You know what our financial situation is. I get Emmanuella every weekend too, remember?

From: Monica
Well that is not my problem! Is it? What do you think is going to happen when people divorce? You chose to move out, so deal with it. All I care about is money for this little girl. Your expenses and what you do with your life are not my concern! Be a man and take care of your responsibilities!

To: Monica
Wow! All of a sudden I don't take care of my responsibilities? I'm a bum now because we are no longer together? When have I been known not to take care of business? Wow! Lol. I chose to move out because we didn't get along—not just because I woke up one morning and decided it was a thing to do! Anyway, I handle my business! *sigh*

From: Monica
You're a joke! I wish I never met you. My life would have been better than this. I hate you and everything you stand for!

To: Monica
Whatever, Monica! You're part of the reason this didn't work out. It's not just me. I hope you know that.

From: Monica

You're the worse mistake of my life. You're pathetic. I shouldn't have fallen for an excuse of a man.

To: Monica

Oh really? Now, I'm an excuse of a man? Aren't you the same one who was drooling all over me not too long ago? You can kiss my ass.

From: Monica

Drooling? You make me laugh. You're not all that, for your information! I shouldn't have gone with you. I don't know what I was thinking when I chose you. You're nothing but a bad dream.

To: Monica

Okay, enough of the name-calling. Show some class! This is the same crap we've been going through for the last two years. We are not even together, and it still won't stop. Get a life!

From: Monica

You get a life! Asshole. Just make sure you feed this damn child.

To: Monica

That has never been and will never be a problem. I love my kid and will always be there for her no matter what.

From: Monica

Yeah, right! And you're complaining about money. Shows how much you really love her.

To: Monica

Why don't you get a real job and help out with money instead of waiting for me to take care of you!

From: Monica

Who says you're taking care of me? The money is for this child. I don't need your money! I'll be fine.

WTF MOMENT

To: Monica
Whatever! You have a nice day. I've tolerated enough of this nonsense for one day.

From: Monica
I hope the bitch you're with now finds out who you really are quickly before it's too late for her.

To: Monica
Who says this is all about another woman? I'm happy to be alone. At least I have peace of mind when I come home from work. And when I do decide to be involved with someone, you can count on it that she won't be crazy and unappreciative like you.

From: Monica
Whatever! Jerk. Loser. You're pathetic.

To: Monica
If that is what makes you sleep at night . . . this never-ending bickering won't stop, will it? At least I admitted I'm part of the problem with why the relationship didn't work, and I am not turning around and making it all your fault. That is what you are doing to me and you are not realizing it. We have chosen to move on since we no longer want to be with each other. That doesn't mean I want to make your life miserable!

From: Monica
Whatever! You're such a fraud. I'm happy without you.

I read the last text and I wanted to respond sarcastically by writing *Good for you. Glad you are happy.* As tempted as I was, I decided against it. The texting rage could go on forever.

Ironically, a few minutes later, I received a call from Ms. Smith, my lawyer. She wanted me to come by her office to go over some paperwork. I told her I could get over there after work so we could try and finalize the divorce. I was mentally drained. *I just can't wait for this to be over!*

4. Curiosity Kills the Cat

Brandon walked into Mood's and headed straight for the bar. I watched as one of the bartenders poured him two shots. The drinks barely touched the counter before he downed them and signaled for another two. A waitress walked by, and I grabbed her gently. "Could you please tell that gentleman at the end of the bar to join us over here?" I asked.

"Sure thing," she replied in a flirting voice. "Let me know if you need anything else."

"Sure thing." I smiled back. As she walked away, Phil was checking her out. "Sneaky chick! They never stop working people to get more tips."

"It's her job, Phil! That's how she makes a living. Get over it already," I said. "Besides you are an up-and-coming top dog in the sports agency field. I'm sure you know a little something about working clients!"

The waitress tapped Brandon and pointed to our direction. He jumped up and walked toward us with his two replenished glasses in hand. I was surprised to see him out.

He gave everyone a quick hug, not saying much. Then he pulled me to the other side of the room away from the rest of the crew. He had met the boys through me so he wasn't as close to them as he was to me. I could feel that he was quite uneasy; his eyes kept darting all the over place.

He was usually an upbeat, happy-go-lucky kind of guy. But he seemed different tonight. He seemed spaced out. His shirt had stains on it; his jeans were wrinkled. He was wearing tennis shoes, but they were the same ones he plays hoops in. He wore a scarf around his neck, but it wasn't a cold evening. Something wasn't quite right.

When Brandon stands next to me, he always looks much bigger though we are the same height. Women called him Big Teddy Bear because he is cuddly and sports a full beard. He played fullback as a senior in high school just

WTF MOMENT

because he was big, although sports were never his thing anyway. He weighed two hundred pounds then and had to be pushing three hundred now.

"What's up, B?" I asked.

He took a seat and looked up at me with dimmed, sunken eyes, as though, he hadn't slept for days.

"It's over!" he said.

"What's over?"

"It's over! Ashley and I are done! Done!"

"Dude! What are you talking about?" I asked, staring at him wide-eyed. "You have got to be kidding me!"

Brandon and I grew up on the same street, and Ashley lived on the next one over. We had all known each other as kids, although they didn't officially become a couple until the eleventh grade in high school.

Brandon started to get agitated, shifting back and forth on his stool; his teeth were clenched. The muscle in the middle of his forehead had popped out.

He sighed and said, "I just found out she's been in a relationship with Yvette for a while now."

"What the . . .," I started to say.

Yvette was supposedly a distant cousin. Ashley's aunt adopted her when she was about ten years old. Technically they aren't cousins, but they are still family in a way.

Yvette was rumored to have a 'Lick her License' As long as she had been around the crew, no one had questioned her. She had been treated the same as everyone else. She came to every function we had. Yvette always hung out with good-looking women for some reason. Some of my buddies had even tried to get in good with her so they could try talking to some of her friends. There's something about bisexual women that makes men drool.

"What? Hold on, hold on, bro! Ashley is a lesbian . . . bisexual now? Are you sure? She doesn't strike me as someone that would go that way. Are you sure you're not overreacting?" I asked, as I stood there frozen, staring at him.

"I'm telling you, man! I caught her red-handed. She has been messing with Yvette all this time!"

"Really?" I was shocked, so I pulled a stool next to him, sat down, and listened attentively as he told me the details about how he had found out.

* * *

Brandon was supposed to be at Lake Batista for the weekend, skiing with some work buddies that fateful Friday, a week prior. Things had

37

changed because John, one of the guys, had a scare—his father had a minor stroke. They all decided to leave the following day so John could go be with his dad.

Brandon arrived back home about midnight, and Ashley wasn't there. *She must have gone out with her girlfriends*, he thought. He got himself a beer and decided to watch TV. A few hours later, he woke up suddenly, realizing he had fallen asleep on the couch. It was 2:30 a.m., and there was no sign of Ashley. He thought maybe she'd gone upstairs to sleep because she didn't want to bother him. *No! That wouldn't be right! She would have woken me up and asked me why I wasn't at Lake Batista*, he thought. He went upstairs to look anyway. As he'd expected, she wasn't there. He paced around for a while wondering where she could be. *She's never stayed out this late.*

He decided to call her phone, but it went straight to voicemail. *Maybe she was staying with one of her friends* because he was supposedly out of town. Then again, Ashley always liked to sleep in her own bed no matter what. He called her phone again as he walked back down the stairs—still no answer.

Then he heard a faint vibrating sound. It was coming from the den, but then it stopped. He pressed the redial button, and there was the noise again. He walked into the den and found her phone on the table next to the computer. *Why would she leave her phone at home? She never goes anywhere without her phone*, he thought.

Brandon was worried because Ashley's new Volkswagen Beetle was in the driveway too. She always drove when she and her girls went out because she never liked to wait around for a ride or to be on someone else's time. Whenever she felt she needed to leave, she wanted to do so without any hassles. Crazy thoughts ran through his mind. *I hope she hasn't been kidnapped.* He didn't notice any signs of a struggle in the car or in the house. Nothing seemed to be out of place.

He paced around some more, thinking, *What would make her leave the house without her car and cell phone?*

He grabbed Ashley's phone and decided to look at the dialed and received call log to see whether he could locate the last person she had spoken to. That person may have an idea where she was. Her most recent call—at 11:00 p.m.—had been to Yvette. He dialed the number, and there was no answer. He tried a few more times with the same results. Something told him to check her text messages. Maybe there was a clue; he was desperately searching for something or someone to assure him that his wife was safe.

WTF MOMENT

The first text message he checked was from Yvette.

From: Yvette
Why are you doing this to me? It's been three years now, and I can't take it any longer! I eat, sleep, and think about you every day. We should be together. We are supposed to be building a family together! I'm tired of pretending. I don't want to share you any longer. I need to know something! I'm dying inside!

Brandon didn't know what to make of the message. It had to be some kind of joke, or maybe it was Yvette's text to a boyfriend she had forwarded to his wife. *What a nagging chick. Some poor guy has his hands full*, he thought, chuckling.

Then, he read a previous message.

From: Yvette
So Brandon kept you in the house again this past weekend huh? I have not seen you in a few days, and you know that doesn't work for me. That is a long time, and you know how restless I get. Ashley, baby, I miss you. When are you going to leave him? I want you in my bed every single night.

"What the . . .," Brandon muttered.

He didn't know what to make of the text, so he double-checked the name and number the text had come from. He thought maybe a guy was masquerading as Yvette. So he compared the phone number to the one he had. It was the same! He decided to go through additional older texts.

From: Yvette
Oh, baby, I love the way you suck on my nipples and how you gently bite them . . . and your kisses! Oh, baby, I can't begin to explain what they do to me! No one knows my body better than you. I have been so happy the last few years. You're the best. I just can't believe you're still wasting all that goodness on a man. You know he has no clue as to what to do with you!

Sweat beads formed over his forehead as he switched over to the sent messages log, curious to see what kind of responses Ashley had sent.

To: Yvette
Baby, you know I love the way you make love to me too. I think your tongue was specially made for my clit . . . I quiver when you lick it. Ecstasy is you. Last night was so great. Cuddled up under that cover with the fireplace lit up was so romantic. God! You do wonders to me.

He went on to read an older text.

To: Yvette
You have to be patient with me, baby. I'm leaving Brandon soon. I just have to figure out the right time. It is you that I want, and it is only you that I want to be with. Give me a little time. Can you do that for me?

He scrolled down further.

To: Yvette
I'm going to call you around 7. I want to come over. Brandon's mother is visiting and I don't feel like being in the house with her! You know how she always wants to rearrange my kitchen. She is so annoying! I can't wait to show you the new lingerie I bought this afternoon. I know you will like it, baby. I got it in the colors you like too. lol.

Brandon was boiling hot now. He was reflecting on how he had cooked dinner a few days before. They had all hung out in the living room. The girls complimented him on the food. He had left them downstairs and gone to bed. He was tired, and Yvette and Ashley wanted to watch a movie. The two women had both snuggled under a blanket. He'd even lit the fireplace for them and poured them more wine. All this time and under his nose, under his roof, they had been eating each other out. He'd heard noises and giggles that night, but he had thought it was the movie that was causing all the excitement. How many other times had they done this?! Mocking him, laughing at him, he thought.

"Freaking tramps!" he mumbled to himself as he hopped into his truck. He soon found himself exiting on Twenty-second Avenue heading toward Yvette's house in West Brookdale.

As he pulled up, he saw Yvette's Chrysler 300 parked in the driveway. Her living room lights were off. "These tramps are going to get it today," he fumed

WTF MOMENT

to himself. He opened the side gate and slowly glided toward the bedroom in the back area. Just as he had guessed, the bedroom light was on. He leaned over a ledge close to an open window, and there he saw them—both naked! Yvette had a king-sized bed in her room. He had helped her put it together the previous summer. He had wondered what a petite woman was doing with such a big bed. *Thinking about it now, she probably uses it for all-girl orgies.*

"Uugghh! Nasty tramp!" he exclaimed. Ashley lay on the bed with one hand on her clit and the other fondling her breast.

"C'mon, baby! Hurry!" Ashley uttered.

Yvette had in her hands what seemed to be a jar. She poured something out of it onto Ashley's midsection and rubbed it all over her body. Then she began to lick whatever it was off Ashley's body. She dipped her fingers into the jar and let its contents drip directly between Ashley's legs, and then she slowly began to eat her out.

That has to be honey! Same stuff we play around with at home, Brandon thought. The vein on his neck started to pop.

I'm going to kill this woman! were the words swirling around in his head. Ashley and Yvette were in a sixty-nine position. Ashley was on the bottom with her palms stapled onto Yvette's two butt cheeks while she slurped upward on her clit. Yvette slowly parted Ashley's lips and licked around her clit, then directly on it. She soon began to suck it.

There were no floodlights in the backyard so they could not see Brandon, but he could see them clearly. He was perplexed and fixated on the ongoing action inside.

Ashley's shrieks jolted him. She was moving her hips vigorously.

"Oh, baby, I love it when you lick me up and down just like that, baby . . . please don't stop! Oh, you got me so fucking wet!" she screamed as she grabbed Yvette's ass tighter.

Yvette in turn began to indulge Ashley as well with more intensity, taking a breather to moan. She repositioned herself, moving her clit up and down on Ashley's tongue while Ashley licked upward in reverse. It was like ballet as they both moved their bodies in slow, synchronizing rhythms.

"I'm about to cum, baby!" Yvette screamed.

"Cum for me, baby!" Ashley shrieked.

Brandon stood there watching the two as they reached their climax, holding each other. They were both covered in sweat. Moments later, Yvette stood up and went over to the foot of the bed. She then opened up what seemed to be a huge treasure chest. She whipped out a double-ended rubber jellied dildo. She lubed it up and hopped back onto the bed. She smiled as she kissed Ashley's navel. She sucked Ashley's clit for a few seconds and then slowly inserted the dildo. Ashley let out a gasp and then she sat up and in turn assisted Yvette as she inserted the other end. They sat face to face, caressing one another with their legs wrapped around each other. They kissed and grinded on each other slowly. Then they turned the tempo up, moving their pelvises faster and in unison.

Brandon's eyes were bloodshot, watching as his wife and Yvette went at it. He wanted to jump through the window and announce his presence, but he was unable to move. He had just witnessed a shocking and life-altering scene. Something came over him; his mind went blank, and like a zombie, he turned around and walked toward his truck. Tears flowed freely down his face. His anger had turned to despair and self-worthlessness.

* * *

I sat with my mouth agape in disbelief as he concluded the story. I didn't know what to say or do. I wanted to embrace him; do anything to make him feel better. Suddenly, he clenched his stomach and said, "Hold on, I think I'm about to throw up!" He got up and disappeared through the double doors toward the restroom.

I walked over to where the guys were. They were probably wondering why we had snuck off to talk and I hadn't clued them in.

"Where's Brandon?" Phil asked.

"I think he had too much to drink. He went to the bathroom to throw up," I replied.

"You both were having an intense discussion over there. Is everything okay?"

"The usual—wifey drama," I replied.

"Oh! That is enough to make a grown man go crazy." Phil sighed.

"Anyway, I'm going to check on Brandon. Maybe we should try and get him home," I said.

The guys acted as if they hadn't heard what I said and kept conversing as though I were invisible.

"That's messed up, guys!" I shouted. "I'll go get him and take him home. One of you assholes will have to help me carry him if he's passed out!" I walked in the direction of the bathroom.

When I got there, Brandon was in the last stall, kneeling over the toilet seat. I was hoping he had thrown up already. I didn't want any smelly half-digested food particles in my car; it takes a while to get rid of that stench!

WTF MOMENT

"Are you all right in there, bro?" I asked.

"Yeah, I'm okay," he replied. "I just want to make sure I get everything out. Give me a minute. I'll be right out."

I felt bad for Brandon. I could only imagine what he was going through. *I'm still dealing with my separation, but it's nothing compared to this. These two have been married for fifteen years, right after their high school prom night. And for it to end like this? Well, I hadn't seen it coming. They seemed as though they'd be in love forever.*

I don't know how I did it, but I got Brandon home. He was wasted. I didn't see Ashley's car. Good thing she wasn't there. How awkward would it be, carrying her husband into the house passed out? I wonder what would go though her mind. Would she be a devilish woman who wouldn't give a damn, or would she be sympathetic? I searched Brandon's pockets, but I couldn't find his keys. *He probably dropped them at the bar*, I thought. I decided to take Brandon to my place instead.

God! I have to drag him up two flights of stairs. I was starting to get mad thinking about it, and then I realized how much pain Brandon must be in. He just caught his wife cheating with another woman! That must be damaging to a man's ego! I don't even know how I would feel if that happened to me!

I glanced at the backseat at Brandon. He was knocked out and snoring heavily. *He will definitely have a bad hangover in the morning!*

I don't know where I got the strength, but I got him upstairs and laid him on the couch. It was a good thing I worked out; it was not an easy feat carrying a man Brandon's size.

I didn't have extra blankets. I walked into my room and yanked the one off the bed and went back to the living room to lay it over Brandon. *I will be fine with layers of sweatshirts and pants.*

Brandon was passed out, curled in a fetus position like a little baby. Poor guy! It was a sad sight to watch. I have been there—heck, I'm still going through it.

I took off my shoes and headed to my room. I didn't even bother to change my clothes; I just jumped into my bed. I was beat.

The next morning, the sun's rays shining on my face woke me up. I tried blocking the light with my pillow to no avail. I could have sworn the sun rose a block away from my bedroom window. I had forgotten to pull the blinds before I went to bed. A darkened room makes me sleep longer. I peeped at the clock on the table, and it read 9:00 a.m. It was Saturday. I would have preferred to sleep in. I can't sleep in like that anymore these days. About five years ago, I could sleep thirteen hours straight with no problem. Nowadays I'm lucky to get six hours. I don't know whether that has anything to do with age. Maybe I just have too much on my mind and I subconsciously wake up. The only times I do sleep past six hours a night is when I'm out of town. I guess vacation eases the stress on the mind.

I slowly dragged myself out of bed thinking about what to do for the day. I had to pick up Emmanuella later on. I planned on taking her to a karate school not too far from my place. She had seen kids practicing when we drove by and told me she was interested. I didn't mind at all. I liked that she knew what she wanted at such a young age. It brought a smile to my face when I imagined her kicking some unruly boy's butt.

The sound of the television startled me as I was walking to the bathroom, and then I remembered Brandon had spent the night.

He was up watching college football on ESPN. He didn't notice me walk up. He seemed to be concentrating on the game. Either the game was really good, or he was working hard to distract himself and keep his mind from wandering.

"What's up, bro?" Brandon didn't hear me, so I said it louder. "What's happening, bro?"

He finally looked up. "Hey, man!" he replied. "Thanks for taking me out of the spot last night and for letting me crash over here."

"Don't sweat it, man," I said, as I gave him a playful nudge.

"Glad I didn't go home. I hate waking up and going to sleep there, especially with her in the other room. I swear to God, I want to go in there and choke the life out of that woman! I'm not even joking."

His voice was really low, and he sounded as if he was going to cry. It's a crazy combination when you wake up with a hangover and you still have to face the reality and hurt of a breakup. I have been there. One just has to hope one has a strong determination to get over it and a good support system.

I gave him a reassuring smile. "It's nothing, man . . . anytime, I got your back. So how are you feeling today?" I continued.

"Yeah, I'm all right. I have to keep it moving, you know? I'm ready to open a whole new chapter in my life."

I could tell he was in pain as he was trying to maintain a strong attitude on his new lease on life.

"I feel you, bro. There is nothing to it but to do it. You're just dealing with some potholes in the road right now. It's going to get better. It has to!" I said.

Brandon shook his head, looked into the distance, and said, "I sure hope so. I do hope so. I feel as though I'm living in the twilight zone."

WTF MOMENT

I gave him a pound, and once more reassured him that everything was going to be okay. We both watched the TV in silence for a while, so I tried to liven up the atmosphere a bit.

"Dude! Did you see the Panthers last night? A number eight team knocking out the number one? That is insane!"

"Yeah," he replied.

"Who would have thought? A bunch of outcast players who had nothing to lose just went all out and made history," I continued.

Brandon was barely listening. He was deep in thought. All he said was "Yeah" after each statement I made. He is a basketball fanatic. He would go watch the Panthers during the drought years when nobody was going to the games. He would buy season tickets and take his nephews and their buddies to the game once or twice a month.

Today basketball was the farthest thing on his mind.

He started to look around the living room. Then he said, "I see you're settling into the bachelor's life again, huh? Got your place hooked up. Did you kick your tenants out?"

"I had to. I gave them two months notice though. I didn't want to go pay rent elsewhere. You know?"

"Did you have to buy all new furniture too?"

"Actually, a friend moved away a few months back, and I bought most of his stuff."

"Man! I can't wait, bro, meeting new chicks and all. How has that been working for you? I bet you have women coming through here like it's a track meet."

"Yeah, right!" I said, as I walked over to the refrigerator. I took the milk carton out, poured some in the blender, and added soy protein powder, bananas, and flax.

"You know what? Actually I'm not even worried about any of these women. When the time comes, I will start dating. I know a couple of hotties I can call when I need to get my tune-up, if you know what I mean," I said, laughing.

"I can dig it."

"But it's really not about that though. Tell you the truth, I'm just working on me, on my issues and trying to get my life back in order. It isn't easy dealing with a divorce. I'm just trying to keep my head above water," I said, as I surveyed his face and handed him a glass of the protein shake I had just made.

"Yeah, I know what you mean. It's crazy for me right now. My life seems to be a different movie scene every day."

"I can imagine!"

He looked a bit calmer this morning compared to the evening before, but I felt his mind was in total disarray, dealing with the reality that a long-term relationship was no more. It's as if one's life becomes meaningless. All roads begin to lead nowhere, and you have to decide whether you want to keep drowning in your sorrows, or get out and search for a new beginning.

Brandon downed his glass and was eyeing the jug on the table, so I poured him another one. I knew he really needed to talk, some kind of a therapy.

"You and Ashley have been together like what? Fifteen years?" I began.

"Yup! Since high school, bro."

"You never saw any signs all this time? Nothing kind of suspicious?" I continued.

"No."

Brandon was beginning to think deeply now.

"But I will take that back. Maybe there were signs now that I'm thinking about it. I wasn't paying attention because I trusted her and didn't think she was ever into anyone else. She's a good actress. I have to give it to her. She was always out hanging with her girls, and I'm never the one to ask her not to go out. I've always thought freedom is needed for a healthy relationship. My father was overbearing and controlling, and I never wanted to be like him. Maybe I was too relaxed. She hung out with her friends way too often. Don't get me wrong, she and I hung out a lot too. But she would be with them when she wasn't with me."

"Humph," I muttered.

"Can you believe it? While I was fast asleep upstairs, someone was eating my wife's pussy in my house, right under my nose. That's really fucked up!" His voice began to crack.

"What did she even have to say about all this?"

"Nothing but, 'I'm so sorry, Brandon.' Can you believe that?" he bleated.

"You think she was curious?"

"Well, curiosity has killed the damn cat. No way am I going to forgive her for what she has done!"

I watched him as he looked out the window in deep thought. Then he let out a sigh and said, "I remember as if it was yesterday how we really started to gel. I would pick her up from school in my little Jalopy. We would go to the mall, holding hands."

"The Datsun 210, huh?" I asked, and we both bursted out laughing.

I reminisced on those days. Not a lot of high school kids had rides back then. Brandon was fortunate to have one. His dad gave him the car. You were a god if you had a set of wheels. You were still the *man* no matter how old your

WTF MOMENT

car was or how horrible it looked. Most students caught the bus or walked home. Very few were privileged.

About six of us would get into that little car and cruise around town doing nothing but wasting time and gas for hours. Thinking about it, kids have it good, no worries about bills or rent. We just went to school, did our homework, and played the rest of the time. Then we become adults, joined the rat race, and life became stressful.

"We had some fun in that Jalopy though," Brandon said, smiling as he went down memory lane.

"Remember when you were racing a guy in a Cadillac on I-240, and he dusted you? Your tire burst while you were driving one hundred miles an hour. We were some dumb kids. I don't know how you kept control of the car, but can you imagine if you had lost it? We would have been some dead knuckleheads!" I chuckled.

"Yeah, I think about some of the things we did when we were young, and I just shake my head," Brandon said, laughing.

"You know, even with your ride, you had no game," I chuckled.

"C'mon, man. No one had much game back then. You weren't having much sex in high school except if you had a steady girlfriend. Even that was hard; we all had to be home by a certain time."

"Speak for yourself. I didn't have that problem in high school, and I don't have it now," I said, giving him a sarcastic look.

"Yeah, whatever! You were no exception either, bro. If I remember correctly, we hung out together all the time, so you were a no-sex-having teenager too," he said, laughing.

"What? I didn't hang out with you all the time. I had a girlfriend in the tenth grade, one in the eleventh grade, and another in the twelfth grade!"

"And they all lasted but two weeks each," he said, laughing.

"Now you're exaggerating! You know they lasted more than two weeks," I said, chuckling.

"Hey, I know what I saw, and I'm only speaking the truth," Brandon continued.

"If someone decides to write an autobiography about me, I will definitely let the person know to stay clear of you. You tell phantom stories and make me look bad," I said, shaking my head.

"As I said." He sighed.

It was good to see him laugh and joke a little even though it was for a few minutes at a time.

Ashley and Brandon had definitely been inseparable after high school. They always played video games together—even recently. She was such a

47

tomboy when we were growing up. She ran track in high school and would even compete with us on the basketball court. All that changed when her body blossomed though.

Some Saturday nights at Brandon's were like Thanksgiving. Between those two, they had enough recipes to write ten cookbooks. When Ashley didn't feel like cooking, she never had to worry about it because Brandon would cook and clean. The house was always spotless.

Suddenly, he looked at me and said, "You know what? I shouldn't have gotten married at such a young age. I should have dated and waited until I was a bit older. I have to admit, it amazes me when a dude walks up to a lady in the club and whispers something in her ear, and ten minutes later, they are walking out together. It's like a magic trick to me. It always blows my mind. One day before I die, I want to be able to do that. I have to read some books about it or something."

I burst out laughing, "Dude, you're killing me!"

"I jumped at the first opportunity I saw. I was glad a beautiful woman like Ashley was into me. She laughed at my corny jokes. She made me happy. I was content with that," he said.

"You shouldn't beat yourself up, bro. You married her then because you were both into each other and loved each other. Maybe something made her do what she did, but that is up to her to reveal. I'm sure she loves you still," I said, trying to be diplomatic.

"Forget that! You don't do that to the person you love! Do you know that Yvette bitch stayed with us for about three months when she was having problems and had lost her job? I gave her food and shelter, and what do I get in return? She turned my woman out! That is the most fucked up shit ever!" he bleated.

"I never for one second thought she was ever into women. I have always thought we had a healthy relationship. Maybe I was too naive," he continued.

"Humph," I uttered.

"My Auntie Jane made a comment way back about Ashley hanging out with Yvette. 'Don't let your wife hang around nasty women,' she said to me. I laughed at her then thinking she was being old school, stuck in the Stone Age."

"The old folks do catch on to things like that," I added.

"Very true. I wish I had paid more attention. I just never thought . . .," He paused for a while. I could tell from his expression that he still couldn't believe what had transpired.

"How could she even do such a thing to me? We didn't have any problems, no fighting or anything like that. What the hell, man?!"

WTF MOMENT

He continued, "You know what? I've been so dumb. Things have been great between us. She never had problems when I wanted to travel or go out with the boys. She hardly had problems with anything. That should have raised some flags right there! I thought I was the guy with the coolest wife."

"She is selfish though," I said, chuckling. "I'm sure if she had mentioned she was into women, you wouldn't have objected."

"Hell, yeah! We would have worked it out. I would've been the happiest dude on earth. Going to bed with two women? Can you imagine?" he asked, chuckling.

"You're crazy."

"But on a serious note, we have been together for a long time you know?" he continued.

"Yeah, I know."

"Fifteen long years down the tube over some bullshit! I can't even understand it," he lamented.

"I know how you feel, man. I still get depressed regularly thinking about my situation. But you know what? You will get over this. It's not going to be easy, but you will look back at this as a learning experience. I'm always here for you if you need me," I said, and I gave him a pound just to assure him he wasn't alone.

Brandon sighed heavily and said, "Thanks, man . . . thanks, man."

I stood up and went to my cabinet in the kitchen for some Malibu rum and Coke.

"To hell with it! We are going to drink our sorrows away. You want some ice?" I yelled from the kitchen.

"More rum and less ice," he replied, laughing.

Although it was still early in the morning, I felt Brandon needed some love, so we drank and joked some more.

The weekend came and went quickly. I had hung out with both Emmanuella and Brandon.

Emmanuella had asked me, "Is Uncle Brandon your roommate now, Daddy?"

"Uncle is just hanging out for the weekend," I responded to her.

I laughed, thinking, *how could a three-and-a-half-year-old little person come up with stuff like that? How did she know what roommate meant?*

* * *

Brandon called me before closing Monday afternoon. He wanted me to pick him up from work. He had gone straight to work from my house that morning.

49

When I arrived, I saw him sitting on the stairs at the high school building where he taught math.

"What's up, man?" he belted out.

"I can't complain. What is going on with ya?"

As soon as he closed the car door, he pulled out a joint and started rolling it.

"Give me some of that good smoke. I had to deal with some crap at the gym earlier today. I need to relax," I said.

He looked at me as though I were crazy. "When did you start smoking again?" he asked as his eyes lit up.

"I smoke every now and then. I just don't go out of my way to buy any. I try not to cultivate a bad habit."

I reminded him of the time we last smoked together. I was driving thirty-five miles an hour on a sixty-five-mile zoned freeway. There was a black Caprice that followed us for miles. I swore it was a cop. The bastard driving the car must have been messing with us too. He stayed behind us the whole time just like the highway patrol would do. I was so paranoid; I almost peed in my pants. All I was thinking was how embarrassing it would have been to be stopped by the police for being too high. I was relieved when the Caprice finally passed us. It was an old lady driving. She must have had some cognitive issues. There was no way she could have been driving as slowly as we were.

"I love this ride of yours, man," Brandon said, as he continued rolling his joint.

"It's all right."

"Just all right? You're driving a hundred-thousand-dollar, top-of-the-line BMW, bro! A 760Li at that! You must be crazy!"

"It's just a car bro."

"Whatever, man, this is a honey magnet right here. Give it to me then if it's just a car. You can keep my old beat-up Chevy truck and let me have your lake-view condo too while you're it," he said, laughing.

"You're nuts," I said, laughing as well.

Brandon then asked me to take him home since he hadn't been there all weekend. We made it in twenty minutes. We walked straight to the den where he had been staying. *How ironic*, I thought. His clothes and things were all over the place. I almost turned an ankle when I tripped on a shoe. I went straight to his computer to browse the Internet. I couldn't find the switch. I turned around to ask him, but he wasn't there. I was about to yell out his name when he returned with two bottles of Snapple. He must have read my mind, as he pointed to where the switch was.

"So how are you and Ashley doing?"

WTF MOMENT

"How are we doing?" he hissed. "I can't stand looking at her! I can't wait 'til we end this. This roommate thing we got going on is not working for me. The fact that I have to wake up and see her every morning sends chills down my spine. She won't move out, and I'm not leaving either. I'm not going to give her any kind of satisfaction. She can kiss my ass!"

"What do you want to do?"

I could see the vein popping on Brandon's head. He walked around the room pacing. I was hoping I would be able to cheer him up by being here, but he seemed to want to vent. I know it had to be hard on him. It had to hurt finding out that his wife was sleeping with another woman. That was too much of a lump to swallow and would be worse if other people talked about it.

The embarrassment would kill most men. Brandon didn't care if she cheated with a woman or man. The fact that she cheated with anyone drove him nuts. He complained bitterly to anyone who would care to listen. I had to shut him up a few times when we were out at the bar. "This is not the kind of laundry you air out," I told him. He must really have been hurting; he was a total wreck. He had been drinking more and had gained at least thirty pounds.

"She is the one who cheated, right? Why is she walking around here as though it's okay? I'm supposed to just forget that it happened? She needs to just move out! I should throw all her things out right now!" he lamented.

"C'mon, you're not going to do such a thing. You have to take it easy. I know your emotions are running high right now. Why don't you stay with me for a while until things calm down?"

"Are you serious? I'm not leaving this freaking house. She should leave!" he barked.

"Okay, I'm just making a suggestion. I don't think it is healthy for you both to continue living under these conditions. You know what I'm saying?"

"Well, I'm not going anywhere!" he added.

"Okay," I said. I wasn't going to push the issue anymore.

"I need to find a good realtor. I need to sell this house ASAP and get out of here."

"It is going to be a tough sell, bro. The market is upside down. Homes have lost considerable value. You would be selling at a loss if you chose to do that now."

"I don't give a damn. I just want to get rid of it!"

I decided to keep quiet, listen, and let him rant on. He was in so much pain; I was really worried for him.

Brandon turned on the TV in the den. We watched in silence. Then I heard the rattling sound of keys at the front door.

Ashley walked in moments later. She'd probably seen my car in the driveway, so she walked over to the den and poked her head in.

"Hey," she said, talking to us both. Brandon wasn't paying attention to her. He was back on the computer working on something. Ashley turned her attention to me.

"How have you been, Devin?"

"I've been good," I replied. "How was work?"

"It has been a long day. They have used and abused me, and I'm getting ready to quit," she replied, laughing.

Brandon suddenly shouted, "You're damn right you're used and abused! Cheat! Why are you in here? Why don't you just go back to where you just came from? Better yet, why don't you just go to Yvette's? Call some other whore friends of yours, and you all can have one big orgy. How about that? You make me sick!"

Brandon was upset now. I was sitting there trying not to look either of them in the eye. It was an awkward moment.

"Good seeing you, Devin."

"Good seeing you too," I said.

She walked upstairs to the bedroom.

I was going to tell Brandon to take it easy but decided against it. I was sure he was more than hurt at the moment. I didn't want to make him feel he wasn't supported. So I sat there watching TV and making small talk.

"Let's go get something to eat," I said, finally.

"Yeah. Good idea. Let's go to Ester's BBQ Joint."

I was elated with his response. It was the best news I had heard all day. We hopped in my car and headed downtown. I glanced in my rearview mirror and saw the upstairs bedroom curtain close. Ashley must have been watching us leave.

5. Along Came Amanda, Part 1

The alarm on my phone started to sound. I reached over and pressed the snooze button hoping for another five minutes of sleep. The time was 6:45 a.m.

It never fails. I always end up pushing the godforsaken snooze button for the next hour until 7:45 a.m. Then I rush in a frantic pace to get out of the house to make it to work on time, which rarely ever happens. I'm not a morning person, but I've always gotten up early for work. Sometimes I wish I could unplug from the real-life matrix.

As a business owner, I could afford to get to work much later, but I try to set a good example by getting there as early as possible. I train a couple of clients who prefer to work out early. I could delegate to other trainers, but I like to be hands on. I think most of my clients appreciate that I'm accessible as an owner, and I also get to listen to their concerns firsthand.

I finally dragged myself out of bed at 7:30 a.m. I turned my phone on and saw a text message. It was from Amanda. We had just started dating recently. I was secretly hoping she would bring some stability into my life. It had been a little over a year since my separation with the ex.

From: Amanda
Thanks for not calling yesterday! I could have been in a ditch somewhere!
Shows how much you care!

Okay? The text was strange! She was aware I had my daughter this past weekend. Why would she even send such a text?

Amanda is a pretty woman and very smart. At twenty-nine years of age she had recently become a project manager at one of the leading pharmaceutical companies in the country. She stands at five eight, with long, toned legs that are to die for. With high heels on, she could easily be six feet tall. As full figured as she is, she attracts attention anywhere she goes.

When I made my quick survey, I estimated her measurements to be 40-28-42. I especially like her smooth, nice skin. It is easy to tell she takes really good care of it. She has a heart-shaped face, complemented with succulent, full lips. She wears her hair short and spiky. Her eyes are deep set, which gives me the illusion she is always trying to read me, watching me.

We had met at a local singer's album release party at Mood's. Tammy, a mutual friend, had introduced us. I noticed Amanda was really striking. She wore a black cat suit. She got plenty of stares all evening. We spoke briefly. She seemed aloof, though, conceited even. She stood in the same corner all night shutting down all comers who tried to hold a conversation with her. I think she only spoke to me because of our mutual friend.

I thought she was good looking, but I wasn't going to jock her. She struck me as one of those women who likes attention and gets a thrill out of turning guys down. The irony of it all is you scratch your head when you see the goofballs these women actually fall for.

I bought her and Tammy drinks and moved on to socializing. We threw each other a few glances here and there, but otherwise, paid each other no mind. At the end of the evening, I asked Amanda whether I could call her sometime.

"We will see each other again," she said smirking, followed by an annoying smile—one of those "Why did you even bother to ask me for my number?" smiles.

"We might," I shot back with a smile, not giving her time to enjoy her little "I just turned you down" charade.

"You beautiful ladies drive home safely," I added.

"You do the same," Tammy responded. Amanda simply waved.

I saw her twice after our initial meeting. We just said hello and kept it moving. A few months later, we ran into each other at a wedding. She was one of the bridesmaids, and the groom was my cousin. *Small world*, I thought. She talked to me more at the reception, as though she had known me for years. I had been the matchmaker for the marrying couple. They had both come to a boot camp class I taught about two years ago.

At the wedding reception, Amanda and I talked about the business idea she and a friend were brainstorming. Our conversation lasted a while. Then she asked me for my number, citing she needed to continue picking my brain about business.

To my pleasant surprise, she texted me the very next morning.

WTF MOMENT

From: Amanda
It was nice chatting with you yesterday, mister! You were different from what I had thought of you initially. Thanks for the pep talk. Chat soon. Amanda

To: Amanda
Different? Whatever that means, lol, but we will talk about it the next time we see each other. ☺ What are you doing right now anyway? I'm thinking of grabbing brunch at Tropicana. Are you free? Perhaps, you could join me if you are? ☺

From: Amanda
Sure . . . sounds good. What time?

To: Amanda
I'm shooting for noon. Work for you?

From: Amanda
Yes! I will be there!

To: Amanda
By the way, do you know where Tropicana is?

From: Amanda
I think I do, sir! If I get lost, I will call you ☺ See you then.

    I arrived at Tropicana at about ten minutes before noon. It was modestly crowded on a semi-chilly day. On sunny days, the spot is usually packed to the rim because of its large back patio. I ordered a mimosa while I waited for Amanda. I hoped she wasn't one of those women who make guys wait just for the hell of it. She had seemed a little stuck up initially, but speaking to her last night, I got a sense she put up a front and persona—the "I don't care about anyone or anything. I'm the bomb. Please don't speak to me!" attitude—but underneath, she is a sweet nice person.
    From where I was standing, I could see everyone walking through the door.
    Before long, there she was, strolling in at about 12:05 a.m. *Good timing*, I thought. She was striking, as usual, and she walked as though she knew it. She flashed a smile when she noticed where I was and walked toward me. This wasn't one of those smirks from our previous encounter.

One thing I do like about her smile is her straight and pearly white set of teeth. Amanda is a voluptuous woman and carries all her assets quite well. It was funny watching an older gentleman next to me grinning from ear to ear as Amanda approached, and then making his face go blank when his wife returned from the restroom.

We hugged, but it wasn't the side hug and light back pat I had gotten from her before. This time, it was a full-on, tight embrace. I could feel her breasts on my pecs. After what seemed to be about twenty seconds, we separated, and she flashed a smile.

"There goes that gorgeous smile again!"

"Well, thank you, sir."

She wore a white, slightly transparent strapless blouse; I don't even know how her breasts remained contained in it. I could see her protruding nipples, and I tried not to stare. I kept looking at her directly in the eyes as we spoke. Her tight-fitting, stretch black pants complemented her thighs and butt nicely. Her inquisitive eyes made her look cute—as though she were a baby. I was almost tempted to pull on her cheeks and say, "You're so cute," but I knew better. Most women hate when you tell them they are as cute as babies.

Without being too obvious, we discreetly sized each other up. I never try to overdo it. I think it makes a man look desperate. Even when a woman is very sexy, the appropriate thing to do is to give her a compliment and maintain eye contact. Never over compliment and gnaw at a woman's body. I think I did a pretty good job keeping my eyes in their sockets, and I remained calm and collected throughout the hangout.

She was even more beautiful than I had thought. She wore open-toe, two-inch-high heels. Her feet were well pedicured with nails polished in a neutral color. I find bright colored toenails like pink and turquoise very unattractive.

"So!" I began. "Why do you think I'm different now from the man you met a while ago?"

"I can't really explain it. I just think you are." She laughed.

"You're still not telling me anything. I think you didn't care to know who I am. You seemed to be uninterested. Maybe if you had taken time out to have a normal heart-to-heart conversation with me without the preconceived notions, you might have thought differently."

"You're right. I felt you knew too many people, and I don't like my business out there. I'm a very private person. No offense, I thought you were a whore too," she said.

"Whoa! That's kind of mean and harsh to say to someone you hardly know!" I responded, sighing.

WTF MOMENT

"I didn't mean it to come out like that. I apologize. I just saw too many women around you whenever I saw you out in public. You're good looking, you have an amazing body, your boot camp class is always full of women, and you own the popular and successful Five Star Gym too. So you see why it was natural for me to think as such." She stared at me with her inquiring eyes, smiling slyly, as though she was saying to herself, *Yeah, player! Let's see how you're going to respond to this one!*

"Well." I gently grabbed her by the hand and pulled her closer looking directly in her eyes. "The kind of work I do requires I'm around lots of women, but that shouldn't make me less of a gentleman. You're a beautiful woman, and I'm sure the minute you walk out of your house daily, there is a guy trying to talk to you—heck trying to sleep with you even—but you don't take every guy up on his offer, do you?"

"Hmm, you may have a point, but guys are not the same as us women," she said, playfully taking her hand away.

"How so?" I asked, sarcastically.

"You guys think with your *you-know-whats*, you all can sleep with many women without any feelings of attachment. Most women tend to be more emotional when it comes to sex. We can't just sleep around."

"Well, I beg to differ. Some women do the same."

"I won't argue, mister. That's why I said *most* women and not *all* women."

"If a guy gets emotional especially after just meeting a woman, he is seen as being sprung, pussy-whipped, needy, and psycho. You women run away from him. It's such a double standard."

"I will tell you what a double standard is, mister! If a woman sleeps around like you men do, then she is labeled a whore, but its okay when a guy does it!" she said, sighing.

"Women want to do it as much as we want to. The only difference is that guys have to do the chasing most of the time. Think about it! A guy has to talk to ten women just to find one who really gives him a chance. He's got a one in ten probability of scoring. So it might appear he is running around trying to get with all these women, but, in actuality, he is casting a wider net to catch one fish."

"You're a philosopher now, mister?"

"I'm just saying it is what it is. I can only relate to what I've seen and experienced. You have to always take a closer look and be less judgmental."

"That is a cop-out statement," she said, sighing.

"No it is not. Listen, I love sex as much as the next man, and I could make a woman sing hallelujah, but it's not that serious. As good as sex feels, I'm not losing sleep if I don't get it every night. If I do, fine. If I don't, that is okay too. I'm too busy to be trying to chase after panties all day."

"Hallelujah, huh?"

"Yup, hallelujah!" I responded, laughing.

She rolled her eyes and said, "Anyway, just because you might be an exception to the rule doesn't change the fact that about ninety percent of men just want to sex women down the first chance they get."

"I will let you tell it," I said, smiling.

I looked at my watch; we had been hanging out for almost two hours. The place was emptying out. We must have sipped six glasses of mimosas between the two of us.

"We don't want to close the spot now do we?" I asked, as I playfully touched her chin. She looked up at me with those seductive eyes of hers.

"So what's next?"

"Well, we can continue the party at my place. I have some new movies I've been meaning to watch. And I do make some mean mimosas too."

"Is that so?" she quipped.

"Very much so," I said, smiling.

"Where do you stay again?"

"I'm over by Lake Morgan in Brookdale."

"Nice area."

"It's all right," I responded, laughing.

"Should we go now then?"

"Let's! You can leave your car here. I can bring you back later," I said, as I guided her out of the restaurant.

"No, I think I'll drive. I don't trust my car would be safe here, and besides, I have to go see my sister in Linden City afterward."

"Whatever works for you, sweetie," I said, smiling at her.

She gave me the look again and hopped into her car. She drove a Volvo C20 coupé. Probably a '08 or '07 edition. *Safe and practical,* I thought.

"You lead the way, and I'll follow," she yelled out of her window.

"Really? You would follow me anywhere?"

"Not anywhere, mister! Don't get ahead of yourself. I'm ready whenever you are," she said, laughing.

I turned my engine on, gave it a little gas, and put the gear in reverse. I heard her honk as my car came close to her front bumper.

"I'm not even close to you, damn it!" I playfully yelled at her, and then I realized she couldn't even hear me because both our windows were up. I kind

WTF MOMENT

of liked this woman. It was refreshing to see a playful woman who didn't take herself too seriously.

I pulled out of the parking lot and headed toward the I-460 freeway. *I hope she keeps up with me.*

I could have sworn we had agreed she would follow me. She was flying on the freeway as if she knew where to go. She would pass me up then slow down for me to catch up, wave and then she would be gone again. *This woman is so silly*, I thought, laughing.

I saw my exit come up, so I sped up to pass her and signaled for her to follow me. I was in the middle lane, so I made my way to the far right lane to get ready to exit the freeway. For a few seconds, I couldn't see her anywhere. Then all of sudden, I saw this car veer from the fast lane on the far left all the way behind me.

It was Amanda! I think a few drivers slammed on their brakes to avoid a collision with her car. *Why did she wait until the last minute to change lanes?* I shook my head. *This woman could kill someone driving like a maniac*!

We made it to my place a few minutes later. I parked on the side street next to my building, and she pulled up behind me.

I sighed as she got out of her car. "I'm glad I wasn't the one following you. Wow!"

She gave me a disapproving look and asked, "What do you mean?"

"That you're fast on the gas."

"I still don't know what you're talking about," she said, smiling.

"Looks like someone here must have amnesia."

"I may drive a little crazy, but don't we all?"

"We all do, but I think you're in a class all by yourself."

"You can tell all this by observing my driving in just a day?"

"What I saw today is all the confirmation I need. I bet you have a lot of speeding tickets too, huh?"

"Well, mister, I will have you know I've gotten one speeding ticket in my lifetime, and I've been driving for ten years. Humph! What do you have to say about that?"

"I've had a few, and most weren't my fault," I responded.

"And what exactly is a few?"

"I think three or maybe four."

"Uh huh? Which one is it? Three or four?" she joked, sarcastically.

"Well, I think it's three. But that's beside the point. As I have said, all those tickets were questionable, with the exception of one."

59

"Why am I not surprised you would say that?" she continued.

"But it's true."

"Most people never want to admit they are wrong. You got caught speeding. End of story," she said, sighing.

"You know what's crazy? I drive carefully most of the time but the moment I stray off once in a while, I get ticketed. Someone as yourself who drives crazy all the time never gets stopped. Life is so unfair." It was my turn to sigh.

"Well, my dear. That's the way the cookie crumbles," she said, laughing.

"Whatever!"

"Oooh! Don't be bitter," she said, pulling my cheeks.

I threw her a disgusted expression in response.

"Let's go upstairs, shall we? I would prefer talking to you while lying on my couch."

"I was getting comfortable down here actually."

"Yeah, okay, if you say so, smarty pants," I said, laughing.

My condo was toasty as we walked in. I ran to open up the windows. I had forgotten to turn the heater off when I left in the morning. It had been a little chilly, and I wasn't trying to catch a cold walking around a freezing house after a shower.

"Sorry it's so hot in here," I said, as I walked to the closet to hang our coats.

"It's okay. I'm anemic; I like it hot anyway."

"I think most women are anemic. You all complain about how cold it is even when it's seventy degrees outside."

"Hey, hey, that is how God made us. We are warm-blooded creatures unlike you cold-blooded men."

"There you go again with your male-bashing business."

"Humph!" she responded.

She took her shoes off and walked around the living room. She examined the paintings on the wall and complimented me on how they looked. She sifted through my DVD collections and then turned her attention to my CDs. She picked out Sade and Prince, and handed them to me to play.

Sade is always a good choice to set the mood right, I thought, smiling.

Amanda started to sway her head back and forth to the music.

"What do you know about Sade?" I asked.

"Please! What do you know about Sade?" she shot back.

"You saw it in my collection, didn't you?"

"That doesn't mean you know anything about her. Someone could have brought it over here and forgotten it," she said, laughing.

WTF MOMENT

"I see you got jokes."

"Humph! I probably can recite the words of each song to you," she continued.

"Yeah?" I asked, as I gazed at her playfully. She flirted back at me with her eyes and smiled.

I watched as she swayed her hips to "No Ordinary Love." She found her way to the window. I crept up behind her and gently placed my hands on her hips and pulled closer. She extended her hands over her head and started to rub the back of my neck and head while still looking out the window. I leaned over her shoulder and kissed her neck gently. She closed her eyes as I moved my hands from her hips up her sides. She let me for a short while, and then she pulled my hands away, turned around, and stared at me without saying a word. We continued to gaze at each other for several seconds, and then I pulled her closer until our noses touched. I could hear both of us breathing. I placed my lips on hers, and they simultaneously parted. The Sade CD playing in the background amplified the seductive moments as we kissed.

We finally came up for air after what seemed to be fifteen minutes of interlocking lips and saliva exchange.

"Phew!" she gasped.

She slowly walked away from me while still holding my hand, so I followed her as she navigated her way to where my paintings hung. She asked me where I'd gotten them from and what they meant to me. One was from Africa and another from Malaysia. I explained to her I liked the uniqueness of each. Amanda had noticed that one of the paintings was slanted, so she readjusted it.

"I really love your place," she said, as she looked around.

"Thanks."

"It isn't cluttered. You have enough space to move around. Most of your things are simple yet classy. Some people have too much going on in their place. You know what I mean?"

"Right," I responded.

"A hardwood floor does it for me every time. I would pay for the killer view you have too. Don't you love it? You can see everything from your window!"

"I guess," I responded, smiling.

She proceeded to sit on the sofa and pulled me down next to her.

"Tell me more about yourself, mister."

"What do you want to know?" I asked, sounding innocent.

"Anything," she said, squeezing my hand.

I turned the music down while we talked for what seemed like hours. We ended up watching a documentary on HBO. She fell asleep first, and after a while, I followed suit, holding her in my arms.

"Devin, wake up."

"What's up?" I asked, startled.

"I don't believe we slept that long. It's 10:00 p.m. already. I have to get going."

"Oh okay," I said, half asleep.

She got up and went to the bathroom, came back, and slid back into her open-toe pumps.

"Is my jacket in the closet over there?"

"Yeah, I'll get it for you in a second."

"No, it's okay. I can get it," she said.

"I got it. I'm getting up to walk you downstairs anyway."

"Okay! You know you don't have to."

"I know I don't have to! But I want to," I chimed.

I walked her downstairs, and before she hopped into her car, she gave me a full, wet, juicy kiss. "Thank you. We should do this again really soon. I really enjoyed being with you today, Devin."

"My pleasure. We should definitely do it again. Drive home safely."

She hopped into her car and sped off into the night.

6. Interlude

Kenny was on the phone with his ten-year-old son, Kenny Junior—KJ. They hadn't talked in over a week. KJ was excited and telling his dad about the new soccer season and how great he had been performing.

"Good job, KJ. Remember it's a team sport, so you have to share the ball with your teammates," Kenny said.

Kenny had the phone pressed to his ear, waiting for a response from KJ when he heard Robert's voice in the background. It got louder which meant he was probably walking toward KJ. The next words Kenny heard were "Get your little ass off the phone! It's all you do all day—stay on the phone. How come you haven't taken out the garbage as I asked you? Your little bitch ass better get off the phone right now and do what I asked you to do!"

Blood rushed into Kenny's brain as Robert's words rang in his ears. Just to confirm he had heard what he thought he'd heard, he asked KJ, "Who was Robert talking to?"

KJ hesitated. Kenny asked him the question again.

"He was talking to me, Dad," KJ finally replied.

"Get your mom on the phone now!" he yelled at KJ.

Moments later, Tracy picked up the phone.

"What?" she asked.

"Did you hear Robert talking to KJ just now? You allow him to do that? A grown man talking to a little kid as such! I'm on my way right now to settle this!" screamed Kenny.

"Kenny, please don't! He probably had a bad day," Tracy pleaded.

"His bad day is about to get worse. Can you believe that? Talking to my kid like that? Who the hell does he think he is? You sure know how to pick 'em," Kenny said, as he hung up the phone fuming.

BOLAJI TIJANI-QUDUS

He ran into his room, tucked an object into his pants, and pulled his shirt over it.

Seconds later, Kenny was screeching out of his driveway.

* * *

Blinded with rage, Kenny sped toward his ex-wife's home. It was normally a thirty-minute drive on a regular day, but Kenny seemed to have made it there in ten minutes. He could see the living room lights as he approached the driveway. The front windows were open. He saw Tracy and Robert arguing.

"This fool doesn't even know who he is dealing with," Kenny mumbled to himself as he stepped out of his car. Seconds later, he kicked open the front door and yelled, "Who the fuck gave you permission to talk to my son like that?!"

"Please, Kenny, let it go," Tracy started to plead again. She knew how angry Kenny could get, and there was no telling what he would do. His angry tantrums had scared her a few times in the past.

"What are you going to do, storming in here like Robocop?!" Robert yelled back, moving forward and rolling up his shirtsleeves.

Tracy jumped in front of Robert and held him back, crying and pleading with both men.

"You're a bitch just like the little bitch over there you call a son," Robert continued.

Tracy's look of fear turned into one of bewilderment and disbelief. "Why do you have to say such a thing?" she asked. Robert took his eyes off Kenny and looked down at Tracy in order to scold her. By the time he looked back up, Kenny was airborne and flying toward him.

The next thing Robert heard was Kenny's closed fist cracking his forehead. Robert fell backward, hitting the back of his head on the floor. Kenny was on him immediately, hitting him in the face with both fists. He kept hammering away before Robert could even comprehend what was happening to him.

Suddenly, Tracy jumped on Kenny's back and held him in a full nelson lock. She had taken some self-defense classes in college so she knew a thing or two about how to apprehend someone. She held on to him with all the strength she could muster.

Robert regained some of his senses and took advantage of the situation. He reached for a table lamp and hit Kenny on the head with it while Tracy was still holding him. Blood flowed from the side of Kenny's head as he fell to the ground. Tracy jumped between the two men as Robert was about to deliver

WTF MOMENT

another blow. Robert gave her a hard shove, and she went flying across the living room floor.

As Robert lunged forward at Kenny, two shots rang out. Robert froze as the first bullet hit him in the chest. He dropped onto his knees as the other shot whizzed past his head. Robert was soon lying on the floor wide-eyed.

"You bitch! You shot me," he whimpered.

The look on Kenny's face had changed from anger to fear. *What have I done?* he thought, as he lowered his gun and stared at Robert.

A scream tore through the still night.

"Wake up KJ! Please wake up, baby!"

KJ had been listening and peeping from behind the kitchen door. The second bullet had dug through the door and had hit him in the stomach. Kenny ran into the kitchen and was in shock to find his son lying on the floor, bleeding. The boy's eyes were beginning to roll to the back of his head. He was having a seizure.

Kenny dropped his gun, moved Tracy aside, and lifted KJ off the ground screaming, "Nooooooo!"

Sirens wailed in the distance.

7. Heat of the Moment

I had just sped across town driving a hundred miles an hour trying to catch up with Kenny. I was watching TV at his house, when the phone drama unfolded in the other room. I overhead most of the yelling and before I could calm Kenny down he was out the door.

The whole time I was driving, my mind was going in different directions. I hoped he hadn't done anything stupid. I kept thinking about the look on his face when he left his house. I had seen that facial expression several times before—good things rarely happened afterward.

Despite all my speeding and crazy driving, I got to Kenny's ex in one piece, and I was glad I hadn't run into any police officers. If I had been stopped, I would have gotten a hefty ticket for reckless driving. Then again, I probably would have told the police officers I was on my way to prevent a homicide, and they might have provided me with an escort instead.

When I arrived at Tracy's house, I expected to see sirens, police cars, ambulances, and yellow tapes.

Instead on the side street, I found Kenny sitting in his car staring into space with his cocked gun on his lap. I swallowed hard, hoping against the worst. I walked over to the passenger side and knocked on the window gently.

"Kenny?"

I was very alert in case I needed to duck and make a run for it. He might have just shot someone. He might still be in a rage. He could turn around and shoot me too and then himself. Perhaps that was what he was contemplating as he sat there.

Kenny slowly looked over at me and pressed the unlock button. I opened the door and cautiously took a seat.

"Umm, is everything okay, bro?" I asked.

"I didn't go in there if that's what you mean."

WTF MOMENT

I breathed a sigh of relief. *I wouldn't know how to deal with the aftermath if this guy had to go to jail for murder. It would be a big mess and too many people's lives would be destroyed,* I thought.

I was glad nothing bad had happened. *The man upstairs must have been watching.*

I asked him what had happened and why he was calm and subdued.

"I had a dream, I think it was an epiphany or divine intervention or whatever you want to call it," he replied.

"Well, that's good, right?" I asked, sounding supportive. Truth of the matter is, I was ecstatic. Whatever religious experience he just had might have saved his life too.

"That was what prevented me from going in there and blasting that idiot to kingdom come," he continued.

"You did the right thing, man; he's not even worth it."

"Yeah, and you know what else calmed me down?"

"What?"

"I thought of KJ. How can I be the best father I can possibly be if I'm behind bars?"

"You couldn't have made a better choice than you did tonight, bro. Tell you what,.I think there are some cold beers at the bar with our names on 'em."

I was really trying to get him out of there as quickly as I could.

Kenny is one of the nicest guys on the planet, but when he gets upset, you'd better hope you're not his enemy. He has no stomach for any kind of injustice and hates when people take advantage of others.

I saw him take on five guys from an opposing basketball team in one day. The guys were roughing Phil and me up because we had been running the courts.

Kenny went off on those guys. We had to hold him and beg him to let it go. The other guys were scared too. They didn't know what to make of him—was he crazy or did he have a death wish?

When it comes down to it, I like to have Kenny around when things go sour. He is the kind of guy who has your back no matter what. If any of the crew gets into a tangle, he jumps in, no questions asked. He doesn't care whether you're right or wrong. His friends are his friends for life. Guys always try to test each other's manhood at clubs, so I am always comfortable whenever Kenny is around.

I remember when a guy grabbed a lady I was dating by the arm. She politely told him she was with me and pointed in my direction. The guy was drunk and didn't care; he was still all over my date. Before I could make up my mind on what I was going to do, Kenny was on the guy like white on rice. He had no choice but to back off.

I was going to ask Kenny what he wanted to do when we saw Robert leaving the house. He slowly drove past us with a disgusted look on his face. I prayed Kenny wouldn't do anything crazy. He still had his gun. Fortunately he kept his cool. Tracy and KJ were standing at the doorway. Kenny stepped out of his car and started to walk toward them.

"Just tell her to keep her husband in check. No need to argue with her."

"Don't worry. We will settle this tonight. I'm going to make sure this doesn't happen again or I will have to go to the court and get full custody of my son," he said, reassuring me.

I hung around in case Robert came back. I didn't want to be on the seven o'clock news, in the middle of a domestic violence report.

8. Introspect

Kenny met me at the gym. and we drove to Mood's. It was nice to catch up. A few months had passed since the episode at his ex-wife's house.

There were a couple of people at the bar when we walked in. The bartender must have been bored out of his mind because he was excited when he saw us. Before we could even sit down, he quickly asked us what we wanted.

"Two Heinekens please," I requested.

"Coming right up, gentlemen."

We soon found a table not too far from a giant flat screen.

"Sorry you had to witness all that craziness the last time, bro," Kenny began.

"Don't worry about it. I know how it is. We are supposed to be there for each other. You're not talking to someone who is new to this kind of thing," I said, smiling.

"Yeah, I know. By the way, what's going on with you and the wifey?" he asked.

"Same bull crap, nothing has changed. It's unfortunate we are still tied together because our daughter. I'm tired of battling with her over money and spousal support."

"Doesn't she work?"

"Not right now, so I have to cough up some dough to support her lifestyle because I'm the only one with an income," I said, sighing.

"I feel for you man! You're over here slaving to support an ex. Did she get the house too?"

"You know she did. Why she is insistent on staying in that huge house is beyond me."

Kenny shook his head. "Damn! Someone else is probably sleeping with her in the house you're paying for."

"Don't even get me started," I said, clenching the beer bottle. If I had held it any tighter, I would have broken it.

"Bro! I feel your pain. You know I have been there and done that," Kenny said, patting me on the shoulder.

"Why can't life be so simple?" I asked.

"I wish I had the answer to your question," he replied.

We were still nursing our drinks and chatting on, when Justin walked in. I had seen him around quite a bit, and we had developed a good rapport. He is the lead singer of the house band at Mood's. They have a pretty nice following. His fiancée is a background singer in the band as well. You hardly ever saw them apart.

Justin walked over and gave us hearty hugs.

Kenny got up and went to the bathroom. I guess the beer was starting to kick in.

"What's up, Justin?" I asked. "What are you doing up here? I thought you guys performed only on weekends."

"I came to pick up some mics I need for rehearsal. We're performing at a jazz festival on Saturday," Justin replied.

"Oh yeah, you guys are opening up, huh? Do you have extra tickets for me?"

"No problem," Justin said, as he looked around. I figured he was trying to locate the bartender.

Kenny appeared from his visit to the men's room.

"I feel ten pounds lighter," he said.

"I was wondering what took you so long in there," I said, laughing.

"I need to replenish though. I could start with a sandwich." He flipped through the menu. He grabbed his beer bottle and gobbled down the remainder.

A waitress approached our table in time for us to get reloaded. I asked her for two additional bottles of Heineken.

"Can I get one of those as well?" Justin requested.

"I would also like the chicken wings and a side order of fries," Kenny added.

"No problem," she said.

"Hey, Kenny!" I said, pointing to Justin. "This young man here is getting married next month."

"Is that right? Another one bites the dust. I'm only joking! Congratulations, man," Kenny said, as he playfully grabbed Justin.

"So what advice do you gentlemen have for a guy who is about to jump the broom?" Justin asked us both.

"I think you're asking the wrong guys here. I'm happily divorced, and Devin is about to be. I don't think you want any advice from us," Kenny said, laughing.

WTF MOMENT

"C'mon, Ken, don't scare the young man. He has a good thing going for himself. Please don't corrupt him. We should be encouraging him," I said, giving Kenny a playful, begrudging look.

Justin pulled a stool over next to us and sat down like a schoolboy about to take some real life lessons.

"I'm sure I can learn a thing or two from you guys," he said.

Kenny asked him how long he had been with his fiancée. He responded by saying they had been together for three years.

"You've got yourself a nice gal there," I said. "I remember when you two started to really hang out. You had an ear-to-ear smile when you both sat over there in the corner practicing your music before the other band members arrived."

"Thanks," said Justin. "I appreciate it. We are excited about the wedding. I'm really elated! I proposed to her on Valentine's Day. We were the opening act at the soul fest. I asked her to marry me in front of the crowd. I stopped in the middle of our set, turned around, dropped down on one knee, and asked her. She said yes, and the place erupted. There had to have been at least seven thousand people cheering us on."

"That was really nice," I said, with an appreciative smile. "Women love romance."

"Can I ask you guys a personal question?" Justin asked.

"Sure," Kenny and I responded simultaneously.

"When did you figure it was time to get married? Sorry, I know it didn't quite work out for you guys."

"Don't sweat it," I told him. "Please don't hesitate to ask all kinds of questions with regard to marriage. For me, I guess it felt good, but I would say it was more of a convenience for us. We had been spending a lot of time with each other, and then we did it. There was no proposal or anything of the sort."

Justin turned to Kenny hoping to get his version. After a minute of reflection, Kenny finally laughed and said, "I don't even remember how it happened. Isn't that something you should never forget?"

Justin and I laughed along with Kenny.

"I think I just asked her one day, and she said okay. It wasn't as spectacular as yours—not even close. We were home in bed, pillow talking and I just asked her to marry me. She said yes, and we did it," Kenny continued.

Justin was smiling awkwardly; our responses probably weren't the affirming answers he was looking for. His proposal had been romantic. I wished I had a grand story to tell him, but I didn't. It is refreshing to hear stories like his.

71

"Something must have made you want to get married though, right?" Justin asked Kenny.

"Actually, when I met my ex—that first night I saw her at a club—I told my buddy I was going to make her my wife. I'm serious. She was so hot. She was the best-looking woman among hundreds. I walked up to her and she ate up the game I spat at her."

Justin laughed. "Oh okay. Besides the physical, were you attracted to anything else in particular?"

"You know what? Truthfully I'm ashamed to say, I married her for all the wrong reasons. She was so good looking; all I could think of was marrying her and getting her pregnant. She was also well off. She had a nice car and her own condo. Her family owned about five McDonald's restaurants across the county. Her dad also owned a local bank. I didn't exactly want her money for me, but I felt our kids wouldn't have to worry about a damn thing if anything ever happens to me. I also felt she would be a good mom. We both talked about wanting our kids to go to private schools. She grew up privileged, and her parents cared for her, so she vowed to do the same thing with her own kids. I grew up in a dysfunctional home. My dad wasn't around. My mom was bouncing from one boyfriend to another. I didn't want my kids to grow up as such, and there was Tracy, talking about the same things I longed for. It was perfect. The women I'd been dealing with before her hadn't been doing anything for me anyway," Kenny said.

Justin adjusted in his chair. "Would you say she was a good wife . . . a decent mom?" he continued.

Kenny rubbed his chin and stared at the ceiling. "I wouldn't say so. She is not as good a mom as I thought she would have been. She would let KJ run around the house doing whatever he wanted. I was always on the road with the group I managed at the time. Whenever I called and asked for KJ, she would say he was at Nana's house while she was at home watching reality TV. It was very upsetting. She was just plain lazy. And it was the same attitude she had when it came to intimacy. She never put any effort into it. Sex with her was sloppy; it was like a job to her. I could count the number of times I got head from her."

Justin sipped his drink and took a deep breath. "Had she always been that way, even before you got married?"

"Actually she was," admitted Kenny. "She was very boring, but we didn't see each other every day, so it didn't really bother me much. Women on the road took care of my needs. Getting her to do anything freaky was like pulling a nail with teeth. I turned on a porno flick one time, and she acted as though that was the most disgusting thing she had ever seen. Do you know how frustrating

WTF MOMENT

it was to beg for pussy? And she had the nerve to ask why I was banging this one chick on the side! Pussy on tap, that's why!"

"Do you think your extra curricular activities contributed to the failure of the marriage?" asked Justin.

"Not really. We worked things out. But truly, we weren't compatible anyway. When things get rough, you will find out whether your love is real. My group's popularity waned off, and I was home more. I started hustling here and there. I got a gig as an artist liaison for a local record company. I didn't make much money, but it was okay while I worked on my own independent record label. I was at home watching TV one evening, and she asked me how much I was expecting to bring home for the month. I told her about fifteen hundred or so. She laughed and told me she earned quadruple of what I was earning. I was glad she was making more money. The extra funds would keep us afloat for a while until my project got off the ground—I had thought. Then she hit me with the bomb."

Kenny reclined in his chair, paused for a while, and stared at the ceiling in deep thought. Those had been trying times for him. I recalled how angry and down he had been.

He sighed and went on with his story, "She said, 'I can do this by my damn self!' I was shocked, so I asked her to repeat what she had said. She did, and then I went berserk. I told her to take those words back. We got into a heated argument. She asked me to leave. My ego kicked in. I told her, if I walked out the door; it would be over! She didn't even blink when I said it. She responded, saying, 'Bye, and don't ever come back.' I was blindsided. I was so angry; I felt humiliated and betrayed. She started making money and felt she had to belittle me. Words can't even describe how I felt. Devin convinced me to go back later in the evening after things had cooled off."

"Humph," I muttered.

Kenny sighed and shook his head. "I reluctantly went back home, and guess what I saw when I pulled up to the house? My clothes and things were in Glad bags in front of the garage. That was the worst moment in my entire life. I sat in my car and cried. Just like that, my whole relationship and life was disposed of, in Glad bags!"

"Oh wow!" said Justin. "You didn't see any of it coming?"

"Not at all," said Kenny. "I guess she was tired of me by then, and she did what she had to do. She left me hanging, broke, and nowhere to go. She dropped me like a bad habit. Our divorce was finalized within three months. To make matters worse, she hit me with child support while she was making way more than I was. A month after we signed the papers, she remarried and had a baby shortly afterward!"

"Marriage is something else!" I added.

Kenny continued, "It took me years to get over it, but she did me a favor. Things were tough at first, but those days are behind me. I'm doing great now. The only part I hate is getting drawn into stupid, occasional drama with her."

"Oh I see," said Justin. "What about you, Devin? I hope yours wasn't as bad."

"Well, divorces are never good," I said. "The ex didn't kick me out, but I had to leave. I was at a point where I knew for a fact it wasn't working. We weren't in love anymore. The arguments were more frequent. She had slapped me twice when she was really angry. Our daughter was picking up on things and saying, 'Stop it, Daddy!' or 'Stop it, Mommy! Please stop fighting!' If we had continued on the path we were on, I don't know what would have happened! I had to bounce. We had tried to work it out and even went to counseling a few times, but we both knew deep inside it was a wrap."

Justin asked jokingly, "Should I even get married?"

"You must be crazy!" I told him. "What you and your lady have is very special. You love and respect each other genuinely, which is a good foundation for a relationship. You are friends first and foremost, and you both share the same interests. I had passion for things my ex-wife didn't, so that was a problem. Your wife has to like the things you enjoy and vice versa. It makes the relationship easier. Things get touchy when you don't have the same interests. I know real love when I see it. My parents have been together for forty years and are still very much in love. I see it in their eyes and I see it in your eyes."

"Devin is right!" Kenny added.

"Thank you, Devin. I really do appreciate it."

"Anytime, bro."

"Would you ever get married again?" Justin addressed both of us.

"Hmm," I said. "I have to think about that one for a little bit. I will say this though—never say never! If I found the right woman, maybe I would. I don't mind starting over and raising a family."

Kenny wasn't too optimistic. He gave an emphatic, "Hell, *no!*"

"Oh okay!" Justin said, chuckling.

Kenny sank in his chair, shaking his head in disapproval. He didn't care; he had been through a hard time with his ex, and I understood his plight and anger. I was going through it too. Getting angry was just going to give my ex more power over me; the best way to handle the situation was to be calm and civil.

"Thanks for the talk, gentlemen. I'm heading to rehearsal," Justin said.

Kenny and I bade him good-bye, and I smiled as we watched him skip out of the bar. Love was shooting out of Justin's pores. *It is a good thing,* I thought. *It sure would be nice to be in love and feel giddy like Justin.*

9. Along Came Amanda, Part 2

Amanda and I went on a few more dates and hung out casually for a couple of months. Being single again is difficult after you are used to being with someone. You find yourself alone and doing everything on your own. I felt awkward trying to cultivate a relationship with another woman; it was quite challenging. I prayed about it often.

I hope with time I'll find the person I can spend the rest of my life with. In the meantime, I have to focus and work on becoming a better man. My daughter is my priority. It is imperative I make up for lost time since she stays with me on the weekends only. A male figure is important in a young girl's life.

I was about to leave the office when I saw Amanda's e-mail inviting me to a restaurant located along the marina in Aqua City. It felt weird because I had just seen her a few days before, and we had planned to meet again the coming weekend. I went along with her plan although I wasn't feeling quite well.

I arrived at the restaurant at 8:38 p.m., eight minutes after our scheduled time. I took a quick drive around the parking lot and didn't see her car. *She must be running late too.*

I was lucky; I found a space right in front. The waiting area was moderately filled. I signed my name on the board and waited. Shortly thereafter, I saw Amanda's car pull up into the parking lot. As she walked in, the waitress called my name and ushered us to our seats.

Amanda looked good. Her hair was done, and she was dressed for the occasion. I had almost forgotten how attractive she was. I walked behind her as we followed the waitress. I watched as she swayed from left to right, in rhythm with her steps. I was sure most of the men in the restaurant had taken a glance. One guy in particular, at a table with his buddies, locked eyes with me and wouldn't look away. I laughed inside because I knew he really wanted to look at Amanda, and I just had to torture him by refusing to look away; I wasn't going to let him get the satisfaction.

BOLAJI TIJANI-QUDUS

She sat in the booth portion of the table. I sat on a chair facing her. We both sifted through the menu. I don't really care much for red meat, but since she said it was her favorite restaurant, I didn't mind coming. I had to do something she liked to do as well.

I could sense something wasn't right when I looked at her.

"What?"

"Just wondering whether you are okay," I said, calmly.

"Oh! I just had a long day at work and I have to prepare for my girlfriend's baby shower next weekend."

A waiter poured us the green tea we requested. He took our order and before he walked away, I requested some sugar.

"You drink your green tea with sugar?" She chuckled.

"What is wrong with having sugar in my green tea?"

"Well, you are not supposed to have sugar in green tea. You miss the taste, mister."

"It's my tea, right? And I can add whatever I want to it. I'm the one drinking it, right? Please leave my tea be. Thank you very much," I said, chuckling.

Our steaks finally arrived, and we started eating. I inspected my meat to make sure it was cooked properly. I can't imagine how people eat raw meat. I remember the last time I ate a partially cooked beef kabob. I was sick for three days; I couldn't eat anything solid. I think I may have lost ten pounds in those short few days. It was one of the most unpleasant experiences I've ever had. I was visiting the bathroom every five minutes, it seemed.

I asked the waiter again, "Are you sure this is cooked well?"

He looked at me and smiled. "Yes, sir. It absolutely is."

"Okay." My tone reflected I wasn't convinced.

"Why are you so paranoid? Go ahead and eat. I promise you it's cooked well, and it's so good," Amanda said.

We made small talk in between bites. Then she asked whether a client she had referred to me had called. I answered no. I almost asked Amanda whether she would be coming back to work out with me anytime soon. I stopped short when I remembered the last time I had asked her the same question. She had cried hysterically and asked in between sobs, "Are you trying to change me, Devin?"

I was startled. *How can she ask me to remind her to work out and then rebuke me for it?* I thought. I'd become the bad guy all of a sudden. She claimed I was attacking her and that I was being insensitive, which was untrue. I was only doing what she had asked of me. The scenario was strange, and it made

WTF MOMENT

me cautious. I knew damn well I was very diplomatic. I train people regularly, and I have to be mindful of their sensitivity.

Amanda still looked like a fit "stallion" to me.

I became full quicker than I had expected, so I sat back to take a break. I watched her and smiled as she ate. I was thinking about how beautiful she looked.

She looked up, a little embarrassed because she had been eating so fast.

"Why are you all in my mouth, mister?" she shot at me.

"I wasn't in your mouth," I said, laughing. "I was admiring you, sweetie."

"Well, I'm hungry today! Is that okay with you? Thank you! Why are you watching me eating anyway?"

I decided not to respond because I was beginning to feel she was getting sensitive. So I smiled and went back to eating my food.

"So what's up with us?" she asked suddenly, breaking my train of thought.

Looking directly into her eyes, I responded by asking, "What do you mean?"

"I mean, what is going on with us?"

Her eyes were already swelling as she tried to hold back tears. I knew she would cry sooner or later. She always did, even when we had little disagreements.

"I thought we are getting to know each other . . . building. No?" I asked.

"My friend Kimmy saw you on Saturday night at Mood's with some other chick. I just want to know where we stand, and I need to know whether you are wining and dining other bitches. I don't want to look stupid around here!" she exclaimed.

I became a little irritated. The past Saturday night she was referring to, I had gone to check out a new restaurant that had just opened up in the uptown area. I also went to a couple of other bars with a college buddy Alex, who happened to be in town. I ran into Angel, a friend and my personal lawyer. At the end of the evening, I walked Angel to her car because I had parked close to her. That was the woman Amanda's friend saw me with, but she had relayed the story to Amanda as though I had been on date.

"Okay! I walked someone to her car on Saturday night. What seems to be the problem?" I asked.

"I just want to know whether I can go on dates with other people too."

I tried not to get more upset than I already was when she made the comment, but I couldn't help it.

"I walked someone I know to her car! I don't understand what the fuss is about!" I continued.

"And I saw your missed call from Sunday 1:00 a.m. She must not have given you any, which may have been the reason you called me. That is a booty call!" she went on.

Now I was agitated. How could she come up with a theory like that? I only called her because she had told me she was going to be out drinking with her girlfriends, and since I was out too, I called her to see whether we could meet up.

She was taking it too far, and I didn't understand why I had to keep explaining myself over and over. I was already not feeling well, and the conversation made my head throb.

"Can we move on please, because there really isn't anything for me to explain? I already told you what happened."

"No, you still haven't told me anything! This is not how you treat your girlfriend."

"Girlfriend?!" I asked, surprised.

"What? You're not going to claim me?"

"Amanda, we just started dating, and nothing is outlined yet."

"Whatever! You need to man up and stop being a bitch about this," she said, raising her voice.

"Okay, I've heard enough, and I'm leaving," I said, getting up from my chair. I didn't see any point in continuing with the conversation, and she had started to throw insults.

"I've wasted these last two months of my life with you! And for what?" she asked, as tears started to flow down her cheeks. She got up as well and raced past me toward the door. People around us, watched, as the drama unfolded.

Nosey people! Why don't they mind their own business? I thought.

I kept my composure, though. I could feel all the women's eyes piercing through my skin. I tried not to make any kind of eye contact. They were all probably thinking, *what an asshole.*

I wanted to get the hell out of there pronto, but I couldn't find the waiter, so I walked over to the front and inquired whether I could pay there.

"We have to look for your waiter, sir," the hostess said.

"Just let me have the bill; I need to go."

She looked at me, and saw I was agitated. She almost hesitated, but produced the bill. It was $31. I left two twenty-dollar bills and walked out the door. I could see some people from the corner of my eyes, looking at me and talking in low tones. I didn't care; they didn't even know me and would probably never see me again.

As I was walking toward my car, I saw Amanda next to it on the phone with someone, making animated hand gestures. Then she turned around and saw me. "I'll call you back," I heard her say to the person on the other line.

WTF MOMENT

"Okay, dude! I was going to go home, but I have to let you know you are a complete jerk! I do so much for you, and all you do is treat me like a whore. I'm a very good woman since you don't know! You know what I've been through in my last relationship. I put my trust in you and gave you my all, but you treat me like trash."

Passersby were now watching us.

"What are you talking about?" I asked.

Tears were now flowing freely down her face. "I could care less about these women you are running around with! All I want is for you to treat me with some respect. I really let my guard down with you, and you can't even tell me to my face what is going on with us. You can't even answer a simple question!" she screamed.

"What answer are you expecting?"

I saw a group of ladies in the distance. One of them turned around and said, "You tell him, girl. You don't have to take that mess, girl."

The comment seemed to fuel Amanda. She responded to them, "Thank you," and continued with her madness.

"What are you trying to accomplish with all this drama? This is unacceptable at all levels! Look around. Everyone is watching us," I said.

"I don't care about these people or what they think. All I'm concerned about at this moment is you and me and what's up with us!"

A waitress came out and walked toward us, "Do you guys need to take the rest of your food to go?"

"No!" we both said, simultaneously. She had probably been sent by a manager to calm the waters. I'm sure they could see everything from inside and were concerned about their customers and the reputation of the establishment. *This isn't looking good*, I thought.

I was upset and embarrassed. One at a time, cars were disappearing from the parking lot. Some slowed down and took a peek at us before driving off.

I opened my car door and said, "This isn't going anywhere. I'm about to go. We have been standing here for about an hour. It's really getting late, and I have to work in the morning."

"Go ahead, jerk! This is how you treat a woman you chased for the longest time? You got what you want and now I'm worthless to you, huh? You know I'm the best thing that has ever happened to you!"

She was now throwing the guilt trip statements at me, and her last statement pissed me off even more.

"Look! I truly care about you and enjoy our time together, but this is not a civilized way of having a discussion," I said.

79

I started to think of ways to clean things up. She was primed to go all out. The situation had clearly gotten out of control. So I had to call a truce even though it meant I had to pretend. I gently pulled her close and wiped the tears with a napkin. It worked, and she calmed down. I had to end the drama then and there, although I wanted to say *Take a hike*, and drive off. It may have backfired on me. As crazy as she was acting, I could just see her jumping in front of the car and making matters worse. She may have even thrown things at my windshield.

"You know I care for you one hundred percent, dude!" Her eyes started to well up again.

"I know you do, and I care for you too. Let's talk tomorrow, okay? Emotions are high right now, and I'm drained."

"I'm drained too," she sobbed. "It just seems as though guys always end up hurting me!"

I hugged her and said, "Please, drive home safely, okay?"

I was relieved when she said, "Okay," and started walking toward her car.

I waited until she pulled out of the parking lot before I started my engine. On my drive home, I replayed the evening's encounter over and over in my head. *This woman must be nuts!* I couldn't even believe it. My headache had gotten worse from all the drama. As soon as I got home, I headed straight to bed. I was exhausted.

The very next day at the office, her e-mail was the first one to pop up in my inbox.

To: Devin Lewis
From: Amanda Jones
Subject: Good Morning!

Good morning, babes, how is your day going?
My boss is out today. I'm going to take an extended lunch to do some shopping. I think I'll go get a facial and get my nails done. Maybe I'll get that nail polish you hate so much huh? Lol
Are you working out today?! You know I love those pecs of yours ☺
Babes, enjoy this beautiful sunny day.
I know I am! Lol

Smooches.

Amanda

WTF MOMENT

I shook my head as I read her e-mail. *She couldn't be serious! She is acting as though last night didn't even happen! How can she go from being hysterical one night and happy-go-lucky the very next morning?* It was so weird and unreal. I didn't know how to respond. I was in no mood to chat. I was still ticked over last night's incident, so I decided to ignore her e-mail, at least until after I got some work done.

About five minutes later, another e-mail popped into my inbox. It was from her. Obviously, Amanda wasn't the one who liked to wait.

To: Devin Lewis
From: Amanda Jones
Subject: Re: Good Morning!

Babes, are you there?
-A

To: Amanda Jones
From: Devin Lewis
Subject: Re: Re: Good Morning!

Oh hey,
It's really busy over here today. Let's chat later.

A few minutes later, I saw an email notification.

To: Devin Lewis
From: Amanda Jones
Subject: Re: Re: Re: Good Morning!

Ok! Don't work too hard, babes.
I'll be in your area this evening meeting up with my friend Cindy.
I should be free around 9 ish . . . Are you going to be home?
Hmmm . . . I want to come over and see you ☺

I didn't feel like being bothered, so I sent her one more e-mail hoping that would be the last one for the day.

To: Amanda Jones
From: Devin Lewis
Subject: Re: Re: Re: Re: Good Morning!

> I have a full day ahead of me and I'm teaching later tonight as well.
> Rain check? ☺

I was hoping she'd read the last e-mail and get the point I wasn't trying to have company.

Sure enough, another e-mail from Amanda came through, but I ignored it.

Three days went by without calls, texts, or e-mails from Amanda. I was enjoying the "me time" I was having. It felt good not to argue for almost a week. This was one of those times I cherish—no women drama. Just chilling with me, myself, and I. Nothing is more satisfying than to have peace of mind. Get up and do things when I want to. No dealing with emotional flare-ups. Just as I was having these thoughts, a text came through from her.

> *From: Amanda*
> I know you have been really busy. I have been too. Can I at least see you soon?
> Work has been really stressing me out. I want to leave, but I want to find something else first, you know? I don't want to be jobless.
> But seriously, babes, I want to see you tonight. It's been soooo long?
> I totally get it when we spoke about the last incident.
> I just want to see you. I miss the times we spent together.

There goes my little peace of mind, I thought as I contemplated whether I should go ahead and see her or still continue to give her space. She reminded me of the ex-wife when she started to fuss over nothing.

I caved in and let Amanda come over the next evening. I didn't even try to bring up the whole drama at the restaurant. We had spoken on the phone earlier in the week. I had explained that I wasn't looking for a full-blown relationship yet, and her acting as though she was my *girlfriend* wasn't going to fly. She told me she understood, and she admitted she had been pressuring me. She promised to tone it down.

Just as I was getting ready to jump into the shower, my house phone rang. It was her. I buzzed her up. Wrapped in a towel, I opened the door and let her in.

"Oooh! Sexy . . . sexy . . . yum . . . yum," she said as she dropped her bags and gave me a tight hug. "Baby, I miss you!"

She moved her head upward and started to kiss me passionately. We kissed for a while. She grabbed my kahuna and massaged it as she moaned.

WTF MOMENT

"I want you now!"

I moved away slowly. "Okay. I have to jump in the shower," I said. "You know I got back from the gym not too long ago. Care to join me?"

"No thanks. I just freshened up before I left the house, sweetie. So I'm all ready for you when you are!" she replied, smiling slyly.

I had been in the shower for a few minutes when I heard the bathroom door open and she peeped in. "You sure are taking a long shower today; you never stay in the shower that long—ever!"

"What?" I asked, laughing. "What do you mean? Can I enjoy my shower without someone trying to time me?"

She stood there at the door with one hand on her waist and the other hand holding a glass of wine, watching me. I noticed she had changed into white see-through lingerie. Her body was shiny and smooth; she must have oiled herself down. Her nipples were erect, and they seemed to me calling for me to massage them. My kahuna began to rise as I looked at her body.

"Do you want me to come help you scrub that beautiful body of yours?" she asked.

"No, thank you. I'm almost done now."

"Are you sure?" she asked, with a grin.

I was beginning to wash my privates and she was still there, watching.

"How long do you plan on standing there, missy?"

She had seen me naked, of course, but I still felt a little uncomfortable. I could stand a little watching, but I need some privacy some times.

"Okay! I'm leaving, but finish up already! I don't think you can get cleaner than you are already, babes!" she replied, as she walked away.

Five minutes later, I wrapped up the shower, picked up my jar of lotion, and headed to the bedroom. She was sitting at the edge of the bed, motioning me to come closer to her. The lights were off, and candles were lit all around the room. She had a miniature bottle of oil in her hands.

"Don't bother with the lotion. I'm going to oil you down and give you a massage," she said, seductively.

"Oh really?" I asked, playfully.

"Yes, really! Lie on your stomach, babes." She pulled me to the bed and gently removed the towel from my waist.

She started to slowly drip the massage oil on my back; it felt warm. She started working her way down to my butt and then to my legs. Her hands were soft and tender.

She worked my back for a while. She was pretty good at it, took her time, and actually targeted the pressure points. She grabbed my butt and started to massage the muscles; then she caressed them. Slowly she parted my thighs, spreading my cheeks.

She'd better not try what I'm thinking she is about to do! I don't play that.

I started to tense up a little bit. I've heard stories. One of my buddies said a woman actually licked his butt hole. He had objected to it initially, but she convinced him, and he admitted to liking it. He said he refused to kiss her afterward though. The guys all made fun of him after his revelation, but he shrugged it off and laughed.

I was relieved when she asked me to turn over so she could work my front side.

This gets tricky; m*y kahuna will get rock hard in a second and start to bob in her face. I wonder if she'll finish the massage.* I closed my eyes. She massaged me for a while, and then she slowly started to work my kahuna. She poured some oil generously on her hands and started to stroke it with one hand while she played with my jewels with the other. It felt good . . . too good actually.

"What are you trying to do?" I asked her, as I opened my eyes.

"Nothing," she said playfully, as she watched, looking for my reaction. It turned her on when I moaned a little.

I grabbed her hands and said, "You know you're going to make me cum soon if you keep that up."

She wrestled her hands away and continued stroking me. "Just relax, babe. I'm here to please you."

I started to feel the tingle at the tip of my kahuna, as I started to move my pelvis faster. *It won't take long before I bust one*, I thought. I slowly moved her hands and gently placed mine on her face and motioned for her to put it all in her mouth. She eagerly obliged. She was good at giving head, and her mouth did feel amazing. She worked me for another fifteen minutes or so until I exploded. She sucked my nutrients out and squeezed my kahuna until she saw the last drop. Then, she got up and went to the bathroom. I heard her spit.

"Why did you spit it out?" I asked, laughing.

"I'll only swallow for my husband," she replied.

"What's the point? You already engage in the act of oral sex, you might as well go all the way."

"As I said, only my husband will get the pleasure of me swallowing his sperm."

"Ain't that a bitch?" I mumbled.

I didn't get it. As much as she loves to give head, downing some protein is just one more step of oral sex.

WTF MOMENT

When she returned, I went downtown and pleasured her as well. We went at it all night until we both passed out.

A couple of weeks went by without any incidents until I received an e-mail from her while I was at the office.

>*From: Amanda Jones*
>*To: Devin Lewis*
>*Subject: Hey!*
>
>Hey babes, Good morning ☺ did you sleep well last night?
>
>Devin—I feel last night . . . you should have called me back or at least told me that you were going out, so I wouldn't have had the expectation that I was going to hear from you again. I feel as though you didn't really hear me during our conversation last night.
>
>What if, after I finished talking to you last night, you called me back a few hours later and I wasn't home but at a club somewhere? Don't you think it would feel weird if I was in bed one minute and in a club the very next and that I never mentioned the possibility of going out while I was on the phone with you?
>
>Amanda

I didn't know what to make of the e-mail! *What is she talking about now?* I was trying to understand why her e-mail sounded as though I had done something wrong!

I had talked to her on the phone the previous night at around ten. We were both in bed at our respective places. I recalled telling her I would call her back later. Then, I got a call from Phil who told me Brandon was at a bar, drunk and acting up. Brandon and liquor don't mix. I felt I had an obligation to go save him from himself. Amanda had called shortly after I arrived at the bar where Brandon was.

"What are you doing? It sounds like you are having a party!" she had said.

"I'm at a bar handling some stuff with Brandon real quick. I'm heading home shortly though. I can't really hear you with all the noise. Let me call you back later or perhaps in the morning," I said.

She had hung up before I could even finish my sentence. I didn't make anything of it. By the time I sorted out Brandon and made it back home, it was past midnight, so I went straight to bed. It didn't occur to me that I should call Amanda back. I was tired.

To: Amanda Jones
From: Devin Lewis
Subject: Re: Hey!
You are making a big deal out of nothing, missy. I only stepped out because I got a call. I needed to go help my boy out. I was already in bed but I had to go handle the situation. Where are you going with this? I'm confused. Should I be asking for permission when I leave home and check in when I return?
Anyway, I'm heading to a meeting. Let's chat later. Okay?
Have a nice day.

I wasn't going to any meeting; I only wanted to prevent an e-mail rage. Wishful thinking . . .

From: Amanda Jones
To: Devin Lewis
Subject: Re: Re: Hey!
I don't even have the slightest idea how to talk to you. You are completely out of line right now. I didn't e-mail you with an attitude. I said good morning . . . asked how you slept, etc. didn't I? I wrote you about how I was feeling, and then I get this rant from you!
I hate it when you say you are going to call me back and you don't. That is my problem!
I'm not deserving of your rant. It's rude. It's mean, and it shows me you are incapable of talking/communicating with me in a civil manner. Maybe you're mad about something else and you are taking it out on me, because if you really read (or reread) what I'm saying below—it's me trying to let you know how I feel and get your thoughts. I'm not upset. I'm a beautiful, grown woman who is thoughtful, caring, compassionate, and smart. Don't talk to me as though I'm someone who is unimportant and irrelevant. It's not about checking in, Devin. We are both grown—it's about communication. This e-mail was never meant to be a sound-off. The last time I was with you at the steak house, I promised myself I wasn't going to ever go through the motions like that again.
If you can't apologize for your tone and your e-mail, I'm out of here. I don't deserve this crap. I'm a quality woman, and that's not the way to communicate with me.

WTF MOMENT

From: Devin Lewis
To: Amanda Jones
Subject: Re: Re: Re: Hey

How was I ranting? I was simply stating. Yes, I said I would call you back, and I would have if I hadn't gone to attend to Brandon. But, you beat me to the punch. You can disguise your e-mail however you want and say you were being polite. Fact of the matter is, you are coming at me as though I should be checking in with you. I get up and do stuff when I have to. Why do you have to be bothered by me stepping out of the house to do what I needed to do?

Every time we get into a little argument, you seem to always dwell on how you are a good, quality woman, how you are beautiful woman, blah blah . . . That has nothing to do with what we are talking about. Do you even know how to be humble?

Soon, I saw the e-mail notification again.

From: Amanda Jones
To: Devin Lewis
Subject: Re: Re: Re: Re: Hey

No, I see it differently. I'm not coming at you as if you should be checking in with me, because that would mean that I would have to check in with you. Too grown for that, sweetie, and like you, I don't enjoy that type of attention. That's some issue you must have had with someone else! It's about the simple act of you calling me back when you said you would.

Disguising what, Devin? If I wanted to sound off, I would have done so last night. If I wanted to play games, I would not have e-mailed you today. What could I be disguising? Please let me know, because I don't get it. I was trying to have a conversation with you, and you are making me feel my conversation is irrelevant, and you make me feel as though my thoughts are unimportant. Who are you to write in this manner to me?

I have to remind you what type of person I am because you don't take the extra step on things when I'm clearly worth it. I'm letting you know from my end, your rant was undeserved, and all I was trying to do was have a conversation with you.

I have to remind you, I'm special and I'm beautiful because you don't always remember that . . . because, if you did, you would take more time with me.

I didn't want to reply to her this time because I had work to do, but then I wouldn't be able to get my point across to her. Finally, I decided to e-mail her hoping it would be for the last time.

To: Amanda Jones
From: Devin Lewis
Subject: Re: Re: Re: Re: Re: Hey

Okay! It seems this is going in a different direction. Let's talk later. I'm at work. I'll have to make this the last e-mail for the day. Have a good one!

Before long, I saw the notification for another e-mail from her. I went to my inbox and deleted it without even reading it. The exchange could go back and forth the whole day. I came to the conclusion—I needed to leave Amanda alone. I hadn't known her long enough for her to be sounding off on me as such. It seemed as if I argued with her every week. I wasn't used to having such intense arguments with women I casually date. She's a nice woman, but there seemed to be some underlying emotional issues that I felt were red flags. As much as I liked her, I had no time to deal with emotional roller coasters. I had enough of that with the ex already.

10. Many Moods

I stared at the invitation to Chris and Nadine's wedding I had received in the mail. Just the other day, I had thought about Chris, my third cousin. We share a great-great-grandparent, but we act more like great friends. He has always been busy, so he never really hung out with my core group of friends, but we made up for it every time we saw each other. We usually picked up from where we'd left off.

It's not as though most of us didn't see the wedding coming. I smiled thinking how they made such a great couple. They had always been in love. I can't recall ever seeing them argue. If they did, it would be resolved rather quickly before it escalated! They were so easygoing. Nothing bothered them. They were so good together. It almost seemed unreal that two people could love each other as much as they do.

My thoughts were interrupted by the flashing light on my cell phone. I wondered how long it had been beeping. I couldn't hear it because I'd left it on the couch, and the ringer was off. Had it been on a table, the loud vibration noise would have alerted me. I picked it up and saw that it was Mom calling.

"Devin!" she screamed. My heart began to beat fast; *I hope she doesn't have bad news for me, perhaps, something happened to Dad, or an uncle or aunt died*, I thought. I braced myself.

"What happened, Mom?"

"Why didn't you tell me Chris and Nadine are getting married on a boat? A cruise kind of thing? I just got the invitation in the mail today! That is going to be nice. I haven't been on a cruise in a long time. I can't wait for your father and I to go somewhere. This is going to be a perfect vacation for the summer!" she said, sounding excited.

"It will be nice, Mom," I said, sheepishly. "I just got the invitation too. We all figured it was going to happen sooner or later, so it isn't much of a surprise."

"I knew those two would get married! They are so made for each other. I'm so happy for them."

"I know, Mom." I sighed.

"What, baby? You don't think it is a good idea?"

"That's not it, Mom. I mean . . . never mind . . ." I was really trying to silence her and change the subject because she would go on and on for the next hour about the upcoming wedding.

"So what is it then?" She mellowed down, sounding a bit concerned. "Are you depressed again about your situation? Are you guys going to work it out? I still don't understand why you guys have decided to end it all."

"Mom! There is nothing else to discuss. That's old news. We are moving on with our lives."

She was quiet for a while, then she said, "I love you very much, son. Everything will be all right."

It felt good to hear Mom say that. I thought she was going to ramble on and start preaching how marriages used to be back in the day. I was already moody thinking about divorce. I didn't want to be reminded of it.

"Thanks, Mom," I said. "I may be bringing Emmanuella over later this evening. You're going to be around, right?"

"Yes, I am. I miss her so much. I can't wait to see my baby!"

"Okay, Mom. I have to go get ready. I'm going to Chris's shortly. We have a basketball game."

"Are you taking Emmanuella with you to play basketball?"

"No. Nadine will be watching her while I'm gone."

"Oh! I was hoping you could bring her here before you go play. It would be nice to have her with me while I go get my hair done. She really loves the flea market too, and I'm making a stop there this afternoon. But it's okay. I can wait until the evening," she said, with a subtle, melancholy tone.

"I guess I can drop her off before the game. Nadine would understand."

"Are you sure?"

"Yes, Mom."

"Okay. Bye, son. I love you." She hung up the phone.

I could tell she was excited. Emmanuella would be too. I was glad I decided to take her to my parents' house. They hadn't been spending as much time with Emmanuella as they wanted to. *I have to do a better job. They won't be around forever.*

I walked over to the dining table where I had dumped all my mail. I picked up the wedding invitation again; it really looked nice. The front of the card had

WTF MOMENT

a beautiful backdrop of the ocean and a sandy beach. The text read, "Join us on this fantastic voyage as Chris and Nadine share their wedding vows."

I thought it was an excellent idea. Since I could remember, there had always been a trip or family reunion every year. Why not get all the family and friends on a boat and have a good time while getting hitched? Plenty of fun on the three-day Carnival cruise, which would feature a casino, lounges, clubs, miniature golf course, swimming pools, spas, and restaurants.

The pricing wasn't bad at $300 per person, which included three square meals a day. *The cruise would make a nice vacation*, I thought.

Chris and Nadine wouldn't have to worry about food and finding accommodations for out-of-town guests. I read there was even a babysitting facility for parents bringing their kids.

I hope the ex doesn't come. I was almost certain Nadine or Chris had sent her an invitation. I hoped we wouldn't be a distraction to each other.

It's about a year away; I need not worry right now.

My phone rang again. This time, it was Chris calling. *Speak of the devil.*

As I picked up, I could hear the sarcasm in his voice.

"What's up, bro? Wake your butt up! It's ten o'clock already! Too much fun last night, huh?"

"What do you want so damn early in the morning? You know it's Saturday, right?"

"You shouldn't be complaining. Doesn't Emmanuella wake you up early anyway?"

"She sure does. Don't worry. Your time is coming soon," I said, laughing.

"So I've heard, but we are ready."

"That's the spirit!"

"By the way, Nadine wants to know whether you're still bringing Emmanuella by so she can plan their day."

"Actually, Mom just called. She wants me to drop Emmanuella off with her. I think she wants to take her to the hairdresser. Please let Nadine know I'm sorry. We can make it happen another time."

"No problem. You don't have to apologize. Nadine will understand."

"Cool."

"So are you ready to get your butt whipped today? You haven't been on a winning team the last few games, you know? I think you have lost a step and a half, bro," he said, laughing.

"What!! I haven't lost anything. I've been on horrible teams lately. Watch me get a triple double today though!"

"More like triple dribble when you handle the ball."

"Keep laughing, but we'll see who gets the last laugh when it's all said and done," I said, scoffing.

"Okay, we shall see. Don't forget to take your energy shot."

"Keep talking mess. Make sure you don't pick me because I want to play against you. I can visualize dunking on you right now!"

"It's on, then," he said, still laughing.

"By the way, I got your invitation in the mail today. It's official huh? Congratulations, I'm proud of you," I said, changing the subject.

"Thank you. It's about time." I could feel him smiling.

"No doubt! The unconditional love you both have for each other is amazing; not getting married would be a travesty. And I mean that with the utmost sincerity."

"I really do appreciate it!"

"There are no two people more made for each other than you both," I continued.

"Coming from you means a lot to me. Let's go play ball before we get too mushy on the phone like two girls," he said, laughing.

"True. True. Let me get ready, and I'll see you in a bit."

"Hey, Devin?"

"What's up, bro?"

"Would you do me the honors of serving as one of my groomsmen?"

I was moved when he asked. For him to even consider me was an honor. I have known Chris all my life. He means a lot to me, and I look up to him in more ways than one.

"Of course, bro, of course," I replied.

"Then it's settled. I'll see you shortly."

"Sure thing," I said, as we hung up.

I sat down on my bed thinking about Chris and his wife to be. Chris is genuine, and one of nicest guys I've ever met. No one has ever come around saying anything negative about him. He gets along with everyone. I always teased him about how he could run for president and win by a landslide. He has the *Will Smith-Ben Affleck* air about him. His charismatic smile and good-looking, boy-next-door image makes him very likable. At five ten and lean, with an athletic build, he modeled men's briefs for a popular company years ago. He stopped because he felt the industry was too pretentious.

Ever since I've known him, he has always been a one-woman guy. Nadine is like the female version of him—a beautiful woman with a great spirit and demeanor. She reminds me of the singer Amel Larrieux. It is almost a crime for

WTF MOMENT

Chris and Nadine to be with each other. It's even more amazing how humble they both were. He is an accomplished architect, and she owns an interior designing company. They were both instrumental in helping me shape the unique look of the Five Star Gym.

I started to think about how wonderful it is to share oneself with another. *Will I ever have something like they have? Waking up every day with someone who is there for me and loves me as much as I love her . . . someone I can talk to and who has my back one hundred percent, I wouldn't mind doing it again, but if it doesn't happen, I could live with that too.*

It never ceases to amaze me when Chris talks about Nadine. There is always a glow in his eyes. He truly believes she is his soul mate. Although they take their relationship seriously, they never take themselves too seriously. They have mutual love and respect for each other. They laugh at each other's jokes and hardly get upset even if one offends the other.

I remember one night when Nadine was late in getting home. It was her turn to babysit Chris's nephew and niece. We were supposed to go watch the Lakers who were in town. I was waiting impatiently. She walked through the door about an hour later. I was expecting Chris to be slightly upset, but he calmly hugged her and kissed her on the cheek.

She said, "Oh! I'm sorry, sweetie. There was an accident on Bullion Road, and I had to take the back roads here. My phone is dead, and I left my car charger in your car last night."

"No worries, babe," Chris said.

The situation could have gone differently had it been Monica and me.

I could see the conversation going awry. I may have started off, "You're late again as usual. No consideration for other people's time! A phone call saying you were running late would have been nice."

Monica would have responded, "First off, I wasn't late intentionally, there was traffic! I have no control of accidents!"

"And you couldn't call?"

"Call how? My phone died!" Then, she'd sigh dramatically and roll her eyes. "What is the rush anyway? It is not a matter of life and death. You're running off to watch basketball. Thirty minutes won't kill you. Anyway, I'm here now, you can go watch your little basketball game!"

"Why do you even have to go there?" I would have gotten really angry by now.

"Go where? You're the one getting excited over some basketball game, not even bothering to ask why I was late."

"Under different circumstances I would have," I'd say, "but I can't because you're always late anyway. Accident or no accident, you conveniently show up late when I have to go do my own thing, and you never view any of it as important. It is always *little this* and *little that*. Now, when you have to be someplace, and I have to watch Emmanuella, you would blow my phone up hours before you leave just to make sure I get there on time. That is what I'm referring to."

"Whatever, Devin," she would have added.

Then I would have stormed out and there would have been tension for a week thereafter. She would probably withhold sex, and I would most likely be sleeping on the couch or in the guest room.

I liked the way Chris and Nadine handled things—no room for miscommunication. They both enjoyed telling the story of how they met in college. She worked at the financial aid office. He had gone in there to check on his grant and loans status. He didn't ask her out until the third time he went into the office. Obviously he wasn't checking on the grant status because he had been told he would get an answer the following week. He was there to scope her out. I look back and laugh at the cute little things they used to do when they started going steady. Sometimes they would sit in each other classes waiting until they could leave together. Most professors allowed them the privilege. Even when I observed them back then, I knew they were destined to be together. It was so natural to be excited for Chris and Nadine. Anyone who knew them was.

I lay back on my bed for no particular reason, staring at the ceiling. My mood had lightened up thinking about Chris. Moments later, I heard tiny footsteps coming toward my bedroom. Emmanuella had woken up. She hopped onto my bed next to me, and I couldn't have been happier at that very moment.

"Good morning, Daddy."

"Good morning. How is my little princess doing this morning?" I asked, as I gave her a hug.

"Fine," she replied, bubbly and smiling.

"Did you sleep well?"

"Yes, Daddy. Did you sleep well?"

"Daddy sure did," I said, laughing, as I gently pulled on her cheeks. She is so funny and smart. The comments kids make at times make one thankful for having them. Kids make life so interesting.

"Guess what, pumpkin?"

"What, Daddy?"

"We're going to see Nana in a little while."

"Yay! I miss Nana."

"Okay, it is shower time. Then, we will have breakfast and then go over to Nana's. Okay?"

WTF MOMENT

"Okay, Daddy. Can I have Corn Pops please, Daddy?"

"You sure can, as soon as we get you nice and clean," I said, playfully tickling her.

"Thanks, Daddy," she said, giggling.

I dropped Emmanuella off at Mom's an hour later. I made a quick dash to a local drug store. I needed pain relief ointment for my stubborn lower back and ankle pain. I was at the first aid section reading directions on a new pain rub when I looked up and saw Brandon and Ashley holding hands walking toward me. There had been so much going on with me in the last month, I hadn't really been able to catch up with Brandon. I thought he was getting over Ashley because he hadn't talked much about her the last time we'd seen each other. Instead, he had talked about a potential new job and apartment hunting.

"Hey, people," I said when they got close. They were both startled to see me, and I was shocked to see them together.

"Hey, Devin," Ashley said, first. Brandon was just standing there. He caught himself and quickly gave me a hug as he said hello.

I tried not to look surprised as I conversed with both of them.

"Shopping, huh?" I asked.

"We have to do a lot of shopping because we have another mouth to feed," Brandon said, happily rubbing his wife's belly.

"Oh!" I uttered, in disbelief.

"We are three months pregnant!" Brandon exclaimed.

"Congratulations," I said, taking a peep at Ashley's protruding belly.

"I'm so excited!" Brandon said, giggling. He was either really happy to be a father or was overplaying the fact that I had seen them together and he hadn't mentioned anything about it over the last few months.

"I'm excited for you guys too," I said.

I felt strange. I should have been happy they were having a baby, but the circumstances surrounding the pregnancy didn't seem right to me. Brandon had just been raving about leaving her after she had cheated on him with another woman! A few months back, he had vowed never to move out or leave her the house. He had eventually moved in with his brother, which I thought was the best move because I didn't know how long the roommate thing was going work between them. I guess it did work after all—a baby came out of it!

I was tempted to ask them both how and when it had happened. They had really been secretive about it, because no one in the crew knew about the latest development.

The following minutes were awkward. I acted as if I wasn't surprised, and they acted as if the drama and the breakup never happened. After many forced smiles and small talk, we said our good-byes and went on our merry ways. I couldn't believe what I had just seen. I was trying to dismiss the recent event as a normal occurrence.

No, this is really crazy! Phil has to hear this!

I dialed his number, but his voicemail came on right away. I hung up and I headed to the basketball court.

I arrived there at eleven on the dot. I saw Chris sitting in his car, his head bowed. He was fiddling with his iPhone. He thinks the gadget is the best thing to happen since sliced bread. I liked my phone the way it was—simple with no frills. I can't even get with the whole idea of browsing the Internet through a phone. The screen is so small. I like browsing the Internet on a big screen. I even connected my laptop to my fifty-two-inch TV just to make sure I can see everything magnified.

I parked next to Chris. He looked up and smiled. We both got out of our cars and gave each other a hug.

"I thought you have a girlfriend already," I said, teasing him. "Why are you always playing with your other girl? Your phone, that is."

"Correction, you're talking about my *fiancée*, not my girlfriend, and you need to get with the program and move with the speed of the world. You need to throw away that garage opener you call a phone."

"I'm okay with what I have, thank you very much."

"Suit yourself, dude," he said, smirking.

"Isn't everyone supposed to be here at eleven?"

"I have no idea what happened this morning. You know there was a time change last night. We were supposed to move the clock forward an hour at midnight."

"Are you telling me all these guys don't pay attention? I knew to change the time back, and apparently you did too," I said, chuckling.

"Everyone isn't like us, my man."

"I guess not! On a different note, congratulations on the wedding once again."

"Thank you."

"It is a great thing that is about to happen to you. I think you deserve it. You are a great person, and God has brought you the perfect woman. Most people aren't as lucky to find a soul mate."

"I'm truly blessed, and I'm thankful for her. I have to pinch myself sometimes because I still don't believe I'm marrying someone like her. All my dreams have come true ever since I met Nadine. When I go to sleep at night, she is the last thing I remember, and she is the first thing on my mind when I wake up in the morning," he gushed.

WTF MOMENT

Before we could get further with our touchy-feely conversation, the other guys started to pull up one by one.

"I guess we can catch up on the wedding discussion later on in the week," I said.

After the game, I called Phil. I thought I would have seen him on the court to tell him about my run-in with Brandon and Ashley, but he hadn't shown up.

He picked up this time.

I yelled into the phone, "You can't believe who I just saw today!"

"What? What happened?" Phil asked.

"I just saw Brandon and Ashley at the store, holding hands! And guess what? She is three months pregnant!"

"Whoa! Are you sure?!"

"Of course I'm sure. I didn't see them from afar. We had a conversation and everything!"

"Oh, wow! Weren't we just talking about Brandon the other day? And you said you were going to call him to make sure he was okay."

"I guess he's been MIA because he's been busy knocking Ashley up!"

"I'm surprised. Then again, I shouldn't be. This is Brandon we're talking about, the same guy who was oblivious to what was going on right under his nose. He has always been soft. He had to go crawling back to her like a spineless fool. What she did was unacceptable. You don't go back to that!" Phil said, in an agitated tone.

"I know. It seems strange to me too. But maybe it will work out. Must be love, right?" I asked, trying to be sympathetic.

"C'mon now, Devin. You know that's a load of crap! It doesn't matter whether it was with a man or a woman. The bottom line is, she did step out on him, a couple of times actually. Give me a break! That isn't curiosity—it's cheating. You know she is going to do it again, and he will be left looking stupid and licking his wounds. I really want to go slap him right now. What is wrong with him? With all these women walking around, he has to go back to Ashley?" Phil asked.

"I wonder how it's going to end," I said.

"You already know how! Not good. Forget Brandon, man! What's going on tonight? I want to get out."

"I'm not sure. I'll ask around."

"I'll do the same. Let's catch up later then," he said.

"Definitely! Later, bro."

Phil hung up and went about his business. He had said his piece about Brandon's situation and moved on. Phil doesn't spend too much time thinking or talking about bad situations. He feels it is a waste of energy dealing with matters he has no control of. He would rather spend time on things that pertain to him. He may seem mean and uncaring, but I like him because he gives it to you raw, no sugar coating. He doesn't beat around the bush. He will tell it like it is. A person's feelings may get hurt, but at least he is one guy who tells the truth.

11. Along Came Amanda, Part 3

I looked out of my office window and I saw Monica's Porsche Cayenne parked in the lot. I didn't know she was coming. I looked at my watch; it was noon. My office phone started to beep. It was my secretary calling. Before I could answer it, Monica walked in with Emmanuella who had her doll in one hand and some candy in the other. Her hair was evenly parted down the middle of her head and drawn up into two puffs.

"I'm going away for the weekend so I thought I should drop your daughter off," Monica said.

"Thanks."

Good thing I wasn't out at a lunch meeting. Whatever happened to calling first?

I wasn't going to go there with her. At least she had done me a favor by bringing my daughter early. I wouldn't have to worry about driving two hours to go pick her up later and dealing with commuter traffic on a Friday evening.

Emmanuella ran over and hugged me. "I missed you so much, Daddy."

"I missed my little muffin so much too!" I said, pulling on her cheek.

"I drew you a picture."

"You did?"

"Yes, Daddy, let me show you."

"Okay."

She produced a sheet of paper with a scribbled drawing of what look like a group of people.

"You are holding my hand here. We are walking to a picnic. And there is Mommy and Nana and Grandpa waving at us."

"You did such a great job with your drawing," I said. I gave her another kiss.

Monica barged in, "I have to get going."

"Okay, have a good one," I responded.

BOLAJI TIJANI-QUDUS

"Her allergy drops are in her backpack," she added.

"Sure," I said.

"Come give Mummy a hug, Emma."

They embraced and then Monica left.

I showed Emmanuella around to some of the remaining staff. They were glad to see her. Most of them hadn't seen her since she was born; some had seen only pictures of her. It felt good to show off my pride and joy.

Emmanuella had turned four a few months ago and was now asking lots of questions. She asked me why we had to take the elevator to the fourth floor. "What are you going to do, Daddy, if the elevator stops working?" she asked.

"I'll take the stairs!"

"But that is a long way down, Daddy. You will be really, really tired!"

I assured her the elevator rarely broke down and if it did, it got fixed quickly. I went on to say the stairs were an alternative that I would take if there was an emergency even though I was going to get tired.

After Emmanuella's tour of the gym, we headed home early. I ran some errands with her. We stopped at the grocery store and also bought some children movies. She was excited when I took my car in for a wash. She liked it when the foam and big brush passed over the car and got excited when it moved through the wash without me driving it.

"Daddy, the car is moving by itself!"

"Yes, I know, sweetie. A machine moves the car for us."

We finally made it home, ate dinner, and started watching our movies. We were on our second DVD when the doorbell rang. I wondered who it may be. I hadn't buzzed anyone up. I got up and looked through the peephole.

"What the . . .," I muttered.

It was Amanda! I couldn't believe my eyes. I wondered how she got in. *Someone who lives on the same floor must have let her up.*

I opened the door halfway and stepped into the hallway, blocking her view of my living room.

She peeped around my frame. "Hi, Emmanuella!" she yelled out, waving.

Emmanuella turned around and waved back. "Hi," she responded. Being the well-mannered girl that she is, Emmanuella went back to watching her movie.

"Aww. She is so adorable! What are you guys watching?"

"*Cinderella.*"

"How cute! She is sitting there like such a big girl. And she's only four?"

"Yeah," I responded as I gently pulled at the door but didn't shut it all the way. I left enough room to let Emmanuella know I was just outside the door.

"What are you doing here?" I asked, in a low tone.

WTF MOMENT

"We need to have closure, Devin! There are still unresolved issues between us."

"What are you talking about?"

"You know exactly what I'm talking about!" she bleated.

"Listen, I'm not going to continue going back and forth with you on this. Obviously we have differences in opinion. This is neither the place nor the time. I need to get back to my daughter."

"I understand you have to be with Emmanuella, but the woman in your life is important too. You can't just shut me out!" she exclaimed.

I shook my head and said, "Who says I'm shutting you out? I do give you attention. We do speak on the phone regularly, and when I'm not with Emmanuella, I'm with you! Even if I can't talk right away, I still send you text messages throughout the day to see how you are doing."

"Texts are not enough. You have to call me. You are supposed to be chasing me. All the guys do!"

I laughed and said, "I'm not just any guy, and please don't compare me. When I take time out of my busy day to text you, it means I'm thinking of you. You could call me sometimes too, you know? You could call me when you think about me. Like today, I got caught up running around with Emmanuella; I haven't had the time to do anything else."

"No, you are the man! You should call me more than I call you," she said.

I sighed. "Here we go again with your phone mythology."

"Whatever! Devin!"

"Well, I have to go. You know I have Emmanuella this weekend. It's rude, you barging in like this! Can we please have this discussion another time?" I asked, trying not to get angrier than I already was.

"When is a good time, Devin? When is there ever a good time?"

"Have a good night, Amanda. I'm going back inside. Talk to you later."

She stood there, tears running down her cheeks, her hands on her hips and her lips quivering.

I turned around and went inside. Being with my daughter was more important to me than standing in the hallway having a dead-end conversation with a stubborn woman.

If I were to introduce her to my daughter, it shouldn't be under such circumstances. The woman who would meet Emmanuella would have to be someone I would be with, for the long term. I'll never bring multiple women around my daughter.

As I closed the door behind me, I thought, *this woman had better not bang on my door!* I walked over to the couch and sat down, but I kept glancing in the direction of the door.

"Daddy, who was that?" Emmanuella asked.

"Oh, that was just Daddy's friend. She stopped by to say hello," I responded, forcing a smile.

"She's not staying?"

I rubbed her head playfully. "No, she isn't staying. She has to be somewhere."

"Okay, Daddy . . . Daddy?" she asked, as she looked up at me.

"Yes, baby?"

"What is the auntie's name?"

"Umm," I paused for second. "Oh, that was Ms. Amanda."

"Oh . . . Is she your friend like Mommy's friend, Uncle Fred?"

"Who is Uncle Fred?"

"Mommy's friend, who comes to fix the dishwasher sometimes."

"Oh yeah?" I asked.

"Yeah, and he stays downstairs and talks to Mommy sometimes when I go to bed."

"Oh okay . . . Have I missed anything in the movie?" I asked, changing the subject. I didn't want to start interrogating the child. It didn't matter to me whether Monica started seeing someone. I didn't think it was a good idea to be hanging out with a man late at night while my daughter was sleeping upstairs! I expected more from Monica. I was going to sleep on it and find a way to diplomatically ask her about it. I didn't want to get into a spat with her. Knowing Monica, she would automatically say I was jealous.

*   *   *

Another week went by, and I still hadn't spoken to Amanda. My voicemail was full, and I didn't bother clearing it on purpose. I hoped to deter some people—possibly Amanda—from leaving unnecessary messages. If people wanted to reach me, they could text me.

Just when I thought it was safe to say I had gotten through to Amanda, I received a text from her.

From: Amanda
Please, Devin, did you get my e-mail? I'm not doing well right now. I really need to see you, talk to you. I have no one to talk to about this . . . I don't know what to do, and you're not acknowledging me. I'm hurt! I'm really getting scared, and I need advice.

WTF MOMENT

A few seconds later, I received another text.

> *From: Amanda*
> I've never been so sad like this before. I've been sick, and I've not slept or eaten for three days and counting. I've not made it to work in a couple of days either. I'm really disturbed right now! Please don't do me like this. Please talk to me, Devin. I don't want any drama, I'm asking humbly.

One more text followed.

> *From: Amanda*
> Please reach out to me. I still haven't seen my period yet. I'm beginning to get scared. It's over ten days late. This isn't normal. Call me!

I wasn't shocked after I read the texts. *How low can this woman go?*

I wasn't worried. She had been late before; the last time she took the morning after pill, she was seven days late. Maybe this was one of the side effects.

I have to really slap myself for going through this crap with her. I shouldn't even have put myself in this situation in the first place!

I had really messed up for not using protection a couple of times. The first time it happened, I was out of condoms. I did it only because we had both been tested recently and had even exchanged proof. Still, it was a bonehead thing to do.

Having a baby mama is not an option.

She was probably overreacting. In just the short while I'd known her, I'd learned she was capable of stressing out over nothing.

I called her on the way home from the office. She picked up.

"Hey," she said.

"What's up with ya?" I was upbeat and extra nice on the phone. I was hoping to deter her from getting emotional.

"Not much. I'm just stressing over work this week, and not getting my period is really getting me worked up!" she said.

I listened hard and tried to pick up her tone and vibe.

"How was work?" I asked.

"It's okay. My boss is on maternity leave. I'm doing her work and mine. How is yours?"

"Same BS, different toilet."

"Isn't that the truth?!" She sighed.

"Are you okay otherwise?" I asked.

"For the most part, yeah, except for not seeing my period yet!"

"I think everything is fine. Maybe it's delayed because of stress," I added.

"I guess you're right. I'm worried because ten days is a long time."

"Aaah, it's nothing! You took the pills when you were supposed to, right?" I asked.

"Yeah, I did."

"There is nothing to worry about then," I said.

"I guess so."

"Don't stress. Everything will be all right either way," I said, reassuring her.

"Okay."

I could hear a little relief in her voice, which was a good thing. We didn't need another outburst of hers. She could cry at the drop of a dime.

I had to really tread water with her because I never knew how she would react. I still scratch my head and wonder how a woman could be so nice and sweet one minute, and then, temperamental and combative the next.

We talked for a while longer, and I bade her a good night.

As I was getting ready for work the next morning, a text came through.

From: Amanda
Hey, we are okay ☺

To: Amanda
Great ☺

I vowed it would be the last time she would stress me over anything. I would be heading to the drug store to buy a forty-eight pack of condoms as soon as I got off work. I would always keep two next to my bed for easy access; a rollover away. No more excuses. We'd had two false alarms already; there was no room for a third.

As much as I liked Amanda, I was strongly leaning toward letting her go. Her emotional flare-ups and our subsequent fights were already taking a toll on me. I was having flashbacks of the ex and me getting into it. I needed to figure out a way to end the relationship and still maintain a friendship.

WTF MOMENT

I avoided her as much as I could for the rest of the week, but then I allowed her to convince me to let her come over. It was Sunday evening. I had hoped she would come earlier in the day. I liked to be in bed by ten on Sundays so I would be ready for the upcoming work week.

She arrived at around 10:30 p.m. She put her things down and went to the bathroom. She came back into the bedroom in a lacy Victoria's Secret minigown. She turned on the music, and she spread her legs seductively on the bed.

"What are you trying to do?" I asked.

"I'm trying to put it on you!"

"Wishful thinking, don't you think?"

"No wishing over here," she replied teasingly.

"There you go! Being conceited again."

I turned the light off and jumped on the bed next to her.

In my head, I was thinking, *you should be ending this relationship instead of entertaining her like this!* The other side of me was saying, *Go ahead and have fun for the last time. Put it on her! Enjoy it while it lasts.* I went with the latter.

I licked her ear playfully. "So you ready for some nice waxing?"

"You know what that does to me," she said, gasping and rubbing my butt as I laid on her.

"So . . . What does it do to you again?" I asked, as I licked her other ear.

"Stop!" She began to push me off playfully. I could feel her shivering. As I caressed her breasts, I felt her moving all over the place. I slightly moved to her left, pulled her panties to the side, licked my middle finger and slid it into her piggy bank. It was wet, and I felt the familiar warmth. Her muscles gripped on my finger as I dipped it in and out of her. She started to moan louder now. I rubbed her clit and continued sucking on her nipple at the same time; my other hand was fondling her idle breast. She was gasping for air, feverishly grabbing me. She found my kahuna. The more excited she got, the harder she squeezed and stroked it. I could feel myself throbbing. She pulled so hard at one point, it hurt. I had to change my position. She probably forgot it wasn't a toy.

The penis is all muscle; women have to remember to be gentle with it.

"Oh god! I can't wait to feel you inside of me!"

"Oh really?"

"Yes! Really!" she responded, gasping.

"I love this instrument of yours, big daddy. I love the way it fills me up!"

"It loves you right back, baby."

I slid farther down and started to perform oral sex on her.

A few minutes later, she grabbed my head. "Stop, Stop, babes! I don't want to cum just yet! Come over here. I want you now!" She began pulling my head toward hers and started to kiss me vigorously. My mouth had just been downtown, but it didn't matter to her.

By now, she had made a little puddle on the bed. My fingers were still doing their magic; I started to nibble her nipples again. She was grabbing and pulling me as if she was going to swallow me whole. Her lava was flowing down the insides of her thighs. I took my finger out of her and she slowly grabbed it and put it into her mouth and sucked on it as though it were a lollipop, watching me as my fingers went in and out of her mouth. She pulled me closer and positioned herself beneath me as we kissed. She grabbed my kahuna, stroked it and moved it closer to her kitty as she slowly spread her legs. She rubbed her clit with it for a few seconds, and as she was about to slide it in, I pulled back.

"I have to get the condoms, sweetie. Hold that thought," I said, as I started to get off the bed.

"Okay," she said, with a disappointed look.

She was hot and ready to go. We were so excited that in the heat of the moment, we could get caught up again. I reflected on how the mood gets dulled sometimes when you have to go look for a condom.

Well, I'm not about to take a chance again. I'm not going to have a scenario where it's "three times a charm," or "three strikes and you're out."

The condom was right underneath my bed, so I strapped it on and was back on top of her in a few seconds. Her face lit up as I gently kissed her. I pulled her legs apart, and then I pulled her hands motioning for her to grab my kahuna and lead me in. She gasped as I entered her. She adjusted her hips, grabbed my butt, and pulled me in farther as she shivered. I could feel her nails on my behind. I kept churning slowly.

"God! You feel so damn good!" she screamed.

"You feel so good too, baby, and so freaking wet! Damn!"

"Right there, baby! Please don't stop!" she screamed.

"No?"

"No! Please don't stop . . . Oh my baby!"

I rhythmically moved in and out. Then I turned up the tempo a bit. She put her hands on my chest and grabbed hard. I slowed down and threw her left leg over my left shoulder. It was as if I was half stroking her missionary style and half doing her from a sideways position. I watched for her reaction as I dug in for a few seconds then relaxed. Her eyes were closed; she was breathing

WTF MOMENT

heavily and shaking. Then I started playing with her clit as I continued to thrust in and out of her.

She started to whisper, "Oh baby," and then screamed, "Oh baby!"

We continued for a while. I moved off the bed while still inside her and pulled her closer as I placed my feet on the floor for more leverage.

I crossed her legs at the ankles while I penetrated deeper.

She opened her eyes and then rolled them back, quivering.

"I'm about to cum again, baby! Oh my god, Devin!"

"Hold on, let's cum together!"

"Okay, baby . . . Come on baby. Cum with me, baby!"

Moments later, I felt the good ole tingle at the tip of my kahuna. I unconsciously churned harder and pulled her as I pushed in as far as I could. She felt me as my rhythm changed. She held me in a tight grip and pulled me in as well.

"I'm gonna cum," I whispered into her ear while licking it.

She moaned, shaking as if she was having a convulsion. I felt myself explode as my life forces flowed out of me. It felt good. She was still shaking and having aftershock moments after I had pulled out.

We soon fell asleep and went another round in the morning before we started getting ready for work. She especially liked early morning sex. She always told me, "All you have to do is roll over and stick it in." It made sense because men wake up hard in the mornings, and some women's kitties are wet in the mornings too, as though, they had marinated overnight.

I took a quick shower after our session, and then I started to iron my clothes. She hopped in the shower, singing as the water ran. I was glad she was singing this time around. A few times when she had stayed overnight, she had woken up in a bad mood. This was the same woman who had been excited the night before, cracking jokes and having fun.

On one occasion, I asked her what was wrong, and she replied she'd had a bad dream. I tried to hug her, but she moved away, and when she looked up at me, she was crying. I was baffled and asked her what the dream was about. She didn't answer, but had an attitude. I finally had to pull it out of her the next day; she told me she had dreamt that I went back to the ex-wife.

She actually believed her dream was a revelation of what I was about to do. It was annoying. *How could she come up with stuff like that?* First off, it wasn't true, and secondly, she probably had the dream because her mind wandered so much.

I finished ironing my clothes and started to look for my shoes. She was fixing her hair in the bathroom mirror when she suddenly said, "I met a guy

BOLAJI TIJANI-QUDUS

in Greensburg yesterday. He told me how beautiful I am. He said he wanted to marry me."

Certain men can't control themselves when they see a good-looking woman. The words that come out of their mouths make you shake your head at times. Some men make the rest of us look bad, I thought.

"Another proposal, huh?" I asked, smiling, but I didn't really know whether it was a joke or maybe she was telling me just to see my reaction. Plus it didn't make sense. Did she mean she met a man yesterday? Or was she really saying she had met a new man?

Some women say things sometime to make a partner jealous. In their minds, it would make him pay more attention to them when he is aware of another man, trying to get into the picture. I never had time for such games and never will. So I went about the business of getting ready for work without saying another word on the subject. I wouldn't have minded if she had met someone new who could take her off my hands.

"I have to go, sunshine," I said. "Please lock up when you're done. I'll talk to you later." I gave her a kiss on the forehead, smiled, and headed out the door. I had a strange feeling it was the last time we would get together. I had tried to cut the ties a few times. She had cried and apologized, and we continued the friendship. But the reality was, she wasn't a woman who would let me be. I wouldn't mind a relationship, but the extremities of her mood swings were mind-boggling and made me suspect that she was bipolar. I was still trying to get to know her, but the arguments grew tiresome.

* * *

A work week went by. There had been some chitchatting here and there between Amanda and me. *Maybe it's slowly fizzling,* I thought.

Saturday arrived, and I played basketball with the guys for most of the morning. On the way home after the game, I checked my voicemail. There was a message from Mom. She wanted to know whether I was coming over for dinner. I was tired and didn't feel like going, but I would have to hear her mouth. Since I hadn't been over in three weeks, I had to go.

I decided to go get a massage first. I headed west on I-380 toward Chinatown, to a nice spot I usually patronized. The Asian massage therapists are good. They would stand on your back and massage with their feet. I made it there in twenty minutes, paid the seventy bucks for a ninety-minute session, and headed upstairs to my assigned room.

WTF MOMENT

The place was really clean and welcoming. The prices were reasonable too. Factor in a twenty-dollar tip, and you still end up with a good massage for less than one hundred dollars. Some of the other fancy spots I had been to charged two hundred dollars for an hour of therapy.

I undressed, put on a robe, and walked toward the bathroom for a shower.

I was back in my room in a couple of minutes. I hopped onto the massage table, lay on my belly, covered my butt with a towel, and waited for my therapist. The background music was soothing. I was falling asleep when I heard the door open.

"You ready?" a voice asked in a whispering tone as if trying not to disturb me. I didn't recognize the voice, so I looked up. It was a petite lady, probably in her late thirties or early forties. She weighed about one hundred pounds. She was not remotely attractive. *I hope she gives a damn good massage*, I thought. *Then again, it is probably for the better. Sometimes the pretty cute ones made it hard to concentrate.*

"Sure," I replied.

She washed her hands. Then she poured oil on my back and asked, "Soft or strong?"

"Medium," I responded. I didn't know why I said that. I should have opted for soft. The last time I got the medium/strong massage, my back was sore for a couple of days. Some of the little Asian women look deceptively delicate, but are really strong.

She hopped up on the massage table and stood on my back. "Okay to massage with feet?" she asked. I nodded in agreement. She started with my heels and moved up to my calves and then to my hamstrings. A few minutes later, she was massaging my butt and then my back and shoulders. Surprisingly she had really good skills. I couldn't tell whether they were hands or feet massaging me. She was really light; I didn't feel as if someone was standing on my back. I would have objected, had a hundred-eighty-five-pound woman asked whether she could stand on my back.

About twenty minutes later, she hopped off and started to massage my neck area. Her hands were tough. I started to cringe as she massaged deeper. I was trying my best to man up, but she was putting the hurt on me. I guess I must have been really tense. I tried to give her hints by slightly moving and twisting my upper body as she massaged me, but she seemed to go harder the more I resisted. I almost screamed at one point. I finally muscled up courage.

"A little softer please."

"I sorry," she responded.

She asked me to turn over and she started to massage the front of my body. Minutes later, she brushed against my manhood while she was massaging my inner thighs.

Oh she thinks she is slick. She needs to focus on the damn massage she is giving me. She isn't going to get me aroused. I came here for a massage, and that is all I'm getting.

Moments later she touched my penis slightly and said, "You want me to massage this?"

No way in hell is she going to massage my kahuna with those strong hands of hers! She will probably peel the skin right off my stuff.

"No, thank you," I politely said.

Some of my buddies love to get *happy endings* after massages. They even rave and compare hand jobs by different therapists. That may be their thing, but it definitely ain't mine.

I don't know how many perverts the woman has jerked off. And then she wants to do the same to me with those same hands? I don't think so!

I feel the same way about strip clubs. Why go in there and pay to watch a woman tease me? I would rather have my lady give me a lap dance at home, in my bedroom, so we can have sex afterward. She could even pretend we were in a strip club, and she could tease me all she wanted. I would even offer to install a pole in my room.

I hopped off the massage table and started putting my clothes on. Then I noticed she was still standing there. I guess she wanted her tip. Some therapists will give you privacy for a few minutes. They will ask whether you need some water to drink, and leave you to get dressed.

I looked at her annoyingly and asked, "Can I have a glass of water please?"

"No problem," she said, as she hurried out of the room.

By the time she returned, I was fully dressed and handed her a fifteen-dollar tip which I thought was generous because she did give a good massage. But her hanging around at the end of the session had rubbed me the wrong way.

I headed home. It was 4:00 p.m. when I glanced at the dashboard. I shot Phil a text to check for any happenings for the evening. Then I called Amanda. Her voicemail came on right away, so I left her a voice message. Moments later I got a text from her.

From: Amanda
I'll call you shortly.

I was on my way out the door when Amanda finally called.

WTF MOMENT

"Hi, Devin."

"Hey."

"Just got around to calling you back," she continued.

"Oh okay. You texted me back instead of calling. Is everything okay?"

"Oh I dropped my phone in water earlier today so I couldn't make calls."

"I'm on my way out."

"Okay. Call me later, or I'll call you. I'm meeting up with Anita, and we are going out. I don't know where though," she said.

"Cool. I'll talk to you later."

I felt I should have told her to meet me somewhere. I wanted to tell her face-to-face that I didn't think things were working out. I was hoping to leave things on friendly terms at least. *Well, I can do it some other time*, I thought.

I made a quick dash to the parents' house. I smiled as I thought about Mom's good home cooking. It always makes the trip worthwhile. She asked me why I hadn't brought her granddaughter over. I explained to her Monica was taking Emmanuella to a birthday party. After dinner, I sat there and listened to Mom rant about why it was a sin not to go church.

"So are you coming tomorrow, Devin?" she asked.

"I don't know, Mom. I'll call you in the morning and let you know."

While I was figuring ways to get out of there, Phil called me. *Perfect timing*, I thought.

"Dude, let's go to San Juan tonight!"

"What's going on out there? It's on the other side of the water and an hour and a half away!"

"A new bar just opened up, and I heard the place has been overflowing with honeys. Besides, let's change it up. I'm tired of the bar scene out here. I want to meet new people," he said.

Phil made sense. It would be nice to go somewhere different for a change. San Juan has always been a tourist attraction with its ocean front condos, restaurants, rows of bars, and clubs. The beach has one of the bluest waters around, and is a mecca for surfers.

"We can even get a room and stay there until tomorrow afternoon. What do you say?" he asked.

"Okay, let's do it!" I responded, juiced up.

I went home to change, and Phil picked me up an hour later. We headed to San Juan. When we arrived, we valet parked his ride and walked toward the multi-leveled, Club Mars. There were a lot of people in line. I told the bouncer we were purchasing a bottle, and he let us in right away. We were sharply dressed, and it was only a matter of time before the ladies started to flock

BOLAJI TIJANI-QUDUS

toward us. Some asked us whether we were pro athletes or recording artists. Phil's spanking new Range Rover might have added to our image too.

"It's on tonight!" Phil said, winking at me.

"And you know this!" I responded.

We drank and danced with a couple of ladies, Lisa and Sonia, who were visiting from London. Being six two, they were a bit short for my liking, but the bodies on them both made up for the lack in height.

About an hour later, Phil said, "We should roll to the next spot. There are so many, we need to hit as many as we can!"

"Okay, I'm game. I'm going to use the bathroom," I said.

The men's room on the floor we were on was congested, so I opted to use the one upstairs. I was hoping it was available because I didn't want to travel up to the third level. My bladder was full, and I needed to unload fast.

The bathroom was at the far end of the floor. I had to weave through heavy traffic. I took a glimpse at a nicely shaped woman in a short black dress with a cloche hat, to match. Her back was turned. *What a rump!* She was slow dancing with a guy who seemed to be enjoying himself. His hands were planted on her luscious rump. Her hands were wrapped around his neck. It was slightly dimmed in there, but I could have sworn I saw them kissing. I didn't want to look like a pervert, so I looked away and headed to the restroom. *Freaks need to take that home*, I thought, smiling.

I was glad I was able to use the men's room with no delay. On my way back, I saw a group of six gorgeous ladies dancing by themselves. I wanted to text Phil to come up and see, but I was sure he was more than satisfied downstairs. The club was filled with the best-looking women I had seen in a long time. I had to feed my lusty eyes, so I navigated through the middle of the floor. The view of the gorgeous six was even better up close. As I was about to leave, I got a good look at the freaky couple. They were now in the back corner, still dancing.

"What the . . .," I started to murmur.

Alas! The woman in the short black dress was Amanda! I inched a bit closer and stared dead at her, but she couldn't see me. Her eyes were closed as she danced with her back to his chest, her arms stretched backward over her head, rubbing the back of the guy's head while he danced behind her, caressing her front side.

Time stood still for a few seconds. I gathered my thoughts, turned around, and left.

She isn't my girlfriend anyway. Actually, this is a good thing. I have an excuse to sever all ties completely!

WTF MOMENT

Something told me to go back and confront her. So I piggybacked to where they were dancing. This time she saw me as I walked up.

"Hey, Amanda. How is it going?" I asked.

She stared at me dumbfounded. If she had had magic that could make her disappear, she would have used it at that awkward moment.

She finally gathered herself and said, "Hey, Devin."

The guy she was with was looking at both of us wondering what was going on. He could sense there was something between us. One could cut the tension with a knife. I finally extended my hand to him and said, "Hi, I'm Devin." He shook my hand and introduced himself as well. I didn't pay enough attention to get his name.

"Well, you all have a good night now. See you around, Amanda."

I could feel their eyes on my back as I walked away. She probably wished the floor could open up and swallow her.

I found my way downstairs and met up with Phil. He was still talking to the ladies from London.

"There goes Devin!" Phil announced.

"So I heard you guys are club hopping," Lisa said.

"Yes, we are! So how is the evening going for you both?" I asked.

"We're having a blast. We would love to go hopping with you, guys, but we're here with some other friends of ours, and they're scattered all over this club. We don't want to leave them, you know?" Lisa added.

"I understand. Let's exchange numbers. The night is still young; we may catch up later," I said.

"Sure," Sonia said.

As we were leaving, Phil asked whether they were staying in San Juan.

"We're both staying at the W Hotel for the weekend," Lisa said.

"Room 402. Hope to catch you later," Sonia added. She winked at me while walking away. They both giggled and soon disappeared into the crowd.

"If all else fails, we might end up in their hotel room when the night is over," Phil said, nudging me on the shoulder.

"You know I'm down," I said, as we walked out the front door.

We headed for Air Bar, a block away. Phil told me it was more of a relaxed atmosphere with plenty of lounge space. "A little change of pace for the moment," he said.

"Guess who I saw in there with another dude?"

"Who? Not your ex, I hope," Phil responded.

"No, dude! It was Amanda! Hugged up on the dance floor."

"Wow! What is she doing way out here? Doing some dirt, huh?" he continued.

"She thinks she is slick."

"Forget her. She is plastic and high maintenance anyway. Isn't she the same person who told you she wanted to get a boob job and booty shots?"

"Yup, that's her. You forgot tummy tuck!" I said, laughing. "You've seen how stacked she is already, right? That's all she talks about . . . cosmetic enhancements."

Phil shook his head. "Some women are just too damn vain. It's so sad."

"What a shame! She is always talking about how pretty she looked and how lucky I was to have her," I added, shaking my head.

"She must have not seen Monica," Phil added.

I sighed, as we continued walking.

"Who says that? If it's all about having a trophy woman on my arms, I would still be married or would have locked down one of these other Barbie-looking women I have met. I'm not shallow, bro."

"Don't even sweat it, Devin. She's cute and all, but you don't need all the drama. You have enough headaches dealing with your divorce. She isn't worth it, bro. Clearly, she hasn't evolved emotionally."

"You couldn't have said it any better," I said, shaking my head.

Phil nudged me and said, "We are here to have a damn good time, so let's get it on."

"Damn right! Amanda who?" I scoffed. "At least I won't have to worry about her leaving hair trails everywhere at my place—in the sink, trash can, bathtub, kitchen cabinets. She had conveniently left her bra in the bathroom and panties underneath my bed. Why do some women behave as such? They think they are marking their territories. It's so juvenile!"

"She is loony!" Phil said. "I'm surprised you entertained her for this long."

"I know, huh? I keep thinking the same thing."

Although I liked her, I was relieved it was over.

Oh well, this one wasn't meant to be. There will be plenty of ladies to serenade tonight, I thought, as we walked into the Air Bar.

12. Haters

I was feeling the Monday blues at the office. It was a busy day, signaling how the rest of the week would go. It was only eleven in the morning. I felt depressed thinking about how many more hours I had to go before the end of the workday. Phil had e-mailed me and suggested we go check out a happy hour spot after work, which I was looking forward to. I was so busy I'd forgotten I had gotten a voice message from Naomi earlier. I had been surprised to get a call from her that early in the day.

Naomi and I had been flirting with each other for the past nine months, but we had never really taken it further. We had been on a date once. I'd tried to get another one, but she wasn't too receptive, so I never really pursued her. I felt she was occupied with someone or something. Granted, she is a single mom with a four-year-old son. I don't know what would have happened between us, but I really thought we liked each other.

Naomi has an average look, but her body is spectacular. I don't know how to explain it, but she oozed a different kind of sexiness. She had eyes that said, *I am going to have my way with you!*

Although we had never dated full on, she's the only woman I had ever kissed on a dance floor who wasn't my girlfriend. I remember her staring at me with those eyes; it felt as if someone had hypnotized me. It was a short, sweet, wet kiss. She is a good kisser like me, which amplified my physical attraction to her. It's rare to find someone who knows how to kiss. I think it is an art form.

Shortly after our quick kissing session, I asked myself, *what the hell just happened? I definitely don't like that kind of attention in public, I operated out of character.* I'm usually in control, but she had an unexplainable pull that drew me in.

We met one night at Legion Bar. I had popped in to see Phil. I wore a powder blue sweater, white collared shirt, dark denims, and brown Kenneth Cole shoes. My attire was simple, yet casual. I thought I was put together nicely.

I was standing in the hallway talking to Phil when I noticed her walking to the ladies room with some of her friends. As they passed us, we instinctively sized them all up. We looked at each other and started laughing. We had completely stopped our conversation just to get a peek. Even when men try not to, the eyes and head wander on their own when a good-looking woman walks by.

"They were nice," I said to Phil.

"Man o man! Did you see the one in the pink dress?" he asked.

"You know I did, they're all bad as hell! Damn!"

We stood there in the hallway half pretending we were talking, but our eyes kept darting in the direction of the ladies' bathroom. Phil had the same thought as I—*we were definitely going to ambush them on their way back.*

Ten minutes later, they were walking toward us. As they drew near, Phil said, "You ladies are some of the best-dressed women in here."

"And I concur," I said, quickly.

"Thank you," one of them responded, giggling.

I noticed Naomi; she had a blue dress on. It held tightly to her body, exposing all her curves.

As we were about to spark a conversation with them, a lady Phil knew pounced on him, and they embraced for a long minute, it seemed. It kind of ruined the moment because we would have each pulled a woman out of the group. Phil was very funny, so we would have had their attention. The ladies started to file away toward the main room. Naomi was the last to walk by me, so I said, "Nice color you have on, ma'am."

"Thank you. And I love that color on you too." She stopped and smiled at me.

"I see you got the memo," I said, smiling as well.

"I sure did." She flashed an even bigger smile. She was very friendly. Although she was with her friends, she motioned to one of them, as they kept walking away, that she would catch up with them. It's annoying when a man tries to talk to a woman, and the first thing she says is, "My friends are leaving; I have to go." It is understandable, but there isn't anything wrong with conversing for a minute, especially if she's approached in a respective manner.

We were in the middle of the hallway, blocking traffic, so I gently pulled her closer to me, to allow people to pass.

"Devin," I said, extending my hand.

"It's nice to meet you. Naomi is the name."

WTF MOMENT

"Did you ladies just come from a photo shoot? I have to say, you're looking exceptionally gorgeous."

"Thank you again. You don't look too shabby yourself. It's nice to see a guy well put together."

"Really? I just threw something on . . . nothing spectacular," I said, laughing.

"No . . . I see plenty of guys in here, and they look as though they just threw something on for real. I like . . . I like," she said, in a flirting manner.

"I like too," I flirted back, scanning her from head to toe.

"It's my birthday today"

"Get out of here! Happy birthday!" I said, as I gave her a hug.

"Thanks," she responded, smiling.

We embraced as if we had known each other before that evening. Her hands wrapped behind my neck, and then she squeezed me when they fell across my back. My hands were on her waist, so I pulled her closer to me as I caressed her hips. I don't know why, but it felt good. When my nature began to swell, I moved away slowly before she noticed.

"How about I buy you a birthday drink?" I asked.

"I don't know. I think we have had a lot to drink already."

"It's your birthday! C'mon. Have just one more, okay?" I asked, playfully, sulking.

"Okay," she responded.

"By the way, who will be driving?"

"My best friend . . . and she doesn't drink."

"It's all good then. Let's go."

We wove through the thick crowd. It took us about ten minutes to get to the bar. We ran into her friends and sister on the way, and I asked them to come along. I bought them all a round of drinks. Her sister wanted water. *I don't understand why a bottle of water would cost $6.* I felt it was a rip-off.

Naomi's drink arrived last. I handed it to her and gave her a kiss on the cheek.

"Happy birthday again," I said.

She gave me a tight hug and thanked me.

"I have to go find my boy. I hope I see you later," I said, smiling ear to ear.

"You will," she said, grinning back at me. The rest of her crew threw quick glances at each other and smiled as well.

*   *   *

That was a nice evening, I reminisced.

BOLAJI TIJANI-QUDUS

I decided to return Naomi's phone call. I dialed her number and she picked up right away.

"Hello?"

"Hey, it's Devin. I got your voicemail. How are you?" I asked in a mellow tone.

"I'm doing well, thank you. Good morning!"

"It's going to definitely be a good morning since I am hearing from you this early," I said, laughing.

"Yeah, it took you a while to call me back. I showered, took my son to school, ate breakfast, and ran some errands, and you're just calling now," she said sarcastically.

"Some of us have to work, you know," I shot back.

"Humph! I do work, smarty-pants. I just happen to be off today. I have a few personal things to do. How is work going for you anyway?" she asked.

"Pretty busy for the most part," I replied. "So what's going on with you?"

"Hmmmm, nothing much. I was calling you earlier because I wanted to talk to you."

I started to wonder what she was trying to say. *Was she in trouble? Did she need to borrow money?* I couldn't quite put my finger on it.

"Okay? You're talking to me now."

"Hmmm . . . I just wanted to let you know I'm someone's girlfriend now, and I don't want you to think I am acting funny or weird if I start talking to you less. You know what I mean? I may see you out, and I might not respond to you the way I normally would."

I didn't know how to respond. It was something out of the blue. We had just hung out the prior Friday. We had talked about everything from raising kids to favorite sexual positions. It had been an enlightening conversation because I could feel she was a very sensual person, and we had a great chemistry.

I was a taken aback with the latest development, though we never really dated. *Why do I feel as if she was calling me to break up?*

"You know what I am saying, Devin?" Her voice echoed through the phone, interrupting my thoughts. I finally found some words.

"Oh okay . . . no problem there!"

"I feel I just want you to know what is going on with me, especially since our talk last Friday. You understand?"

"Absolutely no problem," I said to her, in a reassuring manner.

"Okay, I will see you soon. I have to run some errands."

"Absolutely. I have to get back to work too. Talk to you later, and good luck with everything," I said.

WTF MOMENT

"Thanks . . . Talk to you later."
I walked back to my office thinking, *how bizarre was that conversation?* It kept bothering me. So I texted her.

> *To: Naomi*
> I was caught off guard with your revelation. I had no idea you had so much going on, lol. But thanks for the heads up though. I am saddened and disappointed because I thought we had a great vibe going ☺

I wasn't expecting a text back. Something must have happened for her to want to let me know what she told me. Maybe she was fighting the feelings she was having for me, so she felt she had to nip it in the bud. I wrestled with those thoughts for most of the day. It's funny, I truly felt as if she had broken up with me, and I was asking myself why. *What the hell is wrong with me? Nothing happened between us. Why am I even bothered?* So I snapped out of it and continued working. I received a text from Naomi.

> *From: Naomi*
> It wasn't all of a sudden. I have been talking to him for a while, and we have been best friends for three years. We are giving it another try to see what happens. Sometimes feelings develop and things change.

I wanted to tell her to go shove it! I decided against it, as it would be pointless dragging the conversation on. *It wasn't that serious anyway.* She was talking about getting into a relationship with her so-called best friend who conveniently wanted to have a relationship when she started to go out on dates. It's annoying when a guy stays close to one particular ex-girlfriend or *best friend* who probably had self esteem issues and is attached to him. He controls her life under the pretense of being best/good friends. He goes around and messes with other women and still returns to take advantage of her soft spot for him.

I texted her back and kept it simple.

> *To: Naomi*
> No worries at all ☺
> Have a good one.

> *From: Naomi*
> You as well ☺

No, you won't, I thought, as I read her text. I deleted her number. I didn't need to have her info in my phone any longer.

I walked into the bathroom to empty my tank. Whoever was previously in there stunk it up. I held my breath as I peed. I gagged when I tried to come up for air. *Why do people take a bad dump at work? Why can't they do that at home?*

I was cursing at whoever performed the horrible act. It's funny how you can deal with the smell of your own dump no matter how bad it is, but you can't bear to smell someone else's. I pulled my shirt over my nose, breathed some air in, and held my breath again. I finished and got out of there without even washing my hands.

The work day concluded, and I hopped into my car and headed to a happy hour spot to meet Phil. It wasn't too bad for a Monday. When I arrived, Phil was fiddling with his high-tech phone, perhaps browsing the Internet. In front of him was a loud group talking to each other over the equally loud music. Phil looked up and smiled. I signaled to him for us to head to the other side of the bar where it might be quieter.

"Glad you could make it," he said, playfully.

"What are you talking about?"

"You know, I've been sitting here for almost forty-five minutes."

"Wow! Forty-five whole minutes!"

"Yup."

"Whatever, man," I said, laughing. "I was caught up on the phone with Naomi."

"What's up with her?"

"She called to tell me she was going steady with her best friend again."

"She had to call you to tell you that?"

"That's what I said! She could have stopped taking my calls, and I would have gotten the message. It wasn't as if I had expectations anyway."

"Next please."

"Yes! I wish I tapped that though," I added.

"I thought you did already"

"No, we only hung out once, but nothing came of it. She was kind of elusive, and I didn't really press. It's all clear now. She was trying to date me and be with her ex, Jimmy, at the same time. He goes to Mood's often, always trying to pick up a woman."

"He probably noticed she was out trying to do her own thing, and his jealous ass stepped in," Phil said, sighing.

He placed two bottles of Heineken in front of us.

"It's so lame when guys hang on to ex-girlfriends under the pretense of friendship. In my opinion, it's all a form of control. A guy wants to go have fun,

WTF MOMENT

but as soon as she starts something with someone else, here he comes, wanting a relationship all of a sudden." I sighed as well.

Phil nodded in agreement.

"Speaking of lame dudes, look who just walked in," I said.

"Who?" Phil asked, turning around swiftly."

A fella named Isaiah we knew from around the way walked in with a couple of women.

"That's your boy," I said, laughing.

"He is a sorry excuse for a human being. I hope he stays over there."

"Don't worry. I don't think he will come over here and say hello," I assured him.

"You know, what really gets me is when guys try to seek romantic relationships with another guy's current or past woman. There are unwritten rules regarding that."

"I know what you mean," I said.

"He knew Christina and I were dating for a while. It's funny how he conveniently started to send her messages on Facebook the moment we broke up. He was asking her where she was going to hang out for the weekend and whether they could have lunch or coffee sometime," Phil continued.

"How did you find out?"

"Because Christina called me and told me. At first she was upset, saying she wasn't a whore to be passed around. I asked her why she would say such a thing, and she said my buddy was underhandedly making passes at her. I had to let her know John wasn't my buddy—we just happen to have mutual friends, and I talk to him when I see him out at the social spots. I told her to ignore him, and he would go away. Believe me, if he had persisted, I would have had to put him in his place."

"Unbelievable!" I added.

Phil looked as if he was going to walk over to John and hit him in the face. Just like Phil, I can't stand sneaky people who masquerade as friends or associates when, in actuality, they are full of it.

I recalled the same John actually walking up to a lady I had chatted up at the bar one evening. He warned her to be careful. "He has a lot of women," he told her. What kind of guy would say that to a woman he doesn't even know? Heck, he didn't even know me! Apparently he had seen her a few times in there, but never said anything. But on that evening, he had to say something. I wanted to actually sit him down and ask him whether he really knew anything about me besides seeing me around every now and then. I figured it would have been a waste of my time talking to an idiot.

Phil was agitated when I told him about the episode.

"See! Captain Save-A-Hoe. Why couldn't he just walk up to the woman and tell her what he really wanted to say? That he wanted her for himself. But he has no game or fortitude, so he had to say something negative about you to gain a favor. In his mind, he was being a nice guy, pretending to be watching out for her feelings."

"I can't even believe guys do that," I said, shaking my head.

"Cock blocker! You should have confronted him. He had no business throwing you under the bus. He has to be an insecure pathetic idiot."

"He is not even worth it," I concluded.

I ordered another round of beers and changed the subject as soon as some local associates joined us at the table.

13. The Wow! Experience, Part 1

I was lounging at home watching TV when I started to daydream about Whitney whom I was to meet for dinner later on in the evening. I smiled as I reflected on the night she had come to see me at Mood's six weeks ago. She had worn a red dress that could have started a war. Guys wanted to talk to her, and the women gnawed at her. By the end of the evening, I started calling her Ms. Wow! Her physical attributes triggered the "Wow!" response from people.

Ms. Wow is also short for her full name—Whitney Owen Williams. She's only five six, but she walks as if she's a runway model. Her free-flowing, jet-black hair hangs all the way to her waist. She has a pear-shaped face, big round eyes, and long eyelashes. I always joked she could have her own Barbie doll in stores. I don't care too much for nose rings on women, but hers makes her look especially sexy. Her nose is straight and perfectly follows the line of her forehead. She has the most curvaceous body. Her assets are well proportioned—nice rack, tasty butt, and a tiny waist with a measurement of 36-24-39.

Whitney is definitely a brick house. If she were a vain woman, she could have been in one of those music videos or magazines. She is something to look at, and she never took herself too seriously. As gorgeous as she is, she is equally down to earth. I teased her about her squeaky, little girl's voice, and how her nose twinkles when she giggles. Nonetheless she is all that and then some.

We had met at a real estate seminar a couple of months prior. I wasn't keen on going that day. I only went as a favor for my friend, Lester. He had been bugging me for at least a month about how he'd found the perfect business opportunity. He felt it could make him a millionaire. He had said he wouldn't feel right about keeping all the great information to himself. I made a decision to go to the seminar because I didn't want to disappoint him. He has always carried himself with dignity and is a nice guy.

BOLAJI TIJANI-QUDUS

When I arrived at the seminar, I saw a group of lovely ladies seated behind a rectangular table in the lobby. As soon as someone walked in, they would smile and motion for the person to come over. Then, they asked for the guest list update so they could stay in touch. It was annoying going through the questionnaires, but they were polite enough so it didn't bother me much. I was given a guest tag and ushered into the large conference room. A well-dressed man at the other side of the double doors showed me to an empty chair toward the back of the hall.

I glanced at my watch, thinking about the next five hours of torture I was going to endure.

The host was a bubbly, short, bald man with a protruding stomach. He reminded me of my middle school principal. I could have sworn I saw light reflecting off his shiny head. He made a few jokes and introduced a speaker.

"Ladies and gentlemen, it is my great pleasure to introduce Mr. John Robinson. This gentleman was once homeless but this year alone, he has amassed up to three million dollars in wealth. I will let him tell you how he did it," he said with a wide smile.

Mr. Robinson had been sitting at the back of the hall. As he walked forward, people who knew him were shaking his hands or patting him on the back. He worked the room as if he were a rock star. The roar was deafening as he finally took the stage.

Mr. Robinson milked the attention and applause for a few minutes before he finally spoke. He raised his hands signaling for the crowd to stop. "Thank you, thank you," he said, but the applause continued.

He began his speech as soon as it quieted down. He told the story of how he hadn't had a job and was down on his luck, evicted from his apartment, and living out of his car. The crowd was fixated on him as he spoke; you could hear the oohs and the ahhs! He even choked up at one point during his speech, and he received a standing ovation. He gathered himself and continued.

His wife stood next to him. She beamed and nodded her head in agreement. He went on to talk about how he now makes one hundred thousand in a couple of weeks wheeling and dealing in real estate.

"Now I spend all day with my wife, and I get to take my sons to soccer practice. I bought a 10,000-square-foot beautiful home in Napa Valley just last month," he said. A large overhead projector beamed a picture of the home on the wall behind him. I looked around the room and saw people smiling and clapping as if hypnotized. *Everyone can't be this happy*, I thought.

"If this can change my life, I know it can change yours too," he said. The applause got louder this time, and he received another standing ovation when he left the stage. His wife scurried behind him as they headed to their seats.

WTF MOMENT

"That is one of the most touching stories I have ever heard since I have been with this organization," the host said. "It is amazing! Isn't it? One more time for Mr. Robinson please." The crowd erupted.

Once I had attended a seminar put together by a rival company. I understood the logic behind it. One can make serious money in real estate, but it requires plenty of time, dedication, and a whole lot of networking. It is like being a sales person.

A few other speakers were introduced, and I started to get restless. The next intermission was in fifteen minutes. I wanted to go look for Lester so he would see I had shown up. Then I would sneak out right afterward.

The break time didn't come soon enough. A large number of people spilled into the lobby. Some were discussing how awesome the speakers were, others were making small talk. Lester was conversing with a couple. He saw me and waved, signaling he would be with me shortly. I nodded in acknowledgement. I started to feel a bit claustrophobic, so I stepped outside for some fresh air. There were still too many people around the front. I went around to the side of the building to use my phone. Then I saw her sitting in her car with her door open, smoking a cigarette.

She rose and paced around, stretching I presumed. She wore a business suit, radiating sexiness. Her skirt was short, and her assets were well displayed. I wondered whether she had worn the suit to work. *She must frequently be the object of sexual harassment*, I thought.

I looked her way hoping to get her attention, but she was still on the phone. Smokers usually turn me off, but this vixen was too tempting for me to ignore. So I gathered some courage and walked toward her. I was thankful; she had just completed her phone conversation.

"Cigarettes are so bad for your health," I said, smiling.

"Oh! Ya! Bad habit I picked up from my ex-boyfriend."

"Could be a costly habit, you know?"

"I know, I know. Smoking is a stress reliever for me. But I'm going to stop."

"By the way, I am Devin," I said, smiling.

"Whitney. Nice to meet you."

"What do you think about the seminar?"

"It's okay, but I think the speakers enjoy these events more than the guests do," she said, laughing.

"Very true," I said, chuckling. "I'm here because I'm doing a friend a favor."

"Oh my god! Same here!" she exclaimed.

"These things are so long and boring. I don't know whether I can survive another three hours. I guess it's worth it if you're really into real estate."

"True indeed," she said, nodding in agreement.

I glanced at my watch. "I think there is still about half an hour left before the seminar starts back up. I was thinking of grabbing a bite across the street. You wanna come along?"

She bit her lip. "I want to, but fast food is bad for me."

"I know. I normally don't eat junk either, but I don't have much of a choice now as I'm famished, and I think the break will be over soon," I said, smiling.

"Okay. Let me put my belongings in the trunk."

"You probably don't want to do that. You never know who is watching you," I commented.

"You're right. But I don't want to carry my laptop."

"It's okay. I can help you with that."

"That's very thoughtful of you."

"It is no problem at all. Shall we?"

She smiled at me as she pressed a button on her key chain to lock her car doors.

As we crossed the road, a group of young men drove by, and one of them poked his head out of the car window and screamed, "Goddamn!"

Whitney was startled. When she figured out the outburst had been directed at her, she rolled her eyes in disgust and sighed.

"Perverts!"

"He couldn't help himself," I said, chuckling.

"Some of these guys act as though they have never seen a woman before."

"I can see why they act immature," I remarked.

"And I hate it when guys stare at my breasts during a conversation. Hello!" she said, bringing her hands up. "My face is right *here!*"

I nodded my head, sympathizing with her.

"Men! Uhh," she said, scoffing.

"Well, that's what men do."

"And . . . your point?" she asked, sighing.

"Of course I don't mean it that way. It's a joke."

"I hope so," she responded sarcastically.

We arrived at the restaurant, and I ordered a burger; she ordered the fish and chips. I paid the bill. We stood close to the counter and continued chatting while we waited on our food.

"I feel I would blow up like a balloon, if I eat this," she said.

"Are you kidding me? With a body like yours? I don't think fish sticks and fries will do anything to you in one day!"

WTF MOMENT

"You don't understand. I live at the gym. If I eat horribly for a week, things start going to the wrong places," she said, sighing.

"At least you know what you have to do. I'm a physical trainer, and I'm impressed with what I have seen so far."

"Really? I think I'm getting fat."

"No, no. You call this fat? You can't be serious! I have seen fat, and you're not close to being fat! You have an awesome lean body, and this is coming from someone who helps sculpt bodies."

"Well, thank you! So you're a trainer, huh? Maybe you can help me out sometime," she said, beaming.

"Sure. I can get you a nice membership package. I teach boot camp classes every Tuesday and Thursday in Brookdale."

"Oh, I live in Santa Lima; I don't think I can make it over your way."

"You have been doing well on your own anyway."

"Sometimes I need motivation. God knows I need it!"

We finally picked up our food and sat down to eat.

"Oh, we need to get our drinks. What would you like?" I asked.

"Iced tea, please . . . if they have it."

"Okay."

I returned with our drinks. Whitney was looking out of the window thinking deeply.

"Hey there!"

"Hey," she said, smiling.

"You're not eating?"

"I was waiting for you."

"That's considerate of you," I said, smiling.

"I try."

We ate in silence for a few minutes. I guess we were both trying not to talk with our mouths full.

"So . . . Is that all you do?" she asked.

"Excuse me?"

"I mean, are you a full-time trainer?"

"I train part-time and I manage the fitness center the rest of the time."

"Which one?"

"Five Star."

"Oh wow! I have been there once, and I loved the ambiance. I have been praying they would open one in my area. God knows we really need it!"

"We might just have to make it happen," I said, smiling.

"You have persuasive power as such?" she asked, laughing.

"I would think so. I will talk to my partners and see what happens. We have been talking about expanding."

"You own Five Star?"

"Yup."

"Impressive!"

I felt her gaze penetrating my being while I pretended to be focused on my food, so I quickly changed the focus to her.

"What about you? What do you do?" I asked.

"I'm an industrial engineer with Lotus Oil."

"Engineer, huh? Wow! That's different. You must love math."

"I have always loved math and the sciences from a young age."

"Nice. I wasn't too fond of math in high school or college. That's why I opted for sports management," I said, chuckling.

"I see."

She took her suit jacket off and, voila! Those breasts! I was tempted to ask whether they were real. Maybe she was wearing a push up-bra. *There is no way her breasts could be that firm.* I imagined watching one of those corny porn movies where one of the actresses wears a business suit, glasses, and ponytail. Then she pulls the band out and the hair falls down to her waist. The clothes also fall off revealing a sexy body. I was envisioning Whitney doing the same thing right there at the burger joint.

"Devin!" Whitney said, interrupting my train of thought.

"Sorry, I was thinking about all the stuff I cancelled to be here today. What were you saying?"

"I was asking what you intend to do with this seminar?"

"Probably nothing. As I was saying earlier, I came because of Lester. I'm not too keen on the idea of inviting a whole lot of people and have them invest seven thousand dollars for some classes on short sales and foreclosures. I'm sure the classes are very thorough and worth it, but it is a lot of money. I just couldn't sell it to the people I know."

"I see what you mean," she said, nodding in agreement.

"I understand the whole concept and wouldn't mind doing it and inviting people, but it does require quite a bit of money. What happens if they don't make their money back? I wouldn't feel right. The layer of profit sharing resembles a pyramid. Besides I dabbled in real estate already."

"I share the same sentiments. I think I have learned enough on my own. I have three houses now, all of which I bought as short sales. I live in one and the other two are rentals," she added.

"Nice!"

WTF MOMENT

"I'm just trying to get my hustle on. I hope I can be like you!"

"Trust me; you're not doing too badly at all!"

We continued eating. I was so hungry. I could have finished the food within minutes had I been alone. I didn't want to appear greedy, so I picked on the food and ate slowly.

"As beautiful and smart as you are, you must be taken," I said, sparking off another round of conversation.

She showed off her dimpled smile and looked at me in the eye, while thinking. "Well, I'm thirty-nine and still single. Although I was married once before," she said.

"Whoa! I could have sworn you couldn't be more than twenty-eight!" I said, surprised.

"Well, thank you."

"Any children?"

"Not at all. How about you? Any lucky woman has you tied down?"

"Not at the moment, but up until a year and a half ago, I was married. I do have a beautiful daughter," I said, as I proudly pulled Emmanuella's picture out of my wallet.

"Oh my god! She is so adorable! Awwww."

Before we could get into a discussion about our past married lives, she looked at her watch and said, "I think it's time to get back to the seminar."

"Already?" I asked.

We got up to leave, and she walked in front of me as we exited the restaurant. She suddenly turned around to ask me a question. I knew the trick! She was checking to see whether I was staring at her butt. Fortunately, I was checking the text messages on my phone as we walked.

"Are you staying for the rest of the seminar?" she asked.

"I don't think I am. I hope I can find Lester, and then I will leave. What about you?"

"I might not stay until the end either," she said, laughing.

We made our way back to the seminar. We stopped outside the door. I wanted to give her a handshake, but I opted for a hug instead. Then I asked her whether it was okay for me to call her sometime. She obliged, and we exchanged numbers. I watched her walk away, switching her hips.

I decided not to go back in, so I headed to my car.

I could go spend the rest of the day with Emmanuella.

* * *

I finally got a chance to call Whitney after a few weeks had gone by.

She picked up.

"Hello?"

"Hi, may I speak to Whitney please?"

"This is she. Who am I speaking with?"

"It's Devin. I met you at the Up the Stairs Seminar, a couple of weeks ago."

"Hey, Devin!" she said, ecstatically.

I was encouraged by her enthusiasm. She sounded as sexy on the phone as she did in person. She was polite as well. It's annoying to be on the phone with women who sound rude and don't even know it. It's impolite when some women say, 'Who is this?' on the phone or when you text for the first time and they don't recognize your number. It's such a turnoff. I prefer a woman to answer just as Whitney had. The way a woman handles herself on the phone gives me an idea of the kind of personality I will be dealing with. It is very sexy to chat with a woman with manners. Whitney was on the right track. I liked what I had heard already!

We chatted for about an hour, and I really enjoyed our conversation. We set up a time for the following weekend to hang out. She liked the idea of me cooking.

She arrived around 4 p.m. as planned.

"I don't smell any food," she said, as she entered my condo.

"I wasn't going to cook without you present. I don't want you saying someone else did the work for me. I have my pride," I said, laughing.

She laughed as well. "We shall see. I brought some Pepto Bismol just in case."

"Not funny."

"So what are we having, Devin?"

"Pasta with ground turkey sauce. I'm making mine from scratch."

"Woo hoo!"

I got to cooking, and Ms. Wow kept coming over to see if I needed help. I told her I had everything under control. That didn't stop her from sitting across from me on the high swivel chair. She talked to me, watched TV, and watched me cook.

"So who taught you how to cook?" she asked.

"I learned on my own."

"No, noooo . . . someone had to have shown you."

"Hmmm. I watched my mom, I read a few cookbooks, and I just did the trial-and-error thing until I got it right. I have always liked to cook. I wanted to go to culinary school at one point."

"What don't you want to do?"

"I know, huh?" I laughed.

WTF MOMENT

"Well, it smells good in here. I hope it tastes good too," she said, as she grabbed a few of my cookbooks and flipped through the pages.

"We will have to see now, won't we?" I said, sarcastically.

Thirty minutes later, we were eating, talking, laughing, and joking around. She knew something about everything. It was refreshing actually. She was into politics. She was no slouch in sports either. She knew the starting five players of the top basketball teams. She even broke it down and had decided which team needed to make a trade. I enjoyed her company immensely. Then the evening had to end. She had to be home to get enough rest for work the next day. It was a Thursday evening. I had slightly hoped she would have stayed so the night wouldn't be over. I walked her to the car, gave her a hug, and kiss on the cheek.

"How about you come visit me in Santa Lima next time?" she asked, as she entered her car.

I told her it would be a pleasure.

She was cool and looked good too. *I would drive down to the North Pole to see her.*

14. WTF . . .

I parked in front of Phil's house to pick him up for our periodic game nights. Immediately after I honked, I noticed his window curtain move, revealing his small head. He waved, acknowledging he saw me. I left my engine on, anticipating him coming out shortly. Phil is always punctual. He can always be counted on. I couldn't say that about some of my other inconsiderate friends. At times when I had to pick them up, they'd take forever to get ready even when the time had been agreed upon well in advance.

Phil hopped into the car and threw two twenty-four packs of beer on the backseat.

"You must have been reading my mind," I said.

"I like to be prepared! No more running out of beer, please! Remember the last time?" he asked, laughing.

"Yeah, I remember!" I laughed along. "So . . . what's up with you otherwise?"

Phil sighed and said, "There's nothing going on but the damn rent and these damn bills. I tell you, I have to win the lottery soon. I'm tired of so much money going out and much less coming in."

"That, my friend, is called the rat race," I chirped.

"I'm still trying to figure out my next hustle so I can retire early or move to one of the islands and enjoy the life fit for a king. It would be nice to have my house paid for; have enough money to eat and raise my kids. The last time I was on vacation in St. Thomas, I didn't want to come back home. It was so chill and peaceful there. No one was in a hurry to get anywhere. I long for that kind of lifestyle," he said, sighing.

"Amen to that. Please take me with you when you do blow up," I said, laughing.

"I would need a drama-free, smart, and beautiful woman to complete this fantasy of mine," he continued.

"Don't we all?" I added.

WTF MOMENT

I would be surprised if Phil got married. I don't think he enjoys being in a relationship. His job as a sports agent requires him to travel quite often. It could be a reason why he didn't keep women around for very long. He ends a relationship and moves to the next once he sees trouble signs. I've told him to be more compassionate. Although he is a gentleman, he doesn't fall over himself for women. Perhaps that may be the reason some are captivated by him.

He would always say, "When it comes to women, the nice guy finishes last." He believes a guy could be loving and caring, but must exude confidence and take control of situations. The moment a guy allows a woman to walk all over him, the relationship is doomed. She would take advantage of him in every way.

"My issue is, these women have unrealistic expectations—they want prince charming to sweep them off their feet," he said. "They want to be Cinderella in a fairy tale wedding. I swear to God they live in a fantasy world. They say they want a hard-working man who has something going for himself, and when they find him, they want to flip the script: 'Why do you work so much? What about me?' I just can't entertain any woman's insecurities. I just don't see it."

Phil continued, "The crap about women wanting a gentleman is bogus. What they say is different from what they mean. They run around and date all these bad boys and wonder why their hearts get broken. Then they find themselves in their mid-thirties wondering why they are single. They sit around talking about how men are dogs, cheats, and liars, and so on and so forth."

"For once it would be nice to see some of these women look in the mirror and be honest with themselves," I said. "Angel is a good example. You remember her?"

Phil thought for a few seconds and then responded. "Yeah, I know Angel. She is your lawyer friend, right?"

"Yes, she and I have been friends for a long time. I had to be honest with her the other day and tell her I didn't want to hear all her sad stories about how men messed her over. Every time I turn around, she is dating the same kind of loser. I introduced her to a couple of good guys I know, including Pete. She thought he was too nice and nerdy. She didn't even go out with him to see whether he has another side. He is now a doctor and is well-rounded, travels, loves wine, speaks about five languages, and is an avid reader among other things. Anyway, Pete just got married last month. I invited Angel along with me to the wedding. She had the nerve to ask me why I hadn't convinced her enough that Pete was a keeper! Why would I convince a grown woman about dating real men when one was staring her in the face? Her most recent boyfriend lived with her, wrecked her car, maxed out her credit card, and has three kids from two different women. I think he even slapped her around a little bit. She eventually let him go after an intervention from family and friends."

"It's sad. She is smart, educated, and beautiful. I was also surprised to see the caliber of men she dates. Did you ever date her?" Phil asked.

"No. We're just good friends. I'm not attracted to her. She calls me every now and then to tell me the story of her life. She even goes to see a therapist now. I feel bad for her, but she has plenty to do with the state she is in. Now that she is a single mom, has gotten older, a little chubbier, and the pool of eligible bachelors has dwindled. She is feeling sorry for herself."

Phil shook his head and said, "You know what else kills me about some women sometimes? It's how they want to date unavailable men. There could be about one hundred guys at a bar, and you see ninety percent of the women flocking to only three guys in the room—the extremely good looking, the athlete or entertainer, and the bar owner."

I started to laugh. "You're right! And the rest of the guys are falling over each other trying to catch the remaining ten percent."

"I think some of those ninety percent sprinkle your way too, Devin," he said, laughing.

"I think you're talking about yourself," I said, chuckling.

"I'm tired of dating all these women I meet at the bars though. For the life of me, I can't seem to find a decent one."

"You really want something serious huh?"

"It's not as if I don't ever want anything serious. I haven't come across a really great woman I would want to settle down with. You know?"

I shook my head in agreement. "I hear what you're saying because I haven't had any luck either. You're not alone."

"What is your ideal woman?" Phil asked.

I pondered at his question. There was no easy answer. I tried to word it as carefully as I could.

"I understand there isn't such a thing as a perfect woman. I would prefer an easygoing woman, definitely not high maintenance. She is probably driving a Honda Civic hybrid. She doesn't spend half her salary on weaves and unnecessary wants, but rather spends on what she needs. She dresses well but doesn't necessarily wear all brand names, and she isn't carrying a Louis Vuitton bag. She is beautiful, but very subtle. She isn't meek and can carry a conversation. She is independent, confident and has strong convictions. She can debate with me as an equal, but she doesn't cop an attitude to prove she isn't a pushover."

Phil looked at me as if I had lost my mind.

WTF MOMENT

"Good luck. Let me know when you find one like that, and when you do, please ask whether she has a twin sister," he said, laughing.

"Basically I want a woman that would make a good WTF," I continued.

"WTF?"

"Wife, true love, and friend," I added.

"Right, I see," he said, nodding.

"Seriously, I want a woman who will give me peace of mind. Someone I can talk to after a hard day at the office. If the world is crumbling around me, I want her to be my safety net, you know? Someone I can look forward to seeing. I want to have goose bumps when I think about her. I want to say to myself, 'Damn! I can't wait to see my lady.' I want her to talk *to* me not talk *at* me. I want her to be able to accept my imperfections without judgment. I want someone I can garner strength from when I am at my weakest. I want a woman who will build with me, who finds ways to better us mentally, physically, spiritually, and financially; a soul mate, a life partner—in the true sense of the word."

"I hear you!" Phil said, nodding his head again.

"When that moment comes and I can say I have found my wife, true love, and friend, I will be the happiest man on earth."

Phil smiled and said, "There you have it."

I always enjoyed Phil's company. He is one of the few guys who really helped me through the divorce. He never said, "I told you so." He didn't encourage me to go through with the divorce either. He was always there for moral support. I have to commend him for that. It's not as if some of my other friends didn't care. Most were busy with their own problems and work. You got problems; you deal with them on your own, or go see a shrink. Maybe that is how it is for guys. I know women have tight groups, and they help and support each other through issues.

*   *   *

We finally made it to Kenny's house. The guys were already tipsy, and they jumped for joy when they saw the extra packs of beer Phil was carrying.

Kenny and Dave were discussing the latter's recent love. Each time he got a new girlfriend, he would always say, "I think she is the one." Then he'd find himself single again.

"Hey, guys!" announced Kenny. "Dave is single again."

"Are you serious?" I asked. "C'mon, man. I thought the last one was *the one*."

"I thought so too," replied Dave, chuckling.

"What happened this time?" asked Phil.

"She is an airhead," Dave responded.

Phil laughed and asked, "How so?"

"I don't know where to begin. She talked so goddamn much, she talked in her sleep. I'm not kidding. She would go on and on when we are on the phone. One time I put the phone down, went to the bathroom, took a dump, came back, and picked up the phone, and guess what? She didn't even know I'd been gone because she was still talking! Another time, she started talking about us taking a vacation in the middle of making love," Dave responded.

I laughed. "Oh! It's such a turnoff when a woman talks during sex."

"Another time, while she was giving me head, she paused suddenly while examining my penis and she asked how come some guys' *thingies* are crooked? She calls a penis a thingy. I was upset because I was really enjoying being in the groove. She really killed the mood right then. She picks the worse possible time to talk," he added.

We all started to laugh.

"Then she wanted me to come over and meet her kids, but we had only been seeing each other for a month. I don't want some kids to be attached to me! There is a strong possibility the relationship wouldn't work out. The poor kids would be affected by it all," Dave continued.

"I understand where you're coming from," I said. "I won't let any woman meet my daughter until I'm sure the relationship is serious and long term. I don't want my daughter to see me with multiple women—that would send the wrong message. She might grow up thinking it is appropriate for men to behave as such."

"You know what's funny about some of these single moms?" asked Phil. "Some of them still behave as if they don't have kids. You see them at bars and clubs regularly. When you try to date them, they want to give you rules, regulations, and their expectations of you. I'm not trying to be mean, but a single mom is like a depreciated car. Having a kid throws a wrench in the whole relationship. You can't see her as often as you want to; she has to be home at a certain time. She isn't as readily available as a single woman. I'm not trying to play father to some kid; I want to see what the woman is all about first."

Kenny joined the conversation. "I have no problem dating single mothers. You all know Darlene, right? She has a daughter, and we have been dating for a few months. She's really nice. She lets it be known her daughter is her priority. She is in grad school, so she really doesn't have time. When we do hang out, it is a treat. It works out for me too because I'm pretty busy. We seemed to have struck an accord. She gives me space, and I do the same. I haven't had any drama from her as I have had with women I dated in the past. I dig her because she is very mature."

WTF MOMENT

Dave said, "I did date an older woman with teenage kids, and the relationship worked out well. She was divorced and didn't want to get married again, so I got what I wanted and she got what she wanted. She is the kind of single mom I don't mind meeting—not these young ones who want you to play husband and dad."

Kenny asked, "Devin, do women have issues dating you because you have a kid?"

"I don't think so," I responded. "Most of the ones I've dated don't care. If they did, they didn't show it. Women don't care about stuff like that. They are not as shallow as men are. I'm trying to be open-minded. If I hit it off with a woman who has kids, then so be it. We would have one thing in common."

"So . . . fellas!" Phil began. "At what point do you expect to get some from a woman you have been dating for a three months? I'm getting frustrated with this one honey. I don't mind waiting, but I don't know what we are waiting for. We have kissed, but she is acting as though she is saving it for marriage. I'm thinking about pushing her to the curb, but I want to have some of her kitty though."

"Yeah," said Dave, "some women take the waiting game too far. You know what really baffles me? They would make certain men wait a long while before sexing him. These are usually the nice guys too. Then they give it up to other men within a few weeks of meeting him, and those are usually the ones that could care less about them. Women are so inconsistent!"

"You are on point with that one," Phil added.

Kenny picked up the thread of conversation. "How soon a woman gives it up to me is important somewhat, but it isn't a big deal either. I can hang with waiting two to three months. By the second date, I already know whether she is going to be girlfriend material anyway. So it really doesn't matter how soon or how late we have sex. When a woman starts talking about a six-month rule then she is doing a bit much. It isn't going to make the sex worthwhile to me. It turns me off, actually. And even worse, what happens if she turns out to be horrible in bed? I experienced that with one woman. She was really boring, and she was such a turnoff. I was thinking, *This is what I had to wait six months for? See you later.*"

"It bothers me when I go on dates with some women who keep stressing the fact that we are friends," said Dave. "When we go out, they expect me to pick up the tab all the time. If we are friends, shouldn't we be sharing the tab? That's what friends do, right?"

"Such behavior irks me, and it goes to tell you what kind of woman she is" said Phil. "She is insisting you're friends, but she wants you to treat her as you would someone you were dating. She can't have her cake and eat it too.

I'm a gentleman, but I can appreciate a woman who offers to pay for dinner, or covers the tip at least. Most likely I wouldn't allow her to pay, but just the fact that she makes the gesture, is a huge plus!"

"Some women stand at the bar all night, waiting for guys to come up and buy them drinks," I said. "What happened to having your own money? I think it's rude. A woman shouldn't expect a man to buy her drinks if she isn't remotely interested in him."

"Then, they want to turn around and call guys cheap when we don't fall for their trickery," Phil added.

"Where do you go to find a really good woman?" lamented Dave. "God knows, I've been looking for one, but I haven't had any luck."

"I don't think there is any particular place to look," I said. "You can find one at the gas station, grocery store, bar . . . anywhere. It's all about the vibe and what she is all about. Please don't say church either because that is not even true. You know how many ladies come out to the bar on Saturday night? They get drunk, get their freak on, and wake up to go to church on Sunday morning," I said, laughing.

"I really want a good, drama-free woman," said Dave. "I don't think it should be this hard, should it?"

"You're not going to find that ever!" said Phil. "There is no such thing as drama-free women. They all have drama. The question is, what kind of drama can you live with?"

"I have no patience for overly emotional women," I said. "I seem to always run into those types. It's draining, man. I can deal with a little bit of emotion, but all the time? I'm good. The drama is uncalled for."

Dave laughed. "Women make the world go 'round. You can't live with them, and you can't live without them."

"Isn't that the truth? You know they say the same about us too," I said, laughing.

"Women don't know what they want half of the time," whined Dave. "One minute she is saying one thing, and the next it's another. They never seem to make up their minds. I met this woman, and I told her I really liked her after about three weeks. I couldn't hide it—that was the way she made me feel. I wasn't trying to propose to her or anything of the sort. She started avoiding me soon afterward citing a busy work schedule and school. She also said she just got out of a long-term relationship and wanted to wait a while before getting into another one. It wasn't a problem, but she told a mutual friend I was moving too fast and could be crazy. I was hurt by that. Put the shoe on the other foot—when a guy does the same thing, he is running away from commitment, he is a dog, and he is insensitive."

WTF MOMENT

"I will never tell a woman I really like or I love her until I hear her say it first," offered Phil. "I refuse to play myself. I have to really know she is into me."

"What if she tells you she loves you early in the relationship?" I asked.

Phil sighed and said, "That is your cue—run, brother, run! She is one of the really emotional types . . . crazy even. Then she calls you ten times a day, shows up at your house announced. Don't let her get hurt, she might slit your throat open while you sleep. I'm telling you, guys. Remember what I'm saying. You could wake up with your penis cut off!"

I laughed. "Very true, man!"

"I've had a few of those too," said Kenny. "Once you start having sex with her regularly, you belong to her. She claims you automatically."

"Guys," said Phil, "when you have no intention of keeping a woman and you have sex with her, make sure it happens just once. Continuous sex with most women leaves room for her to get attached to you. Sex is emotional for them. It doesn't matter whether you're ready or not. A woman is sharing and giving a part of herself to you when she has sex with you. Now, if you do it once and leave her alone, then she understands you're not trying to commit. Her feelings are not really deep as of yet. She can live with that. She could call you an asshole in her mind, but at least it saves you the drama. If she asks you why she hasn't been hearing from you, come up with an excuse about your company merging and that you have been really busy lately. That way, you can still maintain the friendship and leave the door open for you to go back and hit it again after a long while. You can keep the loop going as long as you're both single. You get in trouble when you become greedy by constantly having sex with a woman and then acting surprised when she falls in love. Trust me! You have to play by the rules to avoid trouble."

"And that is the lesson of the day," I said, with a chuckle.

15. The Wow! Experience, Part 2

Ms. Wow must have left a message when I was out of service range which explains why calls go straight to voicemail at times. I tried telling the strange scenario to some friends when I got hammered once for not calling back on time.

"You should have seen my missed call," one said to me.

"Sometimes I don't get missed calls," I responded. "My phone may have been turned off," I told another. They both thought I was full of it, but it happens—technology can only be so reliable. It has its glitches.

My voicemail timestamp said Ms. Wow had called at 1 p.m. It was 7 p.m. Her chatty voice rang in my ears as I listened to her message:

> Hey there, Mr. Wonderful!
> It's your girl, Ms. Wow! I hope you still remember who I am since you have so many women on speed dial. (Laugh) I haven't talked to you in a minute. Busy man!
> Give me a shout out when you get this, okay?
> Miss ya . . . ciao

I had entertained Ms. Wow briefly, but I had been so busy, I wasn't able to follow up.

I smiled, recalling the last time I had seen her. I'd made a quick stop at her place while I was in the area. I didn't stay long, but I vividly remember how good she looked. She has the firmest butt I've ever seen, and it looks so good in jeans. One would think they were custom made for her. I walked into her closet before; one side was lined with at least thirty pairs of designer jeans. Most of them were blue and looked the same, so I asked her why she had so many.

"They fit me differently, and I wear each with a different blouse and pair of shoes," she replied.

WTF MOMENT

She had rows of shoes lined up against the closet wall on rows of shelves. Some were in plastic containers like lunch boxes. I could have been told I was in a shoe store and would have believed it. I didn't understand the whole logic behind having so many pairs of shoes. I counted twenty black high heels at one point; they all looked alike to me, but she swore each served a different purpose. I stopped trying to understand and moved right along.

I was intrigued by the prospect of seeing Ms. Wow again. She had been in a relationship since we last hooked up, but it had recently come to an end. We now had perfect timing. She hated the idea of commuting to Brookdale where I lived because she thought it was too urban, not quiet enough for her.

If there was ever an ultimate homebody, it was Ms. Wow. Her commute to work is only ten minutes. Her sister and mother lived a couple of miles from her. I came to the conclusion that her favorite past time was relaxing at home, sipping wine, and listening to music.

Her pride and joy was her beautiful four-bedroom home in a gated community. The grounds were well kept and immaculate inside and out. I could see why she never wanted to go anywhere. I wouldn't either if I had a home as nice as hers. The last time I was there, I had to deter her from cleaning up so much so we could spend a little time together.

I smiled as I dialed her number. She didn't pick up and as I was leaving her a message, a call came in. It was Ms. Wow! I clicked over.

"Hello!"

"Well, hello to you, handsome! Long time no see, no hear."

"You know how to find me," I said, laughing.

"There you go again, acting as though the world revolves around you," she responded.

"You know what I mean."

"You have my number too. You could have called too," she said, sulking.

"I've been really busy."

"We are all busy; you can always make time for people who are really important to you. That's all I'm saying."

"Hmmm, anyway . . .," I sighed.

"See how you're reacting? It's because I'm telling the truth, and you don't want to hear it. Uh, uhhh," she said, laughing.

"What are you talking about? I can say the same thing about you," I quipped.

"No, honey, I stay in touch. You're the one who is too busy. I called today, didn't I?"

"Anyway, moving right along . . .," I said, laughing as well.

"Whatever," she said, sarcastically.

"And how have you been?"

"I've been good. Just working my butt off. I've been getting off work at around ten every night. We need to hire someone else because I can't keep going on like this."

"You know you love it—being a workaholic," I added.

She started to laugh. "That I do, I won't lie. I love my job."

"What are you doing later this evening?" I asked, changing the subject.

"Oooooh! Is someone available?"

"Excuse me, I simply asked what you were doing this evening," I responded, laughing.

"Hmm . . . I could be doing you!" She laughed.

"Oh! Really?! In that case, I should be on my way pronto."

"Why are you still on the phone then?" she quipped.

"Oh like that?"

"Yes, like that," she said, giggling.

"You're crazy! I'll be on my way in a few minutes."

"Okay, I will see you later, alligator."

I hung up the phone, shaved, and jumped into the shower. She liked it when I was clean shaven. She once said my face felt like a baby's bottom.

I wasn't too enthusiastic about the hour-and-a-half ride to her place, but I was looking forward to the action that would take place once I got there. One thing I do like about her is how hospitable she is. The last time I visited, she fed me well. Her motherly vibe made me feel at home. A few times when I called, she was cooking something and inviting her family over.

I called her again as I was leaving home. She professed how much she had missed me and explained why she thought I had made the right choice driving to see her. She was trying to butter me up so I wouldn't complain about how long it was going to take me to get to her.

I hopped onto Highway 480 and headed toward Santa Lima. I was surprised to run into traffic, as it was a holiday Monday. *An accident probably*, I thought. The freeway stretched for miles through hills and mountains, and there weren't alternate side roads to take. There is nothing I hate more than being stuck in traffic. I don't have any patience for it. I breathed in and out slowly as if I was in a yoga class. I kept telling myself I wasn't going to get upset. There is a beautiful woman at her home waiting patiently for me to arrive.

This little hiccup on the road isn't going to deprive me of a good time, I thought, as I tried to weave through the thick traffic. I texted Ms. Wow while I was driving. I know I'm not supposed to; I could a get a ticket or get into a wreck. I went on and did it anyway.

WTF MOMENT

To: Ms. Wow
Traffic is ridiculous right now. I'll be getting to u later than anticipated *smh*.

From: Ms. Wow
Humph! Really? On a holiday? Strange, but no worries, honey. I'll be here when u get here.

To: Ms. Wow
Yeah, there is an accident.
Heard it on the radio. I don't know why people drive crazily on wet roads anyway.
Let me stop before I get more irritated lol.

From: Ms. Wow
Yes I know how u hate traffic lol.
It will clear up pretty soon. Hold on tight.

To: Ms. Wow
I know lol. What r u doing anyway?

From: Ms. Wow
Just sittn here watching TV and drinkn wine.
I'm almost done with a bottle lol.

To: Ms. Wow
Ok now. Don't get drunk n go to sleep right when I arrive lol.

From: Ms. Wow
Sleep? Omg! I'm so waitn for u!

To: Ms. Wow
What r u wearing?

From: Ms. Wow
Lingerie ☺

To: Ms. Wow
Hmm . . .

BOLAJI TIJANI-QUDUS

From: Ms. Wow
U don't understand . . . The thought of u holding me in ur arms has me so excited right now.
Just get here soon and in one piece please!

To: Ms. Wow
No worries. I'll be there shortly. U just b ready.

From: Ms. Wow
U don't hv to say that twice!

To: Ms. Wow
That's what I'm talking about lol.

From: Ms. Wow
Btw, hv u eaten yet? I hope not. I hv some chicken in the oven.

To: Ms. Wow
I could eat. I know how u get down. I saved my appetite for some of ur good ole fashion cooking.

From: Ms. Wow
Awww
U know I got u honey.

To: Ms. Wow
U sure do. D traffic is clearing up a bit. Let me get off this phone b4 I cause an accident 2 lol.

From: Ms. Wow
We don't want that!

From: Ms. Wow
Hey, how far are u?

To: Ms. Wow
Just passing Clifton Road.

WTF MOMENT

From: Ms. Wow
To: Devin
K. c u soon.

About half an hour later, I finally passed the scene of the accident that had been causing all the commotion. An SUV was upside down in the emergency lane. It had hit the freeway divider. Three other damaged cars were piled behind each other. Paramedics were attending to some people while police officers were talking to others. The accident had already been moved to the side of the freeway, but as usual, people were stopping or slowing down to get a glimpse of what was going on. I don't understand why people do that; they don't realize by doing so, they cause a chain reaction. It was the reason we had been bumper to bumper the last ten miles.

I felt relieved as the Golf Way exit came up, though I still had several minutes to drive inland. I always teased Ms. Wow about buying a house close to the freeway.

I saw a drugstore and made a quick dash to get some raincoats. The store was moderately busy. I walked over to the aisle and picked up a six-pack of Trojan Magnums. *This should do it*, I thought. I also bought a can of energy drink, some chips, a magazine, and a bottle of wine. I didn't want people looking at me when I reached the register with just a pack of condoms. I shouldn't care, but it could get a little embarrassing with all those eyes on me. I got to the counter to pay for my purchases.

The cashier tried scanning my box of raincoats, but it didn't go through. She tried a few more times and had to call for a price check. I probably turned red just standing there waiting for someone to come back with another pack. Now my worst fear has been realized! I felt everyone was looking at me. I wondered what was going through their minds.

The woman behind me was probably thinking, *There he goes, about to go sleep with someone's daughter, horny toad!* I kept a straight face and was glad when someone returned with another pack with a bar code label. The cashier was smiling as she rang me up. I paid her without making any eye contact. She handed me my bag, and I could almost hear her say, *Good luck, and have fun tonight!* I scurried out of there as fast as I could.

I breathed a sigh of relief when I reached the cul-de-sac in which Ms. Wow's home was nestled. The gate to her community had been open, so I didn't have to call her to buzz me in. I pulled up behind her black convertible Lexus

SC420. It was probably about four years old but the way it's usually detailed, one would think it just left the showroom. I pressed the bell and waited for Ms. Wow to appear. I could hear her footsteps as she raced to the door.

"Who is it?" she asked.

"Devin your handyman," I responded, playfully.

"Is that so?"

She opened the door and stared at me for a few moments. "I don't believe I'm seeing you again. How long has it been? Over a year?" she asked, as she stroked my face.

"Almost a year, but not quite."

"Same thing. That's still too long. I didn't think this day would ever come."

I touched her chin and said, "Good things come to those who wait."

"Hmm . . . Is that so?"

"Very much so!"

"Well, come on in. I have hot bath water with your name on it."

"Now you're talking," I said, as I playfully kissed her on the lips.

The smell of baked chicken filled my nostrils as I entered her abode. I felt my stomach growl. Whitney's food was definitely good. She was familiar with all the southern dishes. She didn't just whip up things; she took her time with preparation, and I especially appreciated that she seasoned her meats.

"What's for dinner?"

"I'm keeping it simple, honey! I have some baked chicken in the oven; mashed potatoes with gravy—made from scratch by the way—umm, some asparagus too. You like that, right? I couldn't remember whether you do."

"I have no objection. Anything you make is good anyway."

"Awww, thank you."

"By the way, I brought a bottle of Moscato in case you ran out," I said, laughing.

"Oh my god! How did you know I needed another one? I just finished my last bottle."

"I know your choice of drugs, so I had to make sure you had enough."

"Are you trying to call me an alcoholic?" She laughed.

"Never!"

"Maybe you're just trying to get me drunk! You know how I am when I'm drunk."

"That's the idea," I said, grinning.

She grabbed the wine from me and placed it on the table. A loosened, flowery black and red silk robe was draped over her. She wore red, lace panties with a matching bra underneath. Her belly button glistened on her perfectly, flat stomach. She asked me to take my shoes off and motioned for me to sit in the

WTF MOMENT

living room. Then she handed me a filled glass of wine. Soft music was playing in the background; the TV was on, but muted. The house was dimly lit.

I noticed she had changed her living room set. Gone were the white leather sofa and love seat; she now had a double sectional with a table ottoman in dark brown, soft, woven upholstery. There were attached arm bolsters and double-welted, boxed bordered seat cushions along with loose scatter pillow backs. The look was fashionably contemporary. She had also replaced her TV with a fifty-five-inch flat screen. It looked great on the wall.

I complimented her on her home's new look. She didn't hear me. She was fiddling with something in her cabinet. Sometimes I wondered why she did so many things at once. She never sat still. She went back and forth to her room doing God knows what with a glass of wine in her hand.

Then her phone rang; I heard her say Mom. She talked with her for about ten minutes in the kitchen. I could hear the rattling sounds of pots, plates, and cutlery. The oven opened and shut. I figured she was checking on the chicken.

I heard her hang up with her mom. Then she said, "My mom thinks I should have a baby."

"Oh really?"

I'd known her for over a year. She had always been adamant about not wanting any kids. She would spoil her nieces and nephews, but that was as far as it went. She had been married before; she had let her then husband know having kids was not part of the package. They were married for ten years. Her professional life was fulfilling enough for her, she had said.

I didn't ask too many questions about what happened between her and her ex-beau. She did say they fell out of love.

"I'm thinking about it though," she continued.

"Oh yeah?" I asked, not believing what I had just heard.

"Yeah, Mom and some of my girls have been on my case about it, and it's starting to make sense now. I've been spending time with my brother's newborn baby, and she's so cute. I wish she were mine. I'm forty, honey. Since I got the feeling now, why not? I don't have to be married to be a mom. I make good money, and my family is close by. I think I can handle it. You know what I'm saying?"

"I hear you."

Good luck! I thought.

I kept my eyes on the TV screen as if the program was really interesting. I was hoping she would leave me alone so we wouldn't continue the conversation.

I saw steam coming out of a pot on the stove as she checked on her cooking. Her phone rang again, and she walked toward the laundry room next to the garage, her high heels made clanking sounds on the hardwood floor.

She is the only woman who I know that wears high heels everywhere, even at home. It was appropriate tonight because she was dressed to set the mood. But the other time I had visited, she'd worn jeans and still walked around her house in high heels. I asked her why and she said she hated being just five five; all her siblings were five eight and taller. I told her it didn't matter; she had the best body out of them all. I'd seen her three other sisters; they would kill to have Whitney's body.

While still on the phone, she poked her head from the laundry room and yelled out to me.

"Hey, Devin, I saw these nice denim dresses at Macy's last week when my friend Nia and I went shopping. She got one for her daughter who is the same age as yours. It was so cute! I'm thinking of buying the same outfit for your daughter. You think she would like denim?"

I didn't know what to say. Why would she want to buy my daughter clothes? It was a nice gesture, but *No, thank you!*

"She doesn't wear much denim," I responded.

"She doesn't?"

"No, she doesn't," I said, sounding as innocent as I could.

She continued on with her phone conversation. She walked toward the living room with the phone perched to her ear with her left shoulder. Her left hand was holding a glass of wine, and she was dragging a laundry bag behind her with her right hand.

I got up from the couch. "You need help?" I asked.

Before she could answer, I grabbed the bag and took it upstairs to her room. I laid it down in front of her closet next to another laundry bag.

I turned around to head back downstairs and was startled. I hadn't heard her footsteps walking up the stairs. Then I remembered the stairs were carpeted. She came closer and kissed me. She dragged yet another bag behind her with one hand, the other pressing her cell phone to her ear. I playfully smacked her bottom and went back downstairs.

I heard her say, "Nia, let me get off this phone. My man is here!"

Her man? She can't be serious; maybe she is joking, I thought. I pretended I didn't hear her as I slumped into the couch once again. I hadn't seen her in a while, and all of a sudden, I'm her man.

Wow! I'm going to need to be careful.

A few minutes passed, and I started to get restless.

"What are you doing up there, miss?" I playfully yelled out to her.

"I just need to sort out some of these clothes. It's getting on my nerves just having them sit here like this," she yelled back from her bedroom.

WTF MOMENT

As usual, she was doing too much already. I wanted her to come back downstairs and relax with me.

"You know you have a guest, right?"

"I know, honey! Sorry. I'll be down in a minute. You know what? Come up here, I almost forgot I already ran your bathwater."

I walked upstairs. There was a big, red, scented candle burning on a stand in the corner of the room. It almost looked like a lamp. I thought it was nice. Her bed was laid. I liked it because it was fluffy and very comfortable. She had all kinds of pillows—big ones, medium ones, and little ones. She even had a couple of teddy bears. Her blanket was huge. Everything on her bed was designer and expensive.

I asked her why she spent so much money on bed accessories.

"I like to be comfortable, and it starts with the bed I sleep in," she said. It actually made sense. I had slept like a baby the last time I spent the night at the Ritz Carlton.

I slipped into the bathtub; the water was still warm. It was soothing. Scented candles were burning in the bathroom too. I didn't remember the last time I'd had a bath. I wouldn't take one on my own. How would I look if my boys came to visit and I was taking a bath with no woman around? They would let me hear it for years, I'm sure.

I closed my eyes and drifted off. Then I thought I heard footsteps. Before I could open my eyes, I felt Whitney's tongue in my right ear as her hand massaged my chest, slipping farther down until she reached for my kahuna. I could feel myself pulsating as she massaged it.

"Oohh, what do we have here? Very nice!"

She then pulled the drain plug and passed me a towel.

"We shouldn't let all that go to waste. Right?" She smiled, looking at my kahuna mischievously.

"Are you sure you want some of this?"

She turned around, put her index finger in her mouth and licked it. The other hand was caressing her body as she walked backward out of the bathroom staring dead at me. Then she turned her gaze toward my kahuna. It stared back at her, hard as a rock. She smiled and disappeared into the room. *Crazy ass woman*, I thought, smiling. *She is gonna get it.*

I quickly dried off and applied lotion, anticipating a dive in her pool of love. As I walked into the room, she was laid out on the bed. Her robe and bra were off, but her panties were still on. Her vibrator was buzzing away at her clit; her panties were pulled to the side. She was pulling at her hair with her other hand. Her perky breasts were pointed to the ceiling, waiting to be nibbled on. She had been asked so many times whether they were real. They looked damn good for a woman her age.

She sure is getting the party started!

I leaned on the side of the door checking her out and smiling. She slowly opened her eyes and watched me as I watched her. She smiled back. She was normally talkative, but in bed tonight, she was very sensual; she talked less and performed more. I really liked that about her—she was all action.

She moved all over the bed as if she were a belly dancer. She even rolled over and lay on her vibrator and grinded on it. Her movements turned me on, so I finally made my way to the bed. I kissed her calves slowly. Then my tongue made its way up to her back and then behind her neck. She moaned as my body graced hers. I turned her around and moved the vibrator to the other side of the bed. I dipped my fingers into her kitty; it was soaking wet. I kissed her belly button ring, playfully pulling it with my teeth while playing with her clit with my fingers. I gently pulled her panties down. She moved her thighs helping me as the panties slid down her legs. She pulled me closer and kissed me passionately. She then rolled over on me and started to slurp on my kahuna as she played simultaneously with my jewels.

Soft jazz music was playing in the background.

She kept looking at me while she was giving me head. She deep throated for a while and then started to lick around the shaft. A few seconds later, she was down at the base, then back to my jewels. Her eyes were fixated on me while she was doing all this. I didn't know whether I should keep smiling or say something. Maybe she wanted me to moan or cheer her on. I closed my eyes, while I enjoyed the show. I rubbed her face tenderly and moaned a little to show I sure was enjoying the act.

"You like it, baby?"

"Yeah," I managed to reply.

"I can't wait to feel you inside of me."

"Yeah?"

"Yeah, baby, I want to cum all over it," she said, as she squeezed my kahuna lightly.

She leaned forward, kissing my chest and then my lips while her left hand was still stroking me. She seemed to be looking for something with her right hand. Maybe she was grabbing for her dildo again, or the condom I had placed on the lamp stand. I didn't bother to open my eyes; I was in the zone.

Suddenly, I felt something I hadn't felt in a very long time! The raw feeling of a woman's wet and warm kitty. I opened my eyes in bewilderment. She was sitting on my kahuna and riding it. I was dumbfounded for a few moments.

WTF MOMENT

I managed to ask, "What are you doing?!"

"I just want to feel you just a little."

It felt so freaking good, I was tempted to allow her to continue. There is no other feeling in this world that can surpass that of some good kitty.

I regained my senses and started to push her off me.

"Get up, get up! What happened to using a condom?!"

She pinned my hands down and started moaning as she rode faster. "You feel so good, baby! I just want to feel every inch of you, baby! Let's do it for just a little bit, then we can get the condom."

"What?!" I exclaimed.

"Your big meat feels so freaking good. You're the best I've ever had! Oh my god! Please stay right there; don't move. I'm going to cum soon!" she screamed.

She thought I was going to go for all the freaky talk, but I managed to wrestle her off of me.

"What the fuck?!" I could hear the shriek in my own voice.

I looked down at my kahuna; it was covered with her juices. *This is not good*, I thought. I got up and went to the bathroom to pee. I hoped by doing so, I would decrease the chances of any virus taking hold of my penis valve. I wiped my kahuna clean with a wash towel, some soap, and water. I kept staring at myself in the bathroom mirror not knowing what to think or do.

When I returned to the room, she was still kneeling on the same spot on the bed.

"What were you thinking? I don't know where you have been! Heck, you don't even know where I've been. You can't just take chances like that," I said.

"I know! I'm sorry I got carried away. I'm so into you. I just wanted to feel you. And condoms dry me out so quickly. All I wanted was to make it pleasurable for both of us."

"You can't be doing shit like that!" I sighed and sat on the edge of the bed thinking deeply.

"I know. I'm sorry," she said in a remorseful tone.

"I'm not saying you have anything, but you can't be too careful these days and you could get pregnant!" I continued.

"Don't worry, honey, that isn't happening." She gave a forced laugh.

"Okay. This is a very serious issue! Do you sleep with all your dates unprotected?"

"No, I just don't date. I have sex with men I'm in a relationship with."

"It doesn't matter. Just because you don't date casually doesn't mean the men you get in relationships with don't have something! Do you test each and every single one of them?" I stared at her angrily.

She paused for a second and said, "Pretty much."

I didn't believe her. She hadn't asked me whether I had been tested. How was she going to go around trusting guys and endangering herself?

She scooped over and grabbed my hand.

"I shouldn't have done that. It was very stupid of me, and I know that. I'm clean. I get tested regularly. Please forgive me."

We sat there for what seemed to be an eternity. She was probably wondering why I was so angry. I was scared as I thought about the ramifications of the events that had just taken place. I don't want to contract any sexually transmitted diseases. HIV, herpes, and a host of other venereal diseases were running through my mind.

All the baby talk I heard earlier spooked me as well. What if she was trying to get pregnant on purpose? I'm not down with the baby mama, baby daddy drama. I still have issues with the ex-wife; I didn't need any more.

She was trying hard to smooth things out, so she asked me whether I was ready to go grab a bite downstairs. I decided not to keep dwelling on it. I put on my boxers and followed her downstairs. We ate in silence. She turned the TV volume up. A boxing match was on HBO.

"Oh! Boxing is on." She knew I was a fan of the sweet science.

I started to watch the match, but I wasn't paying attention. I still kept replaying the earlier events in my mind.

She tried her best to keep the atmosphere lively. I wasn't too happy. She walked upstairs and came back with a condom in hand. She started to kiss me and was fondling my kahuna at the same time. It wasn't receptive. My mind wasn't right, so my best buddy wasn't going to be right either. She figured out it wasn't happening, so she sat back down next to me looking dejected. She tried everything to ease the tension, but nothing was working.

It was too late; the damage had already been done. My phone went off, so I picked it up. It was Phil calling to say hello. I used the opportunity to get out of there. I told her a story about how Phil needed a ride from the airport. I was sure she didn't believe me, but I didn't care. I wanted to get out of there immediately.

The drive home was a very uncomfortable one. It was excruciating, actually. As much as I tried not to be upset, I couldn't help it. *Why would she be taking chances like she just did tonight?* I wondered how many times she had behaved as such. Now I had to worry about getting tested again. I didn't think she was promiscuous, but you just never know. I didn't live with her, so I didn't know what she did in her spare time. *Nah, I don't need to worry. I'm sure it's nothing. I'm fine.* I consoled myself as I drove home. I knew I wouldn't be seeing her again for sure. She might not think it was a big deal, but it was to me. I value my life.

16. Live and Let Live

I woke up with a little anxiety; it was court date. I didn't know what to expect. I had seen my lawyer the previous evening, and we had gone over the divorce master list. We were going to agree on the child support, but I wasn't interested in paying spousal support and Monica's lawyer fees. I felt she was financially equipped to pay for her expenses. She is educated and capable of having a worthwhile, full-time job that pays more. I couldn't comprehend how someone could live off of child and spousal support only.

Working together on our finances had been a major issue during our marriage. A loving wife would go to work and support her husband when things got difficult financially. It was common sense. I glanced at my Excel sheet with my listed monthly expenses. I'd have to show the judge that the ex-wife's demands were unreasonable.

She was already at the court when I arrived. Her lawyer was a short, stout man in his early fifties. He looked at me up and down as if I was the scum of the earth. I laughed inside. *This man doesn't even know me. He is only trying to make a buck and thinking he is doing the best for his client.*

I don't particularly care for lawyers, although I was forced to work with one for my case. It's an ethics issue with me. Some lawyers will take extreme measures to protect their clients even if it means cooking up a ridiculous assumption and convincing everyone it's a fact.

I don't understand how lawyers can defend murderers, tax evaders, and child molesters. I know it's their job, but how can they sleep at night knowing they're working diligently, looking for loopholes to get a wrong doer off? That is so crazy to me.

A murderer can get off just because the arresting officer failed to read the offender his rights. Defense lawyers can ride the angle and possibly get a case dismissed. It is not about who is guilty or how much evidence is stacked against someone. It's about what the lawyers can prove.

BOLAJI TIJANI-QUDUS

I shook my head thinking how much I wished I were somewhere else. The courtroom was full with all kinds of people. Our number hadn't been called yet, so I sat there and listened to everyone else's problems. I wasn't too thrilled we had to air our laundry to complete strangers. I blocked everyone and everything out and was in deep thought until my lawyer nudged me, indicating it was time to step in front of the judge.

Our case was read, and our lawyers pleaded our cases. I agreed with the child support, but I didn't agree with the spousal support. Why would I? I shouldn't be supporting her, especially when I know she is capable of working. The judge heard both lawyers and decided to think about the case and notify them about his decision via mail. *Great*, I thought. *We have to wait some more.*

My lawyer, Ms. Smith, called me about a week later and said, "They are giving her almost everything she wants."

"What does that mean?"

"Besides the child support, you will be paying her the spousal support for the next year and a half."

"This isn't fair," I started to say.

Ms. Smith paused and then said, "It's pretty close to the numbers Disso Master came up with." (Disso Master is the California child and spousal support calculator.)

"It isn't right," I lamented.

"I know, Devin. You are the bread winner and she keeps the child sixty-five percent of the time, affected the outcome as well."

She has to keep Emmanuella more because I work and live in a different city, one hundred miles from where they were. There isn't a way for me to make the commute daily. I would love to have Emmanuella fifty percent of the time, but it was impossible to do so.

"You know it's going to be rough to survive with what I'm making now, taking care of her household and mine too?"

"I understand. Do you think you can talk to her and see whether you can reason with her? Have you shown her your expenses?" she asked.

"I've tried. I don't know what is wrong with her! She flat-out refused. It's baffling. She knows what kind of financial state I'm in. Her refusal to work put a strain on our checkbook. All of a sudden, she thinks I'm making a truckload of money. She is very delusional. I really feel her friends and lawyer are putting her up to all this!" I exclaimed.

"Devin, I have to run to the court in a few minutes. Give me a call later this afternoon, or I can call you when I get back."

WTF MOMENT

"Okay, I'll call you later," I said, as I got off the phone. I was upset at my lawyer as well. Maybe she did her best, maybe she didn't. I was upset anyway. I didn't understand why I had to suffer because I wasn't married anymore. All I felt was bitterness, despair, and deep regret. I often wondered how my life would have turned out if I had not chosen the marriage path. I turned the TV on loudly and screamed at the top of my lungs for at least ten minutes until I lost my voice. Then I hopped into my bed and cried myself to sleep.

The following weeks and months were very difficult. I was depressed.

Things were especially hard for Emmanuella. She didn't understand why Daddy wasn't coming home anymore. It was strange to her that she was only spending the weekends with me.

I wished things could be different. I hated the situation. I felt like a failure at times. I felt as if I were in a bad dream I couldn't wake up from.

One time when I went to visit her, she said, "Daddy, you know you can still sleep on the sofa downstairs if you want." She remembered I used to sleep in the guest room or on the living room sofa the first year we separated.

It was hard to explain what was happening to Emmanuella.

"Daddy will be staying at his own place from now on. Daddy won't be staying downstairs anymore. But you will be able to stay with Daddy sometimes and Mommy sometimes."

"Why?" Emmanuella asked again.

"Well, because Daddy and Mommy are not getting along right now. Sometimes it is better for one person to leave so things can get better. Remember the one time Daddy and Mommy were arguing, and you were crying?"

"Uh uhh," she responded.

"Well, Daddy and Mommy don't want to fight anymore. That is why Daddy moved out. So things can be better. Okay?"

"Uh uhh," she said again.

"But Daddy loves you so much and Mommy loves you so much too. Okay?"

"I love you too, Daddy," she said.

My eyes filled with tears as I hugged her. I hurt every time I dropped her off on Sundays; she always looked so sad.

* * *

I caught a ride to Queensbury City with Ms. Smith, my lawyer. The two-hour trip wasn't appealing, but I was glad the dissolution was almost finished. We were meeting at the ex's lawyer's office.

We made it there five minutes early. I saw the ex's car packed in front. I hoped everything would go smoothly. I wasn't in the mood to bicker.

We walked into the conference room, and Monica was seated on the lofty chair reading a magazine. Her lawyer wasn't there. She exchanged pleasantries with Ms. Smith and returned to reading her magazine.

For a good ten minutes or so, you could have heard a pin drop. I got my phone out and started to return all the texts I had missed. My lawyer fiddled with paperwork from her briefcase.

Finally, the ex's lawyer, Mr. Johnson walked in. "Sorry, I had to deal with a client on the phone. Crazy day," he said.

"I understand," said Ms. Smith with a forced laugh as if to say, *Yeah, right*.

I guess lawyers try to play silly games. Make the other party wait and sweat it out and then make a grand entry with the stupid line *Sorry to keep you waiting . . .*

I sat there, thinking *We need to get this thing over with*.

Mr. Johnson spoke first. Nothing had really changed much; they wanted what the court temporarily ordered—$4,200, about the same amount I had proposed to Monica in the past, except now she wanted me to foot the bill of the daycare, which would add another $1,000 monthly. I asked why I had to pay an extra amount for day care. Then Mr. Johnson blindsided us with something we hadn't discussed before.

"Well, there is the matter of Mr. Devin's business. We figured he needs to buy out my client," he said.

"And how much is that?" I asked.

"Two hundred and fifty thousand dollars," he replied.

"This is insane! Why do I need to buy her out? When in fact she's already getting paid every month via my salary?"

Mr. Johnson looked at me and gave me a condescending smile.

"Well, you started the business while you were married to my client; therefore, she has a stake in it. You used community funds to start the business."

"That was my money!"

"That is where it stands presently. If you guys want to take time to think about it and let me know," Mr. Johnson said in a dismissive fashion.

I wanted to jump over the table and smack the taste out of his mouth. He and his client were delusional. *Why is she worried about getting bought out? I'm the one slaving, not her.*

I looked at my lawyer. "This is stupid. I don't believe this!"

"You can buy her out if you offer two hundred thousand dollars right now, which is a bargain!" Mr. Johnson said.

WTF MOMENT

"Where am I going to get the money from?" I inquired as I looked at everyone in the room.

"We could have your business appraised, and the court can come up with a number for the buyout. You might end up paying more. Trust me, both of you will spend more money going through the process," Mr. Johnson continued.

"What?!" I exclaimed.

"We also understand you are supposed to earn dividends since your business is a corporation. We will need you to declare the numbers at the end of the year so we can reevaluate what you make," he added.

"Dividends? What dividends? Whatever little we made outside of our salaries was put back in the business last year, and we will be doing the same this year!"

"When the time comes, you will need to show documents indicating that any extra funds from the business were reinvested," he said.

I got very upset, and I signaled to Ms. Smith I didn't have anything else to discuss.

As we got up to leave, Mr. Johnson shook hands with Ms. Smith and said, "Hope to hear from you soon."

I was so irritated I couldn't wait to get the hell out of there.

Ms. Smith tried to make small talk on our way back to Brookdale, but I wasn't even trying to hear anything. I was so angry. *Why is Monica trying to break me? She expects me to go live in the crummiest studio apartment while she keeps the big house to herself; where my meals come from doesn't even matter to her. It's mind boggling how people can think as such. It's so evil. There is no other word to describe it.*

"Let's allow everyone to cool off for a few days. I'll contact her lawyer. I hope we can work this out," said Ms. Smith.

"I still don't feel she is entitled to my business. I slave every day. She despised it, now she wants me to pay her from it! Don't forget she cost me an opportunity to expand the business by depleting our savings."

"After two years, you won't be paying spousal support anymore, but I'll suggest to Mr. Johnson you start paying her in installments for the buyout. That way, you won't have to come up with a lump sum of cash, and you won't have to pay it now. The installments could start right after the spousal support ends. Have patience. It will be over before you know it."

"I have no choice, do I?" I asked, sighing.

I felt like going to a really dark room and crying my eyes out. I never in my wildest dreams imagined I would go through this sort of drama with Monica. Ms. Smith told me not to bother to even go to court and wrestle her there. I was eager to end this and get on with my life too. I was at the point where I was extremely tired and frustrated. It's funny how the stipulations and demands changed every month. My lawyer drafted a final dissolution of marriage letter with all the trimmings. She e-mailed it to me, and I went over it and gave her the go-ahead to send it. She called me the next day. "Good news—they are okay with our offer. One more thing though, Monica wants you pay her the child support even when you have your daughter for the summer months," she said.

"What the hell?" I screamed. I could have bursted Ms. Smith's eardrum.

"I know, I know! They are being unreasonable at this point. They know it won't fly in the court of law."

"You're damn right! I'm already paying her an arm and a leg. Now she wants me to keep paying her the same amount of money monthly when I'll be keeping our daughter for the whole summer? What is wrong with her and her lawyer?"

"It's silly, I tell you. There is always something."

"I can't understand the logic behind this one. Child support means money for supporting a child! If I'm keeping the child for three months, doesn't that mean I should be keeping the money since I will be supporting the child? Right?"

I told Ms. Smith there was no way in hell I was going to go for it. *She wants to keep child support while she has no child?* That thought kept whirling in my head. I just couldn't believe it. I was done. I didn't care whether we went in front of a judge now. I knew I didn't want to spend the money for extended court dates, but I didn't care. I was not going to let her get away with what she was trying to do.

How dumb does she think I am? With all the crap she has been pulling over the last year, she has gone overboard with this one! I thought, fuming.

I got off the phone with my lawyer, and went to the gym for a full-on workout. I had to let out some steam.

A few days later, Ms. Smith sent me an e-mail.

To: Devin Lewis
From: Smith and Associates

The opposing counsel has sent back some of the requested changes to the marital settlement agreement I drafted. The first two changes are minor and grammatical, but the last two will have an effect on your spousal support and child support payments. Under Paragraph

WTF MOMENT

10, I reduced the amount of child support payable to your ex-wife during the period you will have primary custody to half of what she would normally get per month. Under Paragraph 13, I reduced spousal support payments if your ex-wife cohabitates with someone, regardless of their sexual relationship.

I would like to discuss this with you as soon as possible. Give me a call when you get a chance. Thanks.

I didn't even bother to respond immediately. I felt I was the only one who understood the meaning of child support. Why was Ms. Smith even trying to compromise? It was a cut-and-dry situation to me.

I logged unto my online account to check my balance. I noticed my automatic deposit was short. Instead of $7,200, I saw $3,000. So I called the payroll company and asked them what the screw-up was all about. The lady on the other line said, "There hasn't been any mistake. Your wages are being garnished for child support."

"What the?" I mumbled.

I felt fumes coming out of my head. Why would my wages be garnished? I was paying my monthly dues to Monica as the court requested. I had given her more than that before the court order when I was staying with Phil. My wages should be garnished only if I were delinquent.

Here we go again with her mind games.

I tried hard to keep a level head. I started to pace around my office. Then I walked outside and back in. I walked to the bathroom and stayed in the stall for a while. I was a few seconds away from putting a hole in the wall. I sat there for a while and cried. I was so angry. It was the only reflex I had. I dried my eyes, went back to my office, grabbed my cell phone, walked outside, and called my lawyer.

Ms. Smith picked up the phone.

"How are you today, Devin?"

"Definitely not good. Did you know about my wages being garnished?"

"No, I wasn't told. Monica's counsel did not send me any such notice."

"Well, my wages are being garnished right now, and I don't know why. It wasn't as though I wasn't paying my monthly dues, and besides the divorce isn't final, so how does the state know how much to take out of my pay?"

"This is ridiculous, Devin. I'll give the opposing counsel a call shortly."

"You're damn right it is ridiculous. It's all a game!" I said, fuming.

"I know, Devin."

BOLAJI TIJANI-QUDUS

"Anyway, I have to get back to work. I'll talk to you later," I said. I hung up the phone and threw it against the back building where I was standing.

God, please help me through this, I prayed.

My emotions were raging. I stood looking at my phone, shattered on the ground. I just realized I wouldn't be able to reach my clients and vice versa. I wasn't too sure whether I had backed up my phone contacts online. *Now I have to call my phone carrier and cook up a story as to how my phone broke.* It would take a few days for me to get a new phone in the mail. I had just created an inconvenience for myself—all in anger! I picked up the scraps and headed back to the office.

I arrived at me desk, and sent Monica an email.

To: Monica Lewis
From: Devin Lewis
Subject: What is going on?

I'm over here calling payroll asking why my paycheck was short, and I was told it was garnished. How embarrassing! Why would you even garnish my wages? I have been paying you consistently every month and doing all I am supposed to do.

To: Devin Lewis
From: Monica Lewis
Subject: Re: What is going on?

Your lawyer should have informed you about it.

To: Monica Lewis
From: Devin Lewis
Subject: Re: Re: What is going on?

My lawyer should have informed me about it . . . Is your response?

To: Devin Lewis
From: Monica Lewis
Subject: Re: Re: Re: What is going on?

What do you want me to say?

WTF MOMENT

To: Monica Lewis
From: Devin Lewis
Subject: Re: Re: Re: Re: What is going on?

What is your problem? Is all this even necessary? It's always something with you.

To: Devin Lewis
From: Monica Lewis
Subject: Re: Re: Re: Re: Re: What is going on?

Well, I thought your lawyer would have told you that the wage assignment would start so you wouldn't have to worry about transferring money every month. We thought it would be easier that way.

To: Monica Lewis
From: Devin Lewis
Subject: Re: Re: Re: Re: Re: Re: What is going on?

That is a load of crap! Since when has it been a problem for me to transfer money to our joint account? My checking account and the one we share are with the same bank. It takes me seconds to transfer the money, and I've been doing it diligently at the end of every month for the last year. What changed?

To: Devin Lewis
From: Monica Lewis
Subject: Re: Re: Re: Re: Re: Re: Re: What is going on?

I don't see anything wrong with the new setup. I'm sorry you're upset, but your lawyer should have informed you.

To: Monica Lewis
From: Devin Lewis
Subject: Re: Re: Re: Re: Re: Re: Re: Re: What is going on?

What are you talking about? My lawyer didn't know about this. All this is laughable. It is about the principle, Monica. You had no problems getting money every month. You think I'll up and leave my business and disappear? Or you think I'll just stop being a father all of a sudden? We are getting a divorce, that doesn't stop me from being responsible and being a father. These antics of yours, why? You feel empowered by trying to fuck with me? At the end of the day I'll be all right. Keep up with all the shenanigans.

You have a nice day.

I told my secretary I wasn't feeling well and left for the day. I called Ms. Smith on the way home.

"How soon can the divorce be finalized?" I asked.

"It could be done in a matter of a few months."

"Good, whatever it takes. Let's get it done. I just hope they don't throw another curve ball. I'm tired of all this. I need to move on with my life. I really wish she could just live and let live!"

"We are almost there, Devin."

17. Dip and Move

The train dropped me off at my destination after another day at the office. I walked to my car while checking my texts. I looked up every few seconds to make sure I wasn't going to run someone over as I walked. From the corner of my eye, I saw what seemed like a familiar figure walk past me. *I know it's not who I think it is*, I thought. She stopped at the crosswalk and waited for the light to flash. I soon caught up with her.

It was Denise. I hadn't seen her in a few months. She stood at about five six, petite and attractive. I met her at my gym. I had walked up to her and complimented her on how great she looked. I find it sexy when women take exceptional care of their bodies. Her perfectly toned, track-star body probably made a number of women jealous at the gym. She looked as if she could pop out five babies and still maintain her figure.

Every inch on her was firm. Being a gym rat as she is will do that. Denise was wearing a pleated wool skirt, stockings, and a black leather jacket with a scarf around her neck. Her long hair, braided into a ponytail, dangled behind her. Her shoes were surprisingly low. Her attire resembled that of a schoolgirl one might see in a Japanese animated movie. Her style didn't have a sexual overtone, but it was different.

I threw a quick glance at her when I drew near. I could see the tension on her face as she tried to avoid looking at me while she eagerly waited for the light to change. I looked away as well. I wasn't trying to speak to her. We had dated for about a month. Our last meeting had not ended well. Thankfully, we had both parked on opposite sides of the street. I hopped into my car and drove off reflecting on our short relationship.

We had lunch once, and she had complained about the waitress and the service. I asked her why she still ate there and why she recommended the place.

"I can't stand any of the waitresses," she said.

She tried to deter me from leaving a tip, but I did anyway because I felt the service was good.

Another time, she ranted about how she went to a nail shop and the service was horrible. She had been going to this particular place for five years. I was surprised she hadn't found someplace else since she didn't like it so much. Knowing her, I think she patronized the same shop because it was convenient and inexpensive.

Denise called me one night and said she was no longer on speaking terms with Vicky, a friend she had introduced me to. She said Vicky had been stalking her, had waited for her at the train station one evening, and even followed her home. It sounded weird.

"I thought you were both good friends?" I asked.

"Hardly!"

"Why do you think she is stalking you?"

"I don't know. Maybe she doesn't have pretty friends like me. She wants to be around me. She talks about how beautiful I am and wants us to go out all the time. I have a demanding job and don't have time to hang out."

"Were you both in a relationship or something? Because this is strange," I asked jokingly.

"Are you gay?!" she screamed at me on the phone.

"Relax, I was just being funny."

"No one is laughing over here, asshole!"

I was shocked at her change of pace. I was only making a joke. *Besides, you never know these days*, I thought.

I pretended someone was on the other line and got off the phone before she made any more unflattering comments. She called me a couple of days later and greeted me as if nothing had happened. I didn't bring it up, and continued conversing with her. Before long, she started to complain about her crazy coworkers, claiming they didn't appreciate all the work she did. She went on to talk about a certain person wanting her job because it was so glamorous. She was an executive assistant at a consulting firm, and she thought she had the ultimate career. When she spoke of her job, one would think she was the CEO of the company. She had a big ego for a little woman.

Denise was as aggressive in bed as she was in person. We both knew it was purely physical between us. I don't even know why I condoned her horrible attitude, but I enjoyed our little excursion while it lasted.

The first time we had sex was in the gym's back office. I was the only manager around, and I happened to be closing. It was late one Friday night, so the gym was pretty much empty. I think she came in purposely to mess with

WTF MOMENT

me. We usually close at 11:00 p.m., but she had walked in at 10:40 p.m. *How much of a workout is she going to get in twenty minutes?* I thought. That night she wore the sexiest and most revealing workout clothing I had ever seen. Her black yoga pants were tight, showing off her perfect plum, hard ass. She wore a half tank top that showed off her mid-section. Her stomach was flat and ripped. Her breasts were average sized, but her sports bra pushed them up, exposing her nice cleavage.

Denise went to the matted area of the gym and performed a variety of stretches. As the last customer left, I paused at the front door and glanced in Denise's direction. She continued with her stretching as if she wasn't aware it was closing time. I smiled and proceeded to lock the door.

I turned off the main lights and walked to the back office. I was fiddling with some paperwork when she appeared in the doorway smiling. I dropped what I was doing and motioned for her to *come here* with my index finger. She danced toward me as if she were a stripper. Then she mounted me while I was seated on the chair. She slowly grinded on me, then we kissed.

I lifted her tank top, and her beautiful breasts stared at me. I removed her top, and she really got turned on as I teasingly caressed her nipples. She grabbed and pulled on my hair, ears, and anything she could hold on to. She soon ripped my shirt off, then my pants and underwear. Her eyes shone when she saw how hard my kahuna was. She soon took off her pants. I saw the wet, white stains in her crotch area. She wasn't wearing any panties. I was still sitting on the chair when she stepped up to me and whispered in my ear.

"Do you have protection, Devin?"

"Do I?!" I responded.

I got up and searched one of my office cabinets. I remembered I had a few raincoats stashed away in one of the compartments.

When I returned, she was seated, her legs halfway spread, and her eyes beckoned for me to take her. Good thing the chair didn't have armrests. I smiled and raised the chair up a bit so I could have a better entry angle. I peeled the condom wrapper and strapped it on. I kissed her and worked her nipples again while my fingers serenaded her kitty. I stuck my middle finger in her creamy pie. She moaned and moved her pelvis as if my finger was a miniature penis. Then she grabbed my hand, indicating I should insert two fingers. She moaned some more. She removed my sticky fingers and grabbed my kahuna simultaneously. She pulled me closer and guided me in. She was tight and wet. I grabbed her legs by the ankles and stroked her.

"Right there!" she screamed. Those were words of encouragement, so I dug in deeper. As I slowed down to change the pace, she moved faster toward me, basically screwing me back. She knew how to move. I picked her up off the chair while I was still inside her. I walked around the office for several minutes, carrying her and thrusting in and out of her with my hands palming both of her butt cheeks. Her legs were wrapped around my waist. She soon had a jerking orgasm, so I laid her down on the floor. She took a few moments to gather herself, and then she crouched on all fours, inviting me to come in. I obliged her. I held her by the waist and plunged in. I smiled as I observed my kahuna moving in and out of her.

As I glided outward, she pushed her ass toward me, and her kitty muscles grabbed my kahuna, squeezing it. When I pushed inward, she released her kitty muscles, allowing me to slide in deeper. She did this in rhythm with my strokes. It felt so good. *She is a pro*, I thought. We changed positions again; this time, missionary. While I was on top of her, I reached around her and cupped her butt raising her off the floor a bit. I swirled my hips, digging in faster and deeper. She grabbed my butt in return, and her whole body tightened as she climaxed.

All of a sudden, I felt something warm around my groin area. I stood up to examine the situation.

"I think you just squirted on me."

"Sorry," she said, a bit embarrassed.

"No worries."

I grabbed a towel and laid it on the spot.

"We are not done yet," I said, smiling.

"You want to bang my brains out, huh?"

"I think we both want to do that to each other," I said, laughing.

I lay on the floor, and she squatted over me and rode me until we both climaxed. While basking in the afterglow, I said, "You should have been a porn star."

"I think that's you," she said, smiling.

We showered together in the men's bathroom, and she asked me what I was doing for the rest of the evening. Half an hour later, we were at her place.

I lay on her bed naked, staring at my reflection in a ceiling mirror. I noticed some kind of suspenders with circles at the end, directly hanging from the same ceiling above her bed.

Freak! I thought, smiling.

She returned from the bathroom and mounted the suspenders. It was as if she was participating in a ring gymnastic event at the Olympics.

She soon descended slowly with her legs spread wide apart, almost on a straight line, parallel to the bed. *This woman has some skills, but I'm game!*

WTF MOMENT

My kahuna was hard and straight, nodding upward. She must have done this a thousand times because, as she slid down, her kitty was aligned with my kahuna. I was intrigued watching as her kitty found and locked with my kahuna. It was as if they had minds of their own. She rode me up and down as if exercising with my tool, which was completely covered in her juices. With her legs still wide apart, she twisted 360-degrees with me still inside her, pulsating and hard as a rock. I lay back and let her work her magic. She climaxed a few more times and eventually climbed down. We continued our session for a bit longer, both climaxed, and fell asleep.

A month into our brief relationship, I had just made it home from work one evening when my phone rang. Denise was on the line.

"What are you doing right now?" she asked.

"No *Hello, how are you doing?*" I replied, sarcastically.

"Oh, sorry! I didn't know you were going to be sensitive today. So . . . how are you?"

"I'm good, thank you. So what's up?"

"I was just checking to see whether you wanted to hang out. Have you eaten dinner?"

"I was about to eat dinner actually, you could come join me if you like."

"What are you eating?"

"I have some Chinese food."

"I don't know about Chinese food. I saw roaches at this one restaurant by my job. The cooks don't wear gloves or hair nets in the kitchen, and who knows what else they put in the food. The MSG thing is not good for you. I heard they eat anything that moves—snakes, pigeons, lizards, dogs, and cats. Nasty! I don't want to eat that! Those people are not only unhygienic. They are not nice when you visit their restaurant. Someone needs to teach them about customer service." She sighed.

I had almost forgotten how quickly she could exasperate me. I wasn't in the mood to argue with her. She had just made a dumb, general statement. I had never had problems at the restaurants I visited.

One time I made a suggestion about a West African cuisine, and she had said, "I'm not eating African food; they sit on the floor and eat with their hands. It is so unsanitary."

I was irritated when I heard her statement. *She must have been watching too much Discovery Channel. How ignorant can one person be?*

"That's all the food I have, and I don't feel like eating anything else."

"I'm not eating what you're eating. I think I will stop by Big Burger's down the street and eat at your place. Can you meet me there in ten minutes?" she asked.

BOLAJI TIJANI-QUDUS

Oh! She really thinks fast food is healthier than Chinese food?
"Suit yourself. I will see you in ten minutes," I said.
"Okay. See you soon."
Maybe she can shut up long enough for me to sex her up tonight.
I moved things around to make my place look presentable when she arrived. She called my cell phone again.
"What's up?"
"Do you have any good movies?" she asked.
"I have a few, why?"
"I want to relax and just cuddle up; it's been a long day."
"Oh okay."
"FYI, we are not having sex tonight! From now on, I only want to do it if you're going to be my man. Besides, it's that time of the month anyway."

She was definitely trying my patience. Sometimes it's not about sex. I wouldn't mind hanging out with a date when she is on her cycle, as long as she is good company. *Then again, why would I want to hang with a motor-mouthed honey all night if I'm not sexing her?* I thought. I definitely would not want her as a girlfriend. She seemed like one of those women who would disrespect and try to humiliate a man when she is upset.

No thank you. I contemplated dismissing her right then, but I decided against it.

I had told her I would meet her at the burger joint. I grabbed my keys and headed out the door. *Why did I even agree to meet her down there anyway? Why can't she just buy her food and come over?* I couldn't understand how someone could be so brash and demanding.

We arrived at the burger joint at the same time. I noticed my mom was calling, so I answered my phone. Denise honked at me. I rolled down my window and signaled to her I was on the phone.

"Could you go in and get me a Fajita wrap?" she yelled from across the way.

I quickly covered the phone's mouthpiece so my mom wouldn't hear. I signaled to her again pointing to my phone, indicating I was busy on an important call. Mom was having a fit about how my little brother hadn't called her in over three weeks. I had to listen patiently and agree with everything she was saying or else I would have had to feel her wrath. I could already hear what she was going to say *Your brother picked up those bad habits from you. You should lead by example; family is important . . . blah, blah.*

Denise honked at me again; she had her hands up as if to say, *What's up? Didn't you hear my request?*

WTF MOMENT

I ignored her as I continued my conversation with Mom. Denise finally got out of her car and walked in. Five minutes later, she walked out with her food. I was still on the phone and signaled for her to follow me. I prayed for Mom to get off the phone; she could go on and on forever, so I started thinking of a lie to tell her. I pulled up to the basement garage of my complex, slid the access card in, and as I was about to enter, I told her I didn't get reception in the parking garage because it was located in the basement of my building.

I checked behind me; Denise had parked across the street. My parking space was a few levels below. It took me a couple of minutes to walk out of the garage and pop out on the other side of my building. I looked in the direction where Denise had parked and the space was empty. *Maybe she moved to a much closer space*, I thought, as I looked around. I walked around the block a few times, and still there were no signs of Denise or her car. She couldn't have parked down in the garage because she knew she wasn't supposed to. I hadn't seen her follow me in because the gate had closed behind me.

Oh hell, no! This crazy woman didn't just bounce!

I called her phone twice, but it went straight to voicemail. On the third try, she picked up. I could here background music.

"Hello," she said.

The call became static, so she hung up. I called her again, and it went straight to voicemail. I was ticked that I had been home minding my business and she had called me, got me out of the house, and I had to deal with her crap afterward. She had looked angry when she stepped out of Big Burger earlier. Still there was no excuse for her behavior. *How rude! Did she expect me to hop off the phone and run in and get her a burger?*

I finally got hold of her the next day, and I asked her why she had disappeared.

"I just felt like it," she said.

"It doesn't make any sense. It's rude actually. What happened? You wanted me to drop my call and cater to you?"

"Whatever!"

"You're not saying anything."

"I didn't feel like hanging out anymore, so I left," she continued.

"You didn't feel the need to show some respect and let me know?"

"Look! I said I didn't feel like staying anymore, so I left. I'm a grown woman, and I can do whatever the fuck I want to do!" she screamed.

"What's with the hostility now? Why don't you call me when you know how to speak properly to people," I said, indicating I was going to end the call. Before I could finish the sentence, she hung up. So I texted her.

To: Denise
Please delete my number because I just deleted yours.

I hit my contact list, scrolled down to her name, and *poof* her information was gone. Denise was one of those women the boys call *dip and move*. They have nothing to offer, but great sex and a spectacular body. Their drama and attitude usually outweighed everything else. As Phil would say, *You tap it a few times and keep it moving.*

I probably wouldn't have thought about Denise had I not seen her earlier that day. We hadn't spoken for about six weeks. I smiled when I thought about the sex drills we'd had, but that quickly disappeared as soon as I started to recall all the drama and awful conversations I'd had with her. The relationship had too many cons and not enough pros.

When I arrived at the office the next day, my desk phone message button was blinking. So I pushed the button.

Hi Devin, it's Denise. I don't have your cell number anymore. Your secretary directed me to your voicemail. I hope all is well. I was shocked to see you yesterday. We didn't even speak! I've never experienced that before. Give me a call when you get a minute. Thanks (121) 222-4449.

She had to be really loony for even calling me. Yeah, right! I thought. I deleted her message and went on about my day's business.

Situations like that make me miss being married, minus the drama of course. Dating can be challenging, especially when one has to deal with the wrong women back to back. *I hope it gets better, because I'm tired of all the bull.*

I was on my way to lunch when my office phone rang. The call was from an unavailable number, but I picked it up.

"Hey, Devin, how are you?"

"I'm fine. May I ask who is speaking please?"

"It's Denise. You forgot how I sound already? That's a shame," she said, laughing.

"What's up, Denise?" I asked, flatly.

"Don't be like that. You don't know how hard this is for me to say, but I'm sorry for the way I acted the last time. Can we start over?"

"You can't be serious?" I laughed.

"C'mon Devin, can we meet for lunch, please? I really miss you, and I'm truly sorry."

WTF MOMENT

I paused for a long time and then, agreed to meet her for lunch. I didn't know why. *Maybe because I'm trying to make an effort not to quickly write women off.* I figured men and women would always clash, but deep inside, I knew Denise was a no-no. I gave her another shot, and we had lunch.

A few weeks later, I went to her place to visit on a Sunday evening.

"Someone has been misbehaving this whole weekend," she said to me when she opened the door.

"Hello to you as well," I said, as I entered.

"So what happened?" she asked, with her hands on her hips.

"What do you mean by what happened? Saturday, I had to take Emmanuella to Marine Village. This morning, I dropped her off at her mother's. I just finished training a few clients. I'm exhausted right now. Please don't start," I said, as I took of my shoes and slumped on her sofa.

"Someone must have had a good time. You must have been hanging out with the other woman!"

"Whatever, smart ass," I responded, not paying her any mind.

She had just begun to cook when I arrived. I wanted to call Emmanuella before she went to bed. Denise was blasting music in the kitchen while she cooked, so I got up and went to her bedroom to make the call. The ex-wife didn't pick up, so I hung up and returned to the kitchen to keep Denise's company.

"You're so sneaky," she said, under her breath.

I asked her what she had said, and she said it again.

"You're so sneaky, running off to make a call."

I was irritated by the remark, but I kept my cool.

"You're calling me sneaky because I walked away to call my daughter? If I was trying to call someone else, I would have done that before I got here. Your comment is off base."

"No it's not. You're sneaky."

"You should really stop saying that," I said, sternly.

Moments later, my phone rang; it was the ex-wife calling back on behalf of my daughter.

I took her call and walked toward the room again due to the noise in the kitchen. Seconds later, Denise's phone rang as well. I shut the bedroom door as I spoke to Emmanuella. While I was on the phone, the door was pushed wide open, and Denise stood at the door looking at me annoyed.

Then she said, "That is rude."

I covered the mouthpiece of my phone with my hand.

"I'll be right out. Talking to Emmanuella," I whispered.

171

She walked out without listening to what I was saying.

I returned to my conversation, and before long, she popped in again. This time, she spoke louder than before. "That is so very rude," and walked out again.

I wrapped up the call shortly after that. I went to the kitchen to ask her what was up with the hostility. I had been at her place before when she had been on long-distance calls for up to an hour. I hadn't fussed about it. I just watched TV.

"What seems to be the problem?" I asked.

"It is rude to be on the phone."

"Are you telling me I can't be on the phone when I'm with you, even when it's family? Or is it that I can't be on the phone because I'm at your house?"

"That is not what I'm saying, and please lower your voice."

"I'm not raising my voice. You were on the phone with whomever, weren't you?"

"It is not whomever, that was my niece. Get it right! You're ignorant," she said, smirking.

"You're calling me ignorant now. Is that it?!"

"If the shoe fits . . ."

"What?"

"This conversation is over now," was the next statement that came out of her mouth.

I was boiling hot. I had heard enough from this rude, disrespectful woman. I got quiet and stared at the front door for several moments. Then I put my shoes on, looked her in the eye, and said, "I'm done with your crazy ass!"

I didn't wait to see or hear her reaction. I slammed the door behind me and got out of there as fast as I could. *I think I'm going to chill on women for a while*, I thought, as I drove home.

18. After Spring Comes Summer

I was getting my car detailed when Chris called. We weren't supposed to meet until much later to discuss the details of our new gym partnership and the roles two other investors were going to play.

Chris liked my expansion idea. I had been giddy as of late, over the opportunity. I consider Chris a trustworthy person and thought we could maintain a good business relationship without allowing our friendship to get in the way. Neither of us would allow it. That kind of relationship is rare.

I took Chris's call, and he told me he had to cancel our meeting. He was rushing his pregnant wife to the hospital. Although she wasn't due for another three weeks, she was experiencing labor pains.

"No problem, Chris. Nadine is more important right now. Go ahead and take care of her."

"Okay, I will talk to you later."

"Hold on, Chris, what hospital are you guys going to?"

"Belleview."

"I'll come by in a short while, okay?"

"Okay. Thanks," he said and hung up.

I could only imagine how he was feeling. Childbirth is a humbling experience. I recalled when my daughter was born. It was exciting but surreal at the same time—watching another life being introduced into the world.

I called Phil and asked him whether he wanted to go with me to see Chris and Nadine at the hospital. He agreed, and we headed to Belleview.

When we arrived, Chris was outside with his phone pegged to his ear, probably talking to well-wishing friends and relatives. He wrapped up the call, flashed his happy smile, and walked up to us. We all embraced each other, reminiscent of the past year when we had all embraced before Chris wedded Nadine on the boat cruise.

"Congratulations! You're about to be a father soon," I said.

"Thanks. I can't wait! They are checking her now. I can't wait for the baby to come so I can enjoy my wife again. It has been really hard on her," he said.

"Do you know the sex of the baby?" Phil asked.

"We decided to wait and find out when the baby is born. We want it to be a surprise," Chris replied.

"I can respect that," Phil said.

We continued talking about the joys of parenthood, at least Chris and I did. Phil didn't have any kids yet, so he hadn't gone through the ritual. Nonetheless, he was nodding and agreeing with us, giving the impression he had been there already.

A doctor walked in on our conversation and told Chris he had to come with him because his wife's water had broken and they would have to deliver the baby right away. Chris hurriedly followed the doctor while Phil and I stayed behind in the lobby. Neither of us had much to do that evening, so we decided to hang out until we heard the good news so we could give our man a congratulatory hug.

Chris and Nadine had been fun to watch during the pregnancy. They both had started to prep the baby's room as soon as they found out they were expecting. The room was ready two months into the pregnancy, complete with wallpaper and a crib and his-and-her toys. I had asked them what they would do with the other gender toys once they knew what they were having.

"We will put them away in the storage downstairs for next time," Nadine had said.

Sitting in the waiting room brought back memories. Monica and I had packed a couple of bags at least a month out from Emmanuella's due date. We had a few false alarms along the way. We had to have visited the hospital at least four times before the actual birth happened. Three of those times were late in the morning, between 2 a.m. and 4 a.m. I remember being sleepy and driving to the hospital. It was about thirty minutes away from our home. I had prayed every single time that the baby wouldn't come out in the car.

On the final run, Monica was in labor for an hour. The contractions then subsided, but the doctor asked her to stay overnight as a precaution. I was told to go home and rest. I kept my phone charged and next to me the whole time I was gone. Monica said she would call me as soon as she felt she was about to go into labor. I called my job to give them an updated status.

A couple of hours later, as I was settling into sleep, the phone rang. It was Monica. She was in labor again. I made a dash to the hospital, and she was on

WTF MOMENT

the way to the delivery room when I arrived. I was excited and nervous. A few minutes later, Monica was screaming. I tried my best to calm her down.

"Breathe, breathe and push, baby," I said.

"What do you think I'm trying to do? I'm breathing and I'm pushing!" she responded, screaming at me and squeezing the hell out of my hand.

She had refused the epidural because she wanted to have our baby naturally. When the pain was too much to bear, she asked the doctor to administer the drug. I wasn't sure how much it helped because she still screamed the rest of the time.

Finally, I saw the baby's head. I couldn't believe the baby was going to come out of my wife's little kitty. The doctor asked for an instrument. It looked like a little sharp knife. He cut Monica a bit so the baby could have more room to wiggle out. *Oh god! Don't cut up the VJJ some more!* I remember thinking. The baby finally came out after a few more pushes. She was so beautiful. I felt a rush of unexplainable feelings—all of them good. I had finally become a dad. It all seemed surreal.

The doctor then handed me a pair of scissors so I could cut the umbilical cord. I was in a daze for moments looking at the baby. I came back to my senses and took the scissors and did the honors of cutting the cord. Monica lay there, exhausted. A smile came on her face when the baby was placed on her chest. I was so proud of her. She had just performed the greatest and hardest job in the world, the birthing of a child.

I smiled as I walked down memory lane.

Phil and I sat in the lobby and watched the overhead TV. A basketball game between the Lakers and Celtics was on. I was just getting into it when my phone rang. I motioned to Phil I would be stepping out since cell phones weren't allowed inside.

I checked the caller ID. It was Angel.

I wonder whether I should pick up.

Angel had been dating a guy named Wayne for nine months. From what I gathered, it had been a tumultuous relationship. She adored and worshiped the ground Wayne walked on. She thought she was his girlfriend, but his actions said otherwise. He also had a daughter from a prior relationship. She always felt she could talk to me about what was going on in her life. I didn't mind; she was a nice person despite her imperfections. She was instrumental in keeping all the legal workings of Five Star together before we officially opened. She is a very detailed lawyer. We had maintained a good rapport since then.

I decided to pick up.

"What's up, Angel?"

"Hey, Devin."

"Are you all right?" I asked. I could sense something was wrong with the way she sounded.

"I'm okay. I wanted to talk to you about Wayne."

Here we go again! I thought. She had told me on multiple occasions she had ended the relationship with the Wayne guy. Shortly afterward, she would call me saying she was entertaining him again. She had said he had other women, but she thought she was the main one. I told her, if she knew he had other women, she didn't need to be upset. From what she had told me, he didn't deny his side dealings either.

"What did he say you are to him?" I had asked her.

"Oh! He says he cares about me and that I mean a lot to him, but he isn't ready to take it to the next level," she had responded.

"Well, you have your answer right there. He said he isn't ready to be in committed relationship."

"Well . . . that is what he says, but he invites me to meet his family, and he met my daughter too. We took her to Water World just last month! If he is doing all this stuff with me, doesn't that mean we are in a relationship?"

"Not necessarily," I had said.

"What do you mean?"

"I mean he may just be hanging out with you because there is something you do for him that he likes, and since he already said he doesn't want to be in a committed relationship, he must assume you understand too. But I don't like the whole idea of him going on vacation with you and your daughter."

"He does all these things with me and says he wants me in his life. I do things for him I don't usually do for any man. I cook for him. I do his laundry and starch his shirts for work. I help his daughter with her homework. I do all these things, and he is not claiming me!"

I didn't know too many other details regarding their relationship, so I could only add my two cents from what I had heard from Angel. There may be other things she wasn't telling me. Maybe she was infatuated with this guy, and she was the one pushing the issue. Maybe Wayne was one of those guys who like to have his cake and eat it too.

"Look, I'm at the hospital visiting a friend who is having a baby, so I can't talk long. By the way, I thought you and Wayne were over?"

"I know that is what I said, but we have been seeing each other again."

I felt the urge to really tell her about herself and chastise her, but I didn't because she had said she felt I was easy to talk to. Maybe I am, but I had a

WTF MOMENT

lot going on with my life, and I barely had the time to listen to someone else's relationship drama, especially Angel's, which was blatantly going nowhere.

I wasn't trying to play Dr. Phil, but I convinced myself to listen.

"So now what?"

"I'm over at Wayne's house right now, and he is not here. His car isn't here!"

"Maybe he is at work. And why are you over at his house anyway?"

"It's Sunday; he doesn't work on weekends!"

"Maybe he went to church," I said, sounding diplomatic.

"C'mon, Devin, you're not helping. He is an atheist! Come on now!"

"Oh yeah, that's right. Okay, why did you feel the need to pop by his place?"

"I was on the phone with him last night, and he told me he was going to stay up late to study for an exam. He wanted to get off the phone. I just had a funny feeling when I called him an hour later and he wouldn't pick up his phone. I wanted to know whether we could go out to brunch today. I called him this morning, and he didn't pick up either. His phone rings constantly, so I know he would have heard it and picked up if he wasn't doing anything shady. That is why I drove up here, and as I suspected, he isn't here."

"Well, we know he has other women, right?" I continued.

"I know, but since we made up this last time, he told me I was the only one who mattered to him. He said he wasn't messing with the other women anymore. We started on a clean slate."

"Are you sure those words came out of his mouth, or are you assuming?"

"That is what he said. And the bastard is at some other chick's house right now."

"I don't know what to say Angel."

"I know he is with some bitch! I saw a woman's hair in his bathtub when I was over here a few days ago. I also noticed four condoms were gone out of the stack in his drawer."

I wanted to laugh, but I knew it wouldn't be a funny matter to her. *Counting condoms?*

"Okay, Angel. I think we have established the fact that this guy is doing his own thing. Why are you so insistent on being with him when all the signs are indicating you're not the only one?"

"I don't know. He is not only good looking and sexy, but he has it altogether. He is a vice president at his job. He has two master's degrees. I love that he is well dressed like a GQ model. He has done very well for himself. He has it going on, and he is so sexy. I melt when I see him."

"So you're attracted to his accomplishments?"

"Not just that. I can't resist him," she said, as her voice started to crack.

"Okay, then he must be laying it down in the bedroom because I don't know why you would continue to put yourself through all this, knowing it isn't a good situation for you!"

"It's not about the sex, Devin! He's definitely not all that. I just like his swagger."

"Oh. Okay, Angel, whatever! But anyway, you're going to have to decide what you want to do. At this point, I can't really blame this guy. You're not stupid. You know it's all wrong for you, but you still decide to hang on. The writing is on the wall. If you choose to continue doing this, you shouldn't get upset at anyone but yourself."

"You're mean, Devin!"

"Why? Because I am not saying what you want to hear?"

"I know! I just don't want to hear it."

"You know what you have to do. If you want to accept the fact you are the *other woman* and you can live with it, go ahead and do that. If you don't think you can hang with it, move on. It's all up to you, Angel!"

"Oh! He just pulled up! I'll have to call you back, Devin."

"Okay!" I said, shaking my head as I hung up the phone. I hoped she'd really get it together instead of acting desperate. I had told her she had to show her child a better example. It is very important for a single woman to lay the right foundations for her children as to what to accept and what not to accept in a relationship.

I walked back into the hospital lobby and from the corner of my eye, I saw Chris walking toward us. He was still dressed in his scrubs—the gown, head and shoe coverings. As he inched closer, I didn't see his trademark smile. Then I noticed he had tears running down his face.

"She is gone!" he said

"Who is gone?" I asked, with a look of bewilderment.

"My wife is gone!"

"You can't be serious!" I was in shock.

Chris fell to the ground. Phil and I ran forward to catch him. He was crying profusely now. I had never seen Chris like this ever, sobbing uncontrollably. I didn't know what to do at the moment. Phil and I knelt down with him on the floor, holding him, all of us crying.

That was not the news we wanted to hear. He was welcoming a baby at the same time his wife was saying good-bye to the world. The thoughts kept ringing in my head, *why do bad things happen to good people?*

Apparently the baby had been stuck around Nadine's pelvis earlier in the labor. Something else went wrong—her uterus became inverted. Nadine hemorrhaged. The doctors were forced to take her into surgery and performed

WTF MOMENT

an emergency hysterectomy. Unfortunately it was a too late. She was also anemic, which complicated matters. Her blood stopped clotting.

The lead doctor and two nurses walked over to where we were, to hand the baby to Chris. It was a boy. "We are sorry, Mr. Gibson," the lead doctor said, looking sympathetic. The two nurses were teary-eyed as well.

It was the saddest moment of my life. Time stood still. It was as if we were in a movie. Chris took his baby and looked at him through his tears. He was happy he had his baby in his arms, but he was also distraught. He had just lost the woman he loved so dearly. It was a bittersweet moment. I could just imagine what the man was going through. Those feelings could tear someone apart. He sat there with his baby in his arms and cried for a long while. Phil and I just sat there in silence, giving Chris as much moral support as we could.

Amid all this, the baby was quiet. He was sucking on a pacifier and looking around, observing. If someone had said the baby was already a month old, I would have believed it. He was incredibly alert for someone who had just been born minutes earlier.

Chris finally got up and handed the baby to his mother, who had just walked in. Her face was swollen from crying. She had a bottle of baby formula in hand, ready to feed the baby. Nadine's parents walked in shortly thereafter. Nadine's mom wanted to see her daughter immediately, but the doctors told her to wait. She couldn't understand why. The doctors explained to her that they still needed to clean up Nadine before she could be seen. She wasn't trying to hear any of it, and was being consoled by Nadine's father.

It was the most sullen atmosphere I had ever been in. If there was ever a day I wished never happened, that day would have been it. Doctor Margo came back out to get Chris; I guess there was some paperwork he needed to complete. Chris had stopped crying by this time. He had gathered himself. He was consoling the other family members who had just arrived. Nadine's parents disappeared through the steel doors shortly thereafter.

I sat next to Mrs. Davies—Chris's mom. I could see she was really trying to hold back tears while she fed the baby.

"Beautiful baby, huh?"

"Isn't he?"

"Yes, ma'am. And he has great family members around. Everyone is going to lend a hand in raising him," I said.

"That is right. He is in good hands. Thank you, Devin, for being here for your friend . . . you and Phil both."

"It's no problem, ma'am. Chris would do the same for me. He is not the person this kind of thing should happen to," I said, choking up.

"You know what, baby? God has a reason for everything. He giveth and he taketh. We can't really question him. He knows best. As hard as it is for all of us now, we all have to be strong for Chris. Okay?"

"Yes, ma'am," I said. I watched tears flow freely down her face. I started to cry again too. I could see where Chris had gotten his character from. She was a strong woman, and his whole family loved each other unconditionally. Chris was such a genuine guy; I was going to do what I could to help ease this pain.

As the night drew on, more family members came by. Chris and Nadine both had big families, and they were all close.

I started to think back as to how beautiful their wedding was aboard the Carnival cruise ship. It had been simple, yet elegant. Everyone was dressed in his or her best white linen. I remember Chris crying as he watched Nadine walk down the aisle toward him. It was so sweet, so real. They both cried when they read their vows. It was emotional, and everyone was touched. I think most of the guests shed a tear or two, including myself. I couldn't believe the woman I had seen last summer in her beautiful wedding gown was no more!

A few days later, there was an observance ceremony for Nadine. I didn't see one dry eye. I still couldn't believe she was gone—just like that! I had just seen her a few days before. I could still see her angelic smile, those assuring eyes and demeanor.

Chris couldn't have asked God for a better wife. He always said he was the luckiest man on the planet for having a gem like Nadine. She would be quick to tell you she was the lucky one, how blessed she was to have Chris as a husband. I guess they were both lucky to have each other. If there was ever a perfect couple, it was Chris and Nadine, beautiful people inside and out.

How in the world will Chris be able to deal with this awful situation? I thought. Then again, if anyone could, it would be Chris. He is one of the most resilient people I have ever met.

I remember when Chris was out of town many years ago. He had left his car insurance payment for his little brother to take care of while he was gone. His brother forgot to mail it in, and consequently Chris's insurance was cancelled. That very week, a drunken neighbor crashed into Chris's parked car in front of his house. This was a brand-spanking new 325 BMW. Chris got back from his vacation and wasn't even upset. He shrugged it off and said it was only a car and there was no need to go raving about the situation. There was nothing he could do about it.

I had to commend him for having such a great attitude. If that had been me, I know I would have hit the roof and probably skinned my brother alive! I would go nuts; especially knowing I would have to continue making car payments on

WTF MOMENT

a car I would no longer be driving. Chris's attitude about life is one I try to emulate. As hard as this was going to be, I was confident Chris would handle it and raise his son the best possible way he could.

Everyone present at the funeral must have wept. Something of this nature wasn't supposed to happen to people, let alone to Chris.

Chris approached the podium to give Nadine's eulogy. Surprisingly he held it together, more so than I had expected, and remained calm as he spoke.

> Just a few days ago, I thought my life was over and didn't know what I was going to do. But, every time I look at our son, I see Nadine. She is living through our baby, and she will always watch over him. She looked after me all these years. I know she will always be here with me in spirit, helping and guiding me in raising our beautiful son. Nadine made her mark in such a short time. Her body is gone, but I can feel her spirit with me always. I can cry all day, every day, but I have realized she came into my life for a reason. The years we spent together have been and will always be the best years of my life. I am a better man because of Nadine. The love I shared and enjoyed with Nadine in six years is enough to last me a whole lifetime. Please join me in celebrating her life today. It has been the greatest honor and privilege to be able to know and love you, Nadine. Until we meet again. I love you, babe.

I could hear the sobs throughout the room as Chris left the podium. I know he wanted to burst out crying, but he kept it together. He is that kind of man. We all knew he was hurting deeply inside.

I finally got up to say a few words.

"I have known Chris all my life. When he met Nadine, I saw the effect she had on him and the transformation he underwent. All he did was talk about her all the time."

I faced Chris as I continued, "I'm here for you, whatever you need, brother. I know it must be hard for you, but I applaud you on how strong you have been through all this. I think we should all remember how great a person Nadine was and how good she made everyone around her feel. She always smiled and would give anyone a helping hand. I think she would want us to remember her that way. I bet she is looking down at us still smiling. May her beautiful soul rest in peace. Please let's celebrate her life as Chris said. Life is very short and we should all live it to the fullest because no one is promised tomorrow. We think we control our lives, but the man upstairs actually does. So please love every day. Laugh every day if you can. Enjoy your life and spend it with the ones you love. In conclusion, please turn to the person next to you, hug them and say, *I love you*," I said, holding back tears.

Immediately everyone in attendance turned to a neighbor for a hug. Someone walked over to where I was standing and gave me a hug as well. It felt good.

19. Falling In Niagara

An e-mail invitation popped up in my inbox. It was from Phil. We had been talking lately, about going on vacation. He wanted me to visit Toronto, Canada, at the end of the summer for the film festival. It sounded interesting. I thought about how great it would be to get out of the country for a change.

I called Phil, and we spoke on the phone briefly. Finally I confirmed the dates with him. He was going to Quebec a week earlier than my departure date; he would be in Toronto by the time I got there. I was about to book a hotel online when I realized I hadn't spoken about accommodations with Phil. I didn't know whether he was staying with friends or at a hotel. Ideally I always like to get my own hotel room. I value my privacy. I went ahead and booked it anyway; if things changed, I could always cancel. I hadn't been anywhere in a while, so I was looking forward to the trip.

A month later, I was at the airport heading to Toronto. I made it into the terminal in no time. I purchased a book and magazine from a bookstand and walked over to a nearby coffee stand for a grande cup of chai tea and a blueberry scone.

I finished my snack and went back to the terminal. I debated whether to browse the Internet on my laptop or read the book I had just bought. Then I saw her!

She was sitting next to the big windows overlooking the runways. She had big, frizzy hair and big earrings. She wore white New Balance tennis shoes, blue jeans, and a white DKNY hooded sweatshirt. She looked like a free-spirited soul artist. I moved over with my belongings closer to where she was sitting. She didn't notice me. Her head was buried deep in the book she was reading.

I finally said, "That is a nice read there!" I smiled at her.

"That's what everybody keeps telling me," she said, smiling back at me with beautiful, prominent eyes.

"Is this your first one?" I asked

"No, I may have read about seven of his books. I don't quite remember."

"I'm sorry, I'm being rude. My name is Devin," I said, as I extended my hand.

"It's okay, nice to meet you, Devin. I'm Paula."

"Good to meet you as well, Paula. You must have the softest hands I've ever shaken," I said, still holding on to her hand. She laughed at me when I playfully said, "Excuse me, I got carried away for a moment there. You have a special touch."

"Thanks for the compliment." She grinned.

"Enjoying the book so far? I couldn't put it down when I read it," I continued.

"Well, I do like it so far. You're not one of those people who will spoil a good book by telling me what happened at the end, correct?"

"I wouldn't do that!" I said, with a pouting face.

Her laugh was so sincere and real. *Here is this beautiful woman sitting here at the airport talking to a complete stranger*, I thought. She was as real as it gets. *Why can't more women be down to earth as Paula is?*

It was hard to focus and not be carried away by Paula's presence.

"Well, I'm glad you're not reading one of those vampire novels," I said, "if I see one more person reading one of those books, I'll lose it; I swear. What's up with that? It's like the thing to do now. They've even got the vampire TV series and movies. I don't get the infatuation."

"I think women like vampire books because they are very erotic and romantic," she responded.

"Really?"

"Yes, that is why they sell, in case you don't know. They are not that bad. I've read a few, but I'm so busy I don't have much time to read except when I'm in transit as I am now."

"You're reading one of my favorites. That's why I came over."

"So you wouldn't have said anything, had I been reading a vampire novel?"

"Probably not."

"That would have been your loss then!"

"Perhaps," I said, laughing.

"So Devin, have you seen any movies made from John Grisham's books?"

"Yes, and I have to say I liked *A Time to Kill*."

"Oh really?"

"I liked the cast, and the acting was superb. The ending was dramatic and touching. I like how powerful it was, capturing people's emotions the way it did."

WTF MOMENT

She put her book to the side and gazed at me as we continued discussing movies. The more we talked, the more we found we had a mutual love for the same kinds of movies.

"Okay, we are going to have to stop this mutual agreement thing we have going on here," she said, smiling.

"It might be a good thing that our tastes are similar."

"Is that so?"

"Yup," I responded.

"I'm going to have to be careful with you," she said, wiggling her finger at me.

"I'm harmless," I said, playfully biting my lips.

"There you go again," she quipped. She shook her head and gazed at me.

I was mesmerized, so I looked away to clear my head and then returned to her gaze.

"Movies need to be more creative these days, though," I continued. "What's with all these superhero movies, and remakes? Where is the creativity? I don't remember the last time I went to the theater and came out thinking the movie was awesome."

Paula shifted in her seat and adjusted her posture. She folded her legs under herself on the seat as if she were sitting on a yoga mat.

"Best place to look for a good movie is through the independent circuit," she said.

"Yeah, that's right. *Sideways* was a good independent movie which went on to do well mainstream. I hope to catch a few good ones at the Toronto festival this weekend," I added.

"There is a good chance you will."

"So are you heading to Canada on vacation as well?" I asked.

"Yes, I'm visiting some friends in Montreal," she replied, "it's nice to be able to get away sometimes."

"I used to love to travel, but I haven't been anywhere outside the country in the last four years."

"Used to? Why did you stop?"

"I was married, so I couldn't go anywhere," I said, laughing.

"Sorry."

"Oh no, there is nothing to be sorry about. It is what it is."

She smiled again. "So you're free and exploring the world again?"

"You could say that. I have more time to myself now."

"Okay. Toronto is a very nice city. I think you will enjoy it."

"I hope so. I've heard nothing but good things."

I was watching to see whether her mood would change after I mentioned the word *married*. She remained the same, and I liked that she didn't ask too many questions. Some women would have drilled me by now: "What happened? Did you cheat? Do you have kids? How long were you married?" These are valid questions, of course, but I think people should be polite and let others divulge information on their own instead of prying. Divorce can be a sensitive and even hurtful experience for some.

"I think you will like it," she continued. "I have always enjoyed it whenever I visited."

"Cool. I was hoping to bring my little girl but I changed my mind. I'll take her to Disney World later instead."

"Aww, that's cute. How old is she?"

"Five," I said, as I dug into my back pocket and produced my wallet. I browsed through it and gave her the picture of my little girl.

"She's so adorable! What's her name?"

"Emmanuella," I answered, beaming.

"That's a nice name, what does it mean?"

"It means *God is with you*."

"Even better," she said, smiling.

"I'm blessed to have her," I said, proudly.

"I bet you spoil her, huh?"

"Unfortunately, I do."

"There is nothing wrong with that."

"Why did I know you were going to say that?" I asked, laughing.

"You have to pamper us girls, you know?"

"Yeah, yeah, whatever," I said, in sarcasm.

"No?" she asked.

"No comment."

"Are you trying to tell me you don't pamper your women?"

"It all depends."

"On what?"

"Whether she likes to be pampered."

"All women like to be pampered."

"Not all, most. Some women like to do the pampering instead."

"Is that so?"

"Yes! But I do pamper my women though," I said, giving her the most innocent look I could muster.

She laughed and said, "I was beginning to worry about you!"

"You have a beautiful laugh."

WTF MOMENT

"Thank you."

"It is soothing. You laugh from your soul. There is nothing pretentious about you, and that is very rare. Although I don't know you, there is something about you that says, *See me and take me as I am*," I said.

"Well, thank you again," she said, blushing. "You're not too bad yourself."

"Thank you, ma'am."

"You must do this a lot."

"Do what?"

"Put your charm on."

"No charm at all, just being myself," I said, chuckling.

"Oh okay, I can dig that."

"And what is your secret?"

"Secret?"

"For being, *sexycrazycool*."

"Okay, Devin!" she said, laughing.

"I'm serious!"

"I don't know. Just being me, as you've said."

An announcement about our flight interrupted our conversation—our flight would be boarding immediately, first class and those with children first.

I suddenly felt the need to use the restroom, so I told her I would see her shortly. After all, we would be on the same flight to our layover in Calgary, Canada. *I will still have a few opportunities to collect her information*, I thought. I walked as fast as I could toward the restroom. There wasn't one next to our area, so I had to walk several minutes to the next one.

A urinal opened up, and I rushed to it to unload. I washed my hands and hurried back to my departure area; the line was short. *The plane must not be full* I thought. There were no signs of Paula. A few minutes later, I was boarding the plane. I surveyed the cabin as soon as I arrived in the coach area. Paula was seated in the middle section and was looking out the window. She didn't notice me as I walked by and sat in the back row.

I kept thinking about Paula. I wished I were next to her. It felt good to be around her. She had a really good vibe, so I made a bold move. I walked over to where she was sitting and got the attention of the man next to Paula. I noticed she was reading her book.

I whispered to the gentleman, "Excuse me, sir, I don't want to be a nuisance, but would you mind switching seats with me? The beautiful woman sitting next to you is a friend of mine, and I would really love to chat with her."

He glanced at me and then at her. He probably didn't feel like being uprooted from his spot, but then I guess he didn't want to appear to be an asshole since there were a few other seats on the plane. Besides, I had asked nicely. He glanced at us again, and we both flashed him smiles as though we were two kids asking an adult for a favor. He finally smiled and asked, "Okay, where are you sitting?"

"I'm over at 30C, about four rows behind you, sir," I responded.

I was glad he had agreed. I thanked him as he packed his belongings and moved over to my former seat.

A couple sitting in the opposite seats smiled at me as I settled next to Paula. The guy had an approving look on his face as if he was saying, *Nice move. You're the man!* I smiled back as if to say, *Yeah, I know.*

"You didn't think you were going to get away so easily, did you?" I asked Paula, laughing.

"Now, I'm really beginning to worry about you!" She shook her head as she laughed as well.

"You shouldn't. Now that I'm here next to you, you're in safe hands."

"Who said I was in any kind of danger, Superhero?"

"A little bird told me you needed me here to make your flight pleasant."

"Really?"

"Yup," I responded, grinning.

She gave me a curious look.

"You're full of yourself, aren't you?"

"I wouldn't say all that," I said, in a flirting manner.

"Humph!"

I smiled as I observed her. She wasn't wearing any makeup. She could wear a cloak and her beauty would still shine through. She was just one of those people who are naturally sexy and have a warm personality that people are automatically drawn to.

"You smell great. Venus, right?"

"Yes, it is! How did you know?" she asked, surprised.

"I just know these things," I said, with a playful smirk.

"No guy ever mentioned the name of my perfume before. Someone might say you smell nice, and that is about it."

An ex-girlfriend of mine had worked at a boutique store and brought home samples of Venus. I remembered it having a unique and distinctive smell.

"Hmmm . . . what don't you know?" she asked.

"I know a bit of this and a little of that."

"Oh okay," she laughed.

"Do you live in Brookdale?" I asked.

WTF MOMENT

"No, my parents do. I just came to visit them for a few weeks. After this next trip to Canada, I'm heading back home."

"Where is home?"

"I currently live in Dubai in the Arab Emirates."

"Really? What are you doing way out there?"

"I teach high school English. I wanted something different, and I love to travel, so when the opportunity came about, I jumped on it," she said, beaming.

"That's great. How long have you been teaching there?"

"About two years now."

"You like it?"

"Ab-so-lu-te-ly. I love it!"

"You studied English in school I presume?"

"I have my degrees in journalism and English. I like to write and edit, so I would like to get back to that one day. Maybe work for a magazine."

"What don't you want to do?" I teased.

"I would like to do a little bit of this and a little bit of that," she said, laughing.

"So . . . world traveler, where else have you been?"

"Hmm . . . let me see. I've been to parts of Europe—like London, Greece, Italy, Germany, Amsterdam, and Norway. In Asia, I've been to Tokyo, Hong Kong, Malaysia, Thailand, and Bangkok. In Africa—South Africa, Senegal, Cape Verde, Nigeria, and Kenya."

"Okay, wow! Where haven't you been?"

"There are still so many places in the world I need to go visit."

"I'm so jealous. Can I come with you on one of your trips?" I asked, smiling.

"You're more than welcome."

"Why are you passionate about traveling?"

"My parents. They took us on the road with them when we were very young."

"I think that is really great. I would like to travel with Emmanuella. I think it would expose her to different cultures and allow her to see life with broader eyes," I added.

"I agree," she quipped.

"Since you travel quite often, do you speak any other languages?"

"Besides English, I speak Chinese, French and Portuguese. As you know, I've been living in Dubai for a year now, so my Arabic has gotten better."

I was in awe. *She is not only beautiful, she is sharp as well. My kind of woman*! "How long are you going to be in Montreal?"

"I think about two weeks or so."

"You should come to Toronto."

189

"I thought about it, but my friend who lives out there is out of town."

"But you have a new friend there you can visit."

"And who might this friend be?" she inquired, twisting her mouth to the side in a mocking manner.

"Yours truly!" I said boastfully, pointing at my chest with my thumb, and grinning.

"Oh yeah?"

"Yeah!" I replied.

"Hmmm . . . I'll have to think about it. You're a stranger. You know?"

"Now I'm a stranger?"

"Well . . . you still are! In a way . . ."

"I disagree. Although I've just met you, I consider you a friend already."

She smiled and said, "You seem nice enough so far, and we are on vacation. Maybe! Let's play it by ear."

"That's good enough. Can I get your information now?"

"Sure."

I stored her number in my phone. I collected her e-mail address too in case we never got to see each other again in Canada. At least I would still be able to stay in touch, *maybe even look her up on Facebook.*

The flight attendant came around and offered us food. That was the cue that we were halfway to our destination. Paula requested the tuna sandwich, and I opted for the turkey. We both asked for orange juice and smiled as if acknowledging that our taste in beverages was something else we had in common.

As the flight attendant was about to leave, I tapped her on the shoulder. "Would you kindly ask the gentleman in seat 30C whether he wants an alcoholic beverage? If he does want something, please let me know. I would like to take care of it," I said.

"Sure, no problem," she responded.

"Aren't you a gentleman," Paula said, after the flight attendant walked away.

"It's courtesy. He was very nice to let me have his seat. He could have easily told me to scram."

"You have a point."

"He actually made my day. I got to sit with one of the most beautiful and wonderful person I've ever come across. I wouldn't change today for anything in the world."

I could see her blush as she tried to avoid my eyes.

"Thank you. That's very sweet of you. I'm glad I met you today as well, Devin."

WTF MOMENT

We talked all the way through the seven-hour flight. She was pretty sound on every topic from politics to music, films, and sports. We never ran out of things to talk about, which was rare. Neither of us read the books and magazines we had brought with us.

The pilot's voice could be heard over the intercom. "We have now begun our descent; we will be touching down in Calgary International Airport in about ten minutes. Thank you for choosing Air Canada."

We looked at each other as we wondered why the flight had to end. We still had so much to talk about. The layover was short for me. There was a forty-five-minute interval before my next flight. Paula had an hour to kill.

We soon landed and headed to the concourse. We embraced as we were about to separate.

"Make sure you call me, okay?" she said, smiling.

"I sure will!"

"I might just come down there in a few days. Who knows?"

"That is music to my ears," I said, laughing.

She smiled, and we embraced again. Then I watched her walk away until she disappeared into the crowd. I liked the connection we had. I was already missing her.

I walked though the checkpoint, my passport was scanned, and I answered a few questions. Then I was directed to the immigration section of the airport.

I was the only one there. I guessed everyone else was Canadian. I walked over to the nearest window. The officer looked annoyed as if he was bothered by my presence. He put his hands out and motioned for me to tender my passport and itinerary.

I couldn't find my itinerary, but I showed the one I'd used from home to Calgary. *Maybe the ticketing lady forgot to give me the connecting one*, I thought. He asked me for my carry-on and laptop bags, and he started to go through them.

"What is the purpose of your visit to Canada?"

"On vacation," I replied.

"Business or pleasure?"

I was going to say something smart, but I changed my mind. I had already said I was on vacation, so he should know I was there for pleasure.

"Pleasure," I replied, politely.

"Do you know anyone here in Canada?"

"I don't. Basically, I'm a tourist," I said, laughing.

The guy didn't have a sense of humor. He looked at me with a stern face and kept searching my bag.

"Will you partake in any sporting events while you're here?"

"No," I responded. I was wondering why he'd even asked me. Then I noticed he was looking at one of my business cards.

"What is Five Star Fitness?"

"It's a business I own back home."

I was beginning to get irritated. The guy was stripping my bags as if I had drugs in them. I wondered if everyone had to go through the same process. He stared at my passport over and over.

"Are you a citizen of another country?"

"No," I said. I was trying hard not to lash out at the idiot. He seemed to be taking his merry time.

He disappeared with the passport and came back about ten minutes later.

"You don't have your itinerary with you, and it's making my job a little difficult," he said, with an attitude.

"I can always walk back to the airline and get one. I don't want to sound ignorant, but can't you see it on your screen? You have my previous itinerary, and I'm sure you can pull something up with it."

"I can't find anything on here. You should have your itinerary," he said rudely.

"Like I said sir, I didn't notice I wasn't given one. You can give the airline a call to verify."

"I'm not giving anyone a call!" he barked.

I was shocked by his attitude, but I still maintained my composure.

"For your information, my plane leaves in about twenty minutes. What are we doing here? Is there a problem?"

"It doesn't matter when your plane leaves! You're in my country. You leave when I say you leave," he bleated.

I felt like punching him in the face or cursing him out. So as a defense mechanism, I started laughing in his face. *This guy can't be serious!*

He didn't like that, so he sounded off, "Sir! I need you to go sit in the waiting room until I'm done here."

I looked at him and laughed even more. "Are you serious? You're delaying me with no explanation?"

"Sir, I need you to leave right now!"

"Okay," I said, "But I'll need you to put all my stuff back in the bags, and then I'll be on my way."

"I'm not putting anything back. You can do that on your own," he barked.

I could feel the veins in my neck pop.

WTF MOMENT

"Is there a supervisor here I can talk to? Because I don't understand what is going on here."

There were at least three officers flanking him on each side, and they all looked away when I tried to make eye contact.

I shook my head, put my things back in the bag, pulled out my iPod, and walked to the waiting room. There were a few chairs, a table, and a vending machine. It looked like an interrogation room. There was nothing welcoming about it. I looked around for a socket so I could plug my laptop. *At least I can browse the Internet while I wait on these fools*!

I was so upset, but I marveled at how well I handled the situation. I had been so close to throwing a major tantrum, but I would be buying into the drama. They might even throw me in jail. I was on vacation, and no one was going to spoil that for me.

Another ten minutes later, *Officer Asshole* came back and handed me my passport.

"You're free to go!"

I smirked at him and walked off.

I wished I was a famous movie actor. I could get on one of their late-night shows and blast the idiot on TV and also make a formal complaint.

I walked out of there disgusted. *Officer Asshole* had wasted my time just because he could.

When I reached my boarding area, it was deserted, and the gates were closed. I walked back to the main checking point in the lobby, a few stories down. It took me fifteen minutes to get there. I was so upset; I could feel the fumes coming out of my ears. The lady at the counter was nice to me. She apologized for my inconvenience and directed me to another plane which was scheduled to leave for Toronto half an hour later. I was glad I didn't have to wait too much longer.

I arrived in Toronto at 3:00 p.m., an hour later than I was supposed to. I took a cab straight to my hotel. The driver was a pleasant Middle Eastern fellow.

"You from America?"

"Yes, I am."

"Welcome to Toronto."

"Thank you. I hope I like it."

"You will. It's the film festival weekend. Plenty of events to go to, my friend."

He gave me a brochure of the areas to visit while I was in town. He also gave me his card in case I needed a ride sometime.

BOLAJI TIJANI-QUDUS

I thought Toronto looked a bit like Chicago or even Austin, Texas. But I liked how clean the city was. I guess Canada and the United States are alike in some ways; like brother and sister nations.

I took a nap as soon as I arrived at my hotel, and I didn't get up until about ten in the evening. I hadn't expected to sleep that long. *I should have set my alarm.* I wanted to make sure I enjoyed every day I was out there. I checked my phone to see whether I had any messages. There were three missed calls from Phil.

Before I could call him back, I noticed I had a text message as well. It was from Paula. I was elated. Seeing her name sent shockwaves through my body. *Relax, you shouldn't get ahead of yourself,* I thought as I read her text.

From: Paula
Hey there! I arrived in Montréal safe and sound.
I hope you arrived safely too. It was a pleasure meeting you, and I've to say I really enjoyed your company. I hope I get to enjoy it some more when I get out there. Yes! You read it right. lol. I'll be in Toronto in a few days. The friend I told you about will be back tomorrow.
Are you ready?
Xoxo
Paula

I read her text over and over again and smiled, *Whoa! I think she likes me!*

I let out a joyous scream. I don't believe in love at first sight, but I knew I was feeling Paula. I had felt great just being around her earlier that day. I felt I could tell her anything and she would listen without bias or judgment. I responded to her text.

To: Paula
It was definitely refreshing meeting someone like you. I have to say, I had a wonderful time conversing with you. I wasn't expecting you to come down here, but I'm glad you are. See you soon.

From: Paula
See you in a few days if you're not already partied out by then.

To: Paula
I'll definitely make sure I conserve some energy. I wouldn't have it any other way.

WTF MOMENT

I breathed a sigh of relief. I recalled a few times when I had met someone I shared a great connection with, but nothing came out of it. The timing was always off. I had played the meetings over in my head wishing for what might have been. *It seems Paula and I are on the right track.*

I was as elated as a teenager meeting a girl for the first time. I paced around the room, visualizing us hanging out and looking into each other's eyes. *If I'm feeling like this over a woman, I'll have to let her know. A gem like Paula comes around only once in a while*, I thought. *I don't know her quite well, but she was genuine enough, and I dug what I've seen so far.*

When I came down from my Paula high, I remembered I had to return Phil's call. I dialed his number.

"What's up bro? Are you here? I left you two voice messages already," he said.

"What's up, Phil the Great? Dude! I'm here, man! I took a nap. I just woke up. How are you?"

"I'm good and ready to party it up all this week. Are you ready?"

"You know I am. What's the plan for tonight?"

"I called some folks and they are all going to a spot called Palladium. It's in the party district. Where are you staying?"

"I'm at the Hilton downtown."

"Cool. You can catch a cab and you will be there in about ten minutes."

"Where are you staying?" I asked.

"I'm staying at my buddy Tim's place. He rented an apartment in Green Bridge. It's really cool actually. He's got a full kitchen so we can cook—and there is a grocery store down the street."

"Cool. You know I'll be popping in to eat too."

"Anytime, man!"

"Thanks. So . . . what time does this thing start?"

"I'm thinking of rolling out there around eleven. I heard the line is crazy and there are honeys galore in there. You're in for a special treat! Put your game face on, and let's do this. I'm locked and loaded," he said.

"That's what I'm talking about. I can't wait to see some hot new honeys for a change."

"Hot honeys are an understatement. I've been here for four days, and I already got laid. I met this one chick at the mall. You have to see the body on her! We met on Sunday, and I was waxing her on Monday," he said.

"Like that?"

"Dude! She is a freak. We went at it all night. We didn't sleep a wink," Phil bragged.

"I hope she's got some friends!"

"I'm sure she does. I'll inquire. Even if she doesn't, there are too many honeys to choose from. Trust me. And it's only Tuesday."

"I'm ready, man! Let's do this. It's already past ten; I guess I should start getting ready," I said.

"I'm going to get in the shower too. See you around eleven."

"Okay, cool. I'll see you in a bit."

"Later, dude," he said and hung up.

I made it to the Palladium an hour later. I called Phil. He told me he wasn't too far away.

He sure wasn't lying about the talent level. There were so many women in line. My eyes almost fell out of their sockets. There were women of all sizes and shapes. I don't know what it is, but it seems every time I visit a new city, the women always look better. Maybe I feel that way because I'm out of town. Being out of one's element, on a hunt, makes women look especially good.

The venue looked like one of those historic churches from the outside. It was a large white brick building. You wouldn't think it was a club. The taxi driver had told me earlier it had been around for almost ten years, and was still as popular as it was when it first opened.

I stood in line taking in what the city had to offer. Then my mind drifted off to Paula. I wondered what she was doing. *She is coming in a few days*, I thought. *My vacation is starting on a good note. I have a feeling I'm going to enjoy being here. No work, no stress, and no dealing with the ex or crazy dates.* I felt I had been having a nervous breakdown before this vacation.

Phil finally pulled up in a taxi.

"What's up, player?" Phil yelled out of the back window.

He hopped out and walked up to the front of the line. Phil said something to the bouncer who let us in.

The club was really big inside, just as I had expected. It had high ceilings like a cathedral. The DJ was set up upstairs at the other end of the space. The videos of the songs she played were showing simultaneously on huge plasma screens. *Cool*, I thought.

The dance floor was sunken in the middle of the space. I saw nothing but a sea of heads and hands. Laser lights were darting all over the place. Every few minutes, fog was dispensed from above. The crowd went nuts.

"Dude! This place is bananas!" Phil exclaimed.

"Yeah, I know! There has to be at least three thousand people in here!"

"So many fishes to catch," he added.

WTF MOMENT

Phil and I hung with some natives and even ran into some ladies from the States. They were glad to see us. We danced with them for a while and later exchanged numbers and planned on hanging with them if time permitted.

We danced and drank for another couple of hours, it seemed.

By the end of the night, I was lit and ready to fall asleep. We definitely had a blast. I found Phil, whom I had lost after I got held up by a lady who wouldn't let me leave the dance floor. I told him I was ready to leave, and he concurred. Two women who looked as if they could be from Eastern Europe stood behind him. They were dressed alike in short, glittery dresses and high heels. They were both thin, resembled super models one may see on a VH1 reality show. Phil asked me if I liked the friend of the woman he seemed to be with. She was cute, but she wasn't too appealing. She was drunk and wide-eyed, and her mascara was running.

It was four in the morning when we headed out of the club. I flagged down a taxi, and we all sat in the back. Phil started to French kiss his *take away* immediately. Before long, his hand was under her dress. She was moaning loudly, and I wondered what the taxi driver thought. It was funny watching him throw glances at his rear view mirror. The other drunken chick was trying to make passes at me to see if I would make the party double the fun. I wasn't interested, so I ignored her advances.

When we arrived at my stop, Phil looked up at me and said, "You sure? The party is continuing at my place."

"I'm beat," I said.

"Okay, brother. I'll see you sometime tomorrow." He winked at me as the taxi took off. I smiled thinking of how he was probably going to have his way with the two chicks. It could have been really fun if I had gone with them, but I just wasn't in the mood.

To avoid a hangover in the morning, I took a couple of painkillers with a bottle of water before I went to bed.

The next day, Phil and I met up with some of his boys for lunch. We partied for another two days straight.

"You can stay with us, you know?" Phil had said. But I wanted to have my own space while I was on this particular vacation.

*　　*　　*

The ringing of my phone woke me up later that morning. By the time I got to it, the caller had hung up. I check the missed call log. The call had been from Paula.

"Damn!" I exclaimed. I called her right back.

I heard her soothing sweet voice at the other end.

"Hello?"

"Hey, you! Sorry I missed your call. I was still in bed. How are you?"

"I'm good. Thanks for asking. Sorry for waking you."

"It's no problem. I was getting ready to get up anyway."

"Oh okay! I was just letting you know I'm on my way over there. I should arrive around noon if the flight is on schedule."

"Cool."

"I'm out the door as we speak. I'll call you when I get to Toronto, okay?"

"Sure thing. See ya!"

I went downstairs to get some breakfast, but the hotel had stopped serving at nine. So I hopped across the street to a café and ordered a sandwich and coffee. Then it dawned on me. *Maybe I should go surprise her and meet her at the airport. She said her friend would be back in the evening. We could hang out!*

After my meal, I headed to the airport. It was a quarter to twelve. The airport was about ten minutes away. I was sure it would be a surprise when she saw me waiting for her at the arrival terminal with roses in hand, which I had picked up at a flower shop next to the hotel.

I arrived at the airport at noon. I hoped I hadn't missed her. I wouldn't be too thrilled if her plane had arrived early and she had already left.

I was standing outside next to the taxi stand when she walked out. I was on the other side of the street, so she didn't see me. I walked over to where she was standing and crept up behind her.

"Can I help the beautiful lady with her bags?"

She looked back and laughed.

"What are you doing here, Devin?!"

"I came to see you, silly!" I said, as I handed her the roses.

Her eyes shone as she took them.

"They are beautiful!"

"They are, but not quite as beautiful as you."

"Awww, you're so sweet," she said, blushing.

I grabbed her bags, and we hopped into a taxi.

"Since you have a little time to kill before your friend arrives, do you want to do something in the meantime?" I asked.

"I was going to stop by the mall at some point."

"Okay. Let's drop these bags off at my place, and we can go from there. Are you hungry?"

WTF MOMENT

"Sure. I know this place we can go to. It reminds me of the Village in New York. There are some nice shops, restaurants, and cafes. We could take a stroll," she said.

"Sounds good to me. You know this city better than I do."

We dropped her bags off at my hotel and headed to Lexington Street, which stretched about ten blocks. I really liked it. There was a farmer's market-style area at the end of the street. We bought some tangerines and munched on them as we strolled and talked. Phil had called me earlier; I knew he was eager to tell me about his rendezvous the previous evening. I texted him and told him where I was and what I was doing. He responded saying he might join me later.

"So what are you going to be doing when you return home?" she asked.

"Not much. Back to my boring old life."

"Seems as though you stay busy."

"I guess so. It would be been fun to travel to other countries and work while learning the different cultures. What you do is awesome."

"I like what I do. I miss home sometimes. Eventually I hope to publish my book of poems and maybe write another book. That would be ideal. I still would freelance and write for magazines though."

"Nice."

"You could live that life too, Devin. You can have your business run itself while you travel around the world."

"True. I'll eventually get there one day."

We walked around for a while and finally settled into a corner café. We ordered two chicken salads. The portions were really generous.

"This is really good!"

"Hmmm hmmm, yes it is! Do you cook, Devin?"

"Do I? I'm a pro," I said, confidently.

"I should take your word for it?"

"You should! I'm so good I could open my own restaurant," I said, grinning.

"No humility, huh?" she said, laughing.

"You asked, and I answered."

"So what do you know how to cook?"

"A little bit of everything. I can make Italian, Mexican, or whatever."

"Good . . . A man who can cook."

"How about you? Do you cook?"

"As you said, I dabble in everything too. Tell me what you want, and I'll make it," she said.

"You're that of good cook, huh?"

199

"I sure am. I don't eat out much, so I cook for myself."

"Great! We should have a cook-off one day."

"Careful what you wish for. You might get embarrassed," she quipped.

"Says who? The world's best chefs are men, don't you know? Do you watch all those food competition shows on TV? The men run 'em. I'm not making this up either. It's a fact. Do your research."

"Even if that were true, I know I can hold my own," she said, sighing.

"I do not doubt you at all."

Paula had the tip of her fork in her mouth biting it while in thought. Then she said, "This restaurant reminds of the café in the movie *Yellow City*. I've been trying to figure it out. I think it was shot here in Toronto."

"You like that movie too?"

"Yes! It's one of my favorite movies. It might be too slow for some people, but I love it nonetheless!" she exclaimed.

"Good story and even better acting," I added.

She gave me one of her beautiful smiles again and said, "I almost forgot how much of a movie buff you are."

"I have quite a collection too. When I need to relax, I stay home and watch movies all by myself. Watching movies never get old."

"I do that sometimes too. My girls and I organize movie nights at least once a month. We would watch three or four movies in a row. It's always so much fun. I know I won't be bored if I ever come out there to visit you."

That sounded like music to my ears. *I wouldn't mind her coming out to visit me . . . definitely something to look forward to.*

We continued talking into the evening, and finally she received a call from her friend. We wrapped up our hangout and headed to my hotel to get her things.

"What are you guys doing tonight?" she asked, as she peeped out of the taxi window.

"I'm not sure. I have to talk to Phil."

"Maybe we can all get together later. I'm not sure how tired my friend is, but we will see."

"That is a good idea. Call me later, and let's figure something out," I said.

I managed to get Phil to ditch the chick he was hanging out. We ended up going to a local bar with Paula and her friend. It was a good evening. Paula and I continued to build on the connection we had established. We were really feeling each other. Phil and Victoria got along nicely too—although she wasn't one of those women he was going to pull a quick move on. She was too serious

WTF MOMENT

for that. She was cute with a girl-next-door appearance. I was sure Phil had had his fill already on this vacation. He wouldn't mind taking a night off.

The evening concluded, and Victoria offered to drive us back to our hotels. We declined and opted for a taxi instead. Paula and I embraced as I was about to hop in. Then something happened.

Our lips gravitated toward each other, and we kissed passionately. We both seemed surprised, but it wasn't unexpected. It was a genuine, heartfelt kiss.

Phil looked at me smiling. "What is up with you and Paula?" he inquired as our taxi sped off.

"What?" I replied, innocently.

"I think you really like her, dude! You haven't been on the prowl with me the whole time you've been here. You passed on some sure pussy last night too."

"I don't know, man. I'm just chilling, you know? Enjoying the vacation."

"Don't be falling in love in Toronto!" he said, laughing.

"No. I'm feeling her though, but I don't know about the love stuff. It's too soon to tell."

"Okay, brother, if you say so. I know what I see. You don't have to put up a front. It's okay. She seems like a very nice gal. With all the drama you have gone through with women, you sure could use a change of pace. Victoria isn't bad either."

"Yeah, what's up with you and her?"

"There is nothing there. She is cool, but not my type. But you and Paula look good together," he said, smiling.

"You saw all that just from tonight? You're crazy, bro."

"I saw it all. You were over there drooling all evening. I like her energy. She is from Seattle, right?"

"Yes, originally, but lives in Dubai now."

"Dubai? Wow! You have an excuse to travel out of the country now. She does live far though."

"I know, huh? I think she's feeling me as much as I'm feeling her. But we will see. I hope something comes out of it."

Phil looked at me and started to laugh. "I sure hope so, bro. As I said, with your string of bad dates, I've been worried about your state of mind."

"Whatever, man," I said, laughing along.

We soon arrived at my hotel. Right before I hopped out, Phil said, "We have to go out again tomorrow. It's our last day! We have to make it count."

"I'm down!"

BOLAJI TIJANI-QUDUS

I paid the cab driver twenty dollars, which would cover the trip to Phil's place. He and Phil thanked me, and I went up to my room to crash. It had been a good day. I got to hang with Paula and with Phil.

The next day, Paula and I hung out at the mall. Then we took a tour to Niagara Falls, and we had a blast. We visited Niagara-on-the-Lake's Pillitteri Estates Winery. Paula loved the famous ice wine. She even bought a couple of bottles to take home with her. The *Maid of the Mist* journey near the mouth of the falls was probably one of the most breathtaking views I had ever seen. We saw the rainbow, and since we were close to the falls, we were showered on pretty well. It was an exhilarating experience. Sharing those moments with Paula couldn't have been more ideal. When I looked in her eyes, I knew I had fallen for her, there, in Niagara.

We arrived back in Toronto in the early evening, tired, but we still spent more time walking around the city, talking and philosophizing about life. I totally enjoyed every single moment. The kind of chemistry we exhibited was indescribable. I hadn't expected to click with someone that quickly—and in a different country for that matter. It all seemed unreal.

Phil called and told me he was going to take a nap and would call me later to go out. I doubted it; he had been caught up with a woman and had gotten drunk. It worked out for me anyway. It meant I would spend more time with Paula. We caught a few movies at the festival and attended an after-party.

The next time I looked at my watch, it was six in the morning. My flight was leaving in a couple of hours. We hopped into a taxi, and Paula was dropped off first. I walked her up to her place. We embraced and kissed. Every time I turned around and tried to leave, we embraced and kissed again.

Finally, she said, "I don't want you to miss your flight."

"I know," I said, holding her hand.

I mustered the strength and finally left. I stared at her from the backseat of the taxi. She was standing by the stairs, arms folded, watching the taxi drive off.

I asked the taxi driver to wait while I packed. I checked out, and headed to the airport. The time I spent before boarding was torturous. I kept replaying the sight of Paula on those stairs.

The announcement to board snapped me out of my thoughts. But instead of walking toward the plane, I turned around and headed outside the airport. I hopped into a taxi and headed back to Paula.

It started to drizzle. I heard on the radio rain was expected, which was surprising since it was late summer.

Twenty minutes later, the taxi pulled up at the Victorian. Paula was standing next to a big window as if she had been waiting there all along. She drew closer

WTF MOMENT

to the window, watching in disbelief. I stepped out of the taxi and waved to her. She dashed out of the house, and we met by the stairs. We started to kiss passionately. Rain started to pour heavily. We stood there for several minutes, lost in each other, without a care, kissing away, even though we were drenched. The taxi driver finally came over with my bags. I collected them and paid him.

We went inside, and before the door closed behind us, we started to tear each other apart. It was as if we were in a different dimension—all that mattered were the feelings we had for each other. It was as if we were in a cloud. We peeled each other's clothes off our bodies.

We were soon on her bed, and I felt myself entering her. She held me tightly. I have had sex plenty of times in the past, but for the first time in my life, I was making love. It felt as if we were in a state of euphoria. All my senses were heightened. Each stroke was pleasurable. Several minutes later, I felt the most intense orgasm I'd ever had. It lasted forever it seemed. She reached her climax at the same time. We were both covered in sweat. I saw tears flowing down the sides of her face. I kissed her, as I wiped the tears away.

"I've never felt this way before," she said, breathing heavily.

"Neither have I," I responded, teary-eyed.

We continued caressing and kissing passionately. Within minutes, I felt myself pulsating, and we continued making love as if it were our last days together.

A couple of hours later, she looked at the clock on the wall.

"You missed your flight," she said, laughing.

"I know. I'll head back tomorrow. I just have to pay a little extra."

"Sounds like a plan!"

"I want to enjoy the rest of this day with you. Nothing else matters," I said, as I held her in my arms, smiling.

"I hope today never ends," she said, pulling me closer.

20. Pieces to Peaces

It has been exactly three years since that fateful evening when I left the house and my marriage. The divorce has been finalized for about a year. My daughter, Emmanuella, just turned six, going on ten it seems. It never ceases to amaze me how fast kids grow. Emmanuella is getting ready to enter the second grade in a few months. *How time flies.* I recently had a similar conversation with my mom—one minute kids are crawling all over the place in diapers and the next minute the same kid is walking, talking, and starting school.

"You know that means we are really getting old too," I told Mom, laughing.

"Speak for yourself," she said. She never likes to mention her age, and she doesn't like people saying she is older. When her birthday rolls around, everyone says happy birthday without bringing up her age. If we give her a card, it has to be one without her age on it.

My cousins brought her a card last spring for her surprise party. It read, *Life begins at 60!* I had to make them get rid of it before she saw it; I drove down to the store to get another one. My cousin Lesley wasn't too happy, but I knew better. My mom would have an attitude if she saw those dreaded numbers.

I really do hope she never ages. Deep in my heart, I know she will get old and pass one day. I don't know what I will do when that happens. Mom is the pillar of the family. She has held the family together all these years. My father did too, but he was more of the provider, working two jobs or long shifts just to make sure the kids had enough to eat and had materials for school. He was always gone for work. We spent more time with Mom when we were growing up, so it was natural for all the kids to be drawn to her. We appreciate and respect Dad as well for all he did for us.

Mom pampered us but in a good way. You can talk to Mom about anything, and she is never judgmental, though she does lay the law down whenever we

WTF MOMENT

get out of hand. She is nice and sweet. We have never taken her for granted. She wouldn't allow it. You never want to get Mom upset.

My father was a disciplinarian, and we would feel his wrath immediately. Mom would take away our fun privileges for a month or longer and smile at us while doing it. I shake my head whenever I think about how Mom and Dad spoil Emmanuella so much. I don't even think they've ever punished her once since she was born. Grandkids have it the best!

* * *

Why is it that other women seem to want to come around when I'm cultivating a new relationship . . . old friends and random new ones alike? Where were you all when I was in a drought? I wonder!

Amanda left me a text message a few nights ago. I hadn't spoken to her in about a year. I'd purchased a new phone and hadn't added her number. But I was almost certain it was her. She was the only one I knew who had a number with so many three's—(121) 333-3339.

I started to smile replaying our conversation in my head:

From: 121-333-3339
Hey. Just wanted to let you know I have your blue jean jacket. Not sure if you have been looking for it. I have it!

To: 121-333-3339
Hi, who might this be?

From: 121-333-3339
Amanda! You don't have my number?

To: 121-333-3339
Sorry, new phone ☺

From: 121-333-3339
How come you don't have my number? I still have yours!!!!!!!!!!

To: 121-333-3339
Hello and happy New Year to you too ☺ long time. How have you been?

205

From: 121-333-3339
Happy New Year to you as well. I'm well and thank you for asking. Yourself?

To: 121-333-3339
I'm good as well. What's new?

From: 121-333-3339
Nothing much, sir. Did you get my message earlier about your jacket? I have it. If you need it, I can always get it to you.

To: 121-333-3339
Oh yeah, I haven't thought about that jacket in a while. I guess I haven't had much need for it ☺

From: 121-333-3339
Okay. Just let me know if you do ☺

To: 121-333-3339
Sure thing.

From: 121-333-3339
K.
TTYL

From: 121-333-3339
P.S. you should save my number!!

It had been a while, and I hadn't expected to hear from her. She could have easily sent me a text checking to see how I was doing instead of pulling the "I got your jacket" card.

I looked at my text log and thought long and hard about saving her number again. As much I was tempted to do it, I decided not to.

Besides, Paula is coming to town. She is all I want to be occupied with since we had been hitting it off so well. She has mentioned moving back to the States. That is one of the topics we are going to discuss on her visit. I wouldn't mind if she moves to Brookdale or even cohabitates with me. I think I'm ready for a relationship. I'm normally hesitant, especially when I haven't known a woman for a long time.

WTF MOMENT

Something is different about Paula though. I haven't had a relationship to really write home about over the last few years. I have a strong feeling something great is brewing between Paula and me. The connection is amazing. I feel we are kindred spirits. I hear people talk about unexplainable connections all the time, but I've never believed in it. I didn't think I would meet a woman like Paula, but I'm glad I did. The times we have spent together have been great.

I see a lot of me in her. She doesn't spend too much time arguing or having small fights. We both understand we can agree to disagree, which actually helps when we converse. Neither of us takes it personally if we don't share the same view on a topic. That is one major thing I appreciate about Paula. I'm learning to believe people come into our lives for different reasons. I really do feel it was meant for us to cross each other's paths. I never get tired of seeing her or talking to her. I used to get bored rather quickly when a lady I was dating didn't have much in common with me. I can recall a time we talked on the phone from ten in the evening until five the next morning. I had to get up and go to work a few hours later. I was really tired, but I didn't mind because the conversation had been well worth it.

I don't know what the future will bring, but I am willing to ride out whatever feelings I am having. I feel our relationship is going to turn out to be fulfilling.

* * *

I realized I'd been sitting on my couch for almost an hour in thought. I started to get up and be productive. My phone started to ring. I ignored it and went into the kitchen. The whole time I was fixing something to eat, my phone kept ringing. *Who could that be?*

The continuous ringing got on my nerves, so I walked over to the living room to see who had been blowing me up. I checked my missed call log. Brandon had called me about ten times in a row between 11:00 and 11:30 p.m. It could be an emergency, so I called him back. He picked up on the third ring.

"What's up, bro? Everything okay?" I asked.

"Are you home?"

"Yeah, I am. You okay?" I asked again.

"I'm down the street. I'll see you in a minute." He hung up the phone.

I stood there looking at my phone wondering what was up with Brandon. He hadn't sounded frantic on the phone, but something was definitely on his mind. *I'll find out soon enough.*

Brandon popped up at my door a few minutes later. I knew it was all bad from the look he gave me as he walked in.

BOLAJI TIJANI-QUDUS

"What happened?" I asked, as I watched him pace around the living room.

"I can't believe it!" he bleated.

I was starting to ask him whether he had caught Ashley cheating again, but I decided to wait until he told me what had happened. I didn't want to jump the gun. He could be going through something totally different. Since Brandon had gotten back together with Ashley, he hadn't been hanging out with any of us. He probably felt embarrassed about the whole episode.

There is nothing wrong with getting back with an ex if the love is there. I supported Brandon in whatever decisions he chose to make. Matters of the heart are very hard to explain at times. Some of my other friends weren't forgiving; they couldn't believe he'd gone back with her after all she put him through emotionally. Then he went on and had twin girls with her, further complicating an already strange situation.

"She is leaving, Devin!"

"Why? I thought you guys had worked things out?"

"She told me she finally figured out she prefers women, and she wants to be with one exclusively," he said, as his eyes welled up.

What a selfish heifer. Now she wants to go ahead and be with a woman exclusively? When Brandon was going crazy and losing it, she was the one who had come back and convinced him they should get back together. She said she couldn't live without him. She said she'd made a mistake and she had taken her experiments too far.

In my book, what she had done was no experiment! Had she forgotten she had confessed to Brandon that she had had a few other long-term relationships with women? One took place a year after they had gotten married.

She was a serial cheat. I was surprised Brandon had gotten back with her after knowing all about that. As angry as I was, and as much as I wanted to slap Brandon out of his denial state, I had supported his decision to go back to her, hoping things would be different. *Everyone deserves a second chance*, I had thought back then.

"So she has decided this is what she wants to do?"

"She told me she wants to go be with Yvette and start a family, and she wants to take my daughters with her!"

"Whoa! She came out and told you all this?"

"She said she was tired of suppressing her feelings all these years, and she wanted to be honest with me. She said she didn't want to raise her kids with lies and deceit."

"Wow! Now she wants to be honest? What a freaking load of crap," I said, shaking my head.

WTF MOMENT

"I thought she had given all that up as she promised. Why does she have to do this now? She is not taking my kids anywhere! I will kill that woman!" he said, angrily.

"Don't talk like that, Brandon. I know you are angry, but you have to really think things out. You are my friend, and I love you dearly—like a brother—but I have to be really honest with you. Did you really believe her when she said she had changed? No one turns emotions off and on as such. The bottom line is she has always loved women, and that is who she is. She stayed with you all this time because she was comfortable with you and you are a great guy. Women have always turned her on, hence the many relationships she has had with other women in the past while you were married. C'mon on bro, you should know this. No one is that stupid! I know you love her and all, but you have to face the fact that though she may love you as a person, you are not who she wants physically and emotionally. You need to realize you have to move on with your life accordingly."

"How am I going to pick up the pieces and move on with my life? She is all I know. We have one-year-old twin daughters!" he exclaimed.

"As hard as it has been for me, I picked up the pieces and moved on. We all have to move on at some point. I've been there. I've gone through the transition. I like my life now. I've stopped beating myself up, and I have overcome depression. I've accepted what life has dealt me. You have to do the same. We all knew the situation wasn't good for you when you went back with her. She feels what she feels, and that is just it. As much as you want to be mad at her, and as much as I despise how she went about things, her feelings are her feelings. She wants to go be happy with someone else, and you have to let her go. You are a good man, and some other woman will see you for who you are and appreciate you. Trust me—there is a woman out there. You just have to put yourself in a position to recognize her when she comes along. You can't continue living life, loving someone who doesn't love you back."

"Okay!"

"Okay what? Okay, you hear what I'm saying? Or okay, you're done hearing me talk?" I inquired sternly.

He paused for a while, looking at the ground like a schoolboy getting ready to go to detention. I didn't want to be harsh with Brandon, but I had to be. No one else would tell him the truth except me. Our other mutual friends had left him alone because he had stopped calling everyone when he got back with Ashley.

"Deep down, I kind of knew this day would come. I wanted to believe it would be me, her, and the twins—one big happy family," he said, teary-eyed.

"I'm sorry to say this, but you shouldn't be surprised about the recent development. It may have been a calculated move by her to have kids by you and then go be with the one she really wanted to be with. You have all the characteristics of a good man, and she wanted her baby to come from you. Ashley is so cold. I don't understand why she didn't just leave when you found out about her and Yvette."

"This is all a bad dream."

"The good thing about bad dreams is you wake up from them! So, my friend, I'm here for you, whatever you need to get through this. It's not your loss."

Brandon nodded in agreement to what I had said. He was insecure and unsure of himself. I assured him things were going to be fine. I told him he just had to find himself and believe in himself. Yes, looks, money, and status quo are the variables some women look at, but for most, a confident, responsible, caring man is all they want. I thought of rallying the guys to give Brandon the support network he needed. It might take a while for him to bounce back, but I was sure he would be all right. Chris's situation was a little different, but he is strong and surviving. I've gone through a divorce and Kenny, also. One way or the other, we all picked up the pieces of our lives and found the internal peace to forge ahead.

* * *

I feel energized and motivated because Chris has taken me up my offer to partner with me on a new Five Star Gym, which we'll open in the blossoming Fulton City, about fifty miles from Brookdale. I couldn't be happier. Because he is an architect, I know he will conjure up an amazing design for the place. I found an old building that served as a power plant for many years. I think we can have indoor rock climbing, which would be another fun type of workout. Chris agrees with me.

Five Star is at a point where it runs itself. I don't have to be there all the time. With the experience I have gathered from running it, it will be easier to set up shop again. I am enjoying the fact I can have a tightly run ship and spend more time with Emmanuella.

Surprisingly Chris is doing great. A year has passed since the loss of his wife, and he has rebounded. At least that is how it looks from the outside. I know she has left a big void in his heart. Chris has always been an optimistic guy and has always found ways to make positives out of negatives. I guess coming from a religious family has molded him into someone who believes we can't really do anything about what we can't control. I saw him break down at the hospital when Nadine passed, but he has since held it together.

WTF MOMENT

Chris is also a naturally funny guy. Even at Nadine's wake, he was the one consoling people and cracking jokes to keep things light. Nadine's passing touched a lot of people. You would think she was a celebrity actress with the number of people who showed up at her wake and funeral. She and Chris had touched so many people's lives. They were both active in helping out in the community. Chris's dad is a pastor, and Chris and Nadine were permanent fixtures at the church. They ran the Sunday school together and even started other programs to help the homeless and underprivileged. They started a group home where they helped runways and young mothers. Chris still keeps the programs going. He was back at the church the week after Nadine passed, running the Sunday school.

"Life continues. Nadine wouldn't want to me to stop helping people because she is gone," he tells people. He feels he would disrespect her memory if he dropped everything. I admire him for his strong conviction and the way he carries and handles himself. He is also an excellent father. He isn't a single dad by choice, but he has been doing a great job raising his son.

Kenny has settled down with a young, twenty-something-year-old woman. The last time I saw them both, they seemed happy. He even told me his ex-wife Tracy had divorced her husband Robert, met another guy, and was planning to get married again. We both laughed when he told me the story. Guys like Robert meet a new woman and act as if they are better than the last man . . . as if they are the best thing since sliced bread! He was so condescending to Kenny; it was ridiculous. Now, he has gotten the boot too.

Phil is still Mr. Casanova. He prefers the single life, and it seems to work for him. *Maybe some people are not meant to be married.*

Monica and I have finally developed a cordial relationship. We actually get along quite well and have made peace with one another.

It has been a rough road. I am now beginning to see the light at the end of the tunnel. As much as she tried, I didn't give Monica the opportunity to break me. I had to deal with all the crap that could easily have pushed someone else over the edge. The period after the breakup was the worst time in my life, emotionally. I was a wreck.

Nonetheless, I managed to survive. I knew I had to keep my sanity—for my daughter's sake at least. After the initial back-and-forth spat between us, I just stopped engaging in those wars of words because they took so much out of me. I was in danger of becoming a really angry person because I didn't understand why she wanted to hurt me. She probably realized I was determined to move on with my life and wouldn't let her destroy me. Meeting someone she liked may have helped too. Her boyfriend is also divorced, and they seem to hit it off well. *I'm happy for her.*

There were things I despised about my ex-wife. And some of those things seemed to change once we were not together. It's funny; I have heard many people say that about their exes too. She is the most cost-saving person I had seen lately. Gone is the Porsche Cayenne and in is the Toyota Camry. She acknowledged that maintenance on the latter was definitely cheaper. She even told me how she cut her cable expense down from $200 to $39 a month, for basic service. *I wonder why she wasn't acting as such during the time we were together.*

Monica has finally agreed to joint custody of Emmanuella. My little girl is the most important person in my life, and being able to spend more time with her and being a part of her upbringing is priceless. Monica and I get to switch off every other week. I guess over time, she has been able to mellow down and realizes how beneficial it is for us to see eye to eye. She has recently gotten a job as a financial consultant. Her schedule allows her to work a few days from home, which works well for her and allows her to spend more time with Emmanuella as well.

I am looking forward to seeing Paula. She said she was coming to see me in a couple of weeks. She decided to fly out to Brookdale to celebrate my thirty-fourth birthday. I was surprised she was coming. I hadn't taken her seriously when she mentioned it a month earlier. But she recently sent me her itinerary, which got me excited!

We have been talking on the phone on a daily basis for nine months straight. I'm not too much of a phone person, but I feel comfortable talking to Paula for hours without blinking an eye. I don't even remember all the stuff we talk about, but we just enjoy talking to each other.

Life isn't too bad these days! I have a potential soul mate on the horizon . . . I think she may be my WTF. Things are looking up for this man . . .

Excerpt from 'Inside Looking Out'

It was an early evening on a Sunday; the store was full when I arrived. I waited fifteen minutes for a car to leave so I could get a parking spot. As I was walking into the store, I noticed her five-foot-nine frame in black sweat pants and a white "Just Do It" Nike T-shirt. She looked athletic but very womanly. She wore a baby bob hairstyle, which revealed her beautiful facial features. She had high cheekbones and a slender neck.

I said, "Hello."

She smiled and responded, "Hi."

She seemed genuinely nice.

I ran into Sarah again in the frozen food aisle. I saw her pick up two big bags of chicken. There was barely enough room left in her cart to fit them. *She probably has a big family*, I wondered.

"You might need another cart soon," I said to her jokingly.

"Yeah, I know," she said, laughing.

"I like to shop once so I don't have to worry about it for a while," she continued.

"Understandable, I do the same thing."

"Smart man!" she quipped.

"By the way, my name is Phil."

"I'm Sarah. It's nice to meet you."

She picked up a few more items, waved, and moved on to another aisle. I watched her as she walked away. I thought, *Should I go talk to her a little more and possibly ask for her number?*

But I decided not to. She was there to shop and probably didn't have time to continue chatting away at the grocery store. As she walked away, I hoped she would look back, which would be my cue to follow her. She didn't, and I was disappointed. We ran into each other again in the canned food aisle. She was transfixed on the food list she held in her hand, so she didn't see me. I didn't want to seem like a pest, so I walked the other way.

I finished loading my bags of groceries into the trunk of my car and saw she had made it out too. I had parked not too far from her. I noticed she was staring at the last item in her cart. It was a shrink-wrapped twenty-four pack of water. I walked over.

"Those are heavier than they look. Let me help you."

She smiled and obliged me. After I had loaded her pack of water, she thanked me and smiled again. As she was about to get in her car, I said, "We do have a few things in common."

She looked at me confused.

"I'm sorry?"

"We seem to have the same taste in cars," I said, as I pointed to where my SUV was parked. Our Range Rovers were identical, except mine was black, had tinted windows, and was a couple of years newer. I could tell from the slight variations in her back lights. Below her plate number read Blue Lagoon Motors.

"Oh, I see." She smiled. "You bought yours from Blue Lagoon too?"

"I sure did, from a gentleman named Thomas."

"You know Thomas? It's a small world," she said, beaming.

"Yeah, he is a friend of a friend. He gave me a good deal I couldn't pass up. He is really cool. I referred at least four of my buddies."

"He sure is a nice guy. I'm usually skeptical about salesmen because of their fast-talking and conniving ways, but he is a different breed. My car was used, but he still gave me a two-year warranty instead of a six-month one."

I nodded in agreement.

"He did the same for me! You should have hooked him up with a friend just for being nice," I said, laughing.

"Or I could have hooked myself up with him," she said, rolling her eyes.

"That isn't possible."

"How so?"

"Because you're already taken!"

Smirking, she asked, "And how do you know this?"

"You and I were supposed to meet today and live happily ever after."

"Oh really?"

"Yes really. I knew today was the day," I said, laughing.

"Wow, you see into the future too?"

Still smiling, I said, "Maybe you should give me your number and you can find out more about me."

WTF MOMENT

"Sorry, I can't right now. I'm kind of seeing someone at the moment."

"Oh!" I said disappointedly.

"I'm sure we will meet again since you can see into the future anyway," she said as she got into her car.

"I'm sure we will," I said, smiling confidently. It was wishful thinking. *Women like her don't stay single for too long!*

I watched her drive off, hoping I had gotten lucky. *But she has a man. There is nothing I can do.*

I hopped into my ride and frisked quickly through a classified ad I had picked up from the store. I wasn't looking for anything in particular, but I had hoped something would catch my eye.

A few minutes later, I headed home. As I pulled onto the freeway, I saw a familiar sight! It was Sarah on the side of the road. She was standing behind her Range Rover, and her trunk was open. I pulled over in front of her and stepped out. She got off the phone as I walked toward her.

I smiled at her and asked, "May I be of assistance?"

"As you can see, I have a flat. I have never changed a tire before." With her hands on her hips, she looked like she was about to cry.

"Not to worry, Phil is here to the rescue."

Her smile slowly resurfaced. I looked in her trunk and found the jack; the tire was screwed tightly to the bottom. The bolt was challenging. After about five more tries, I finally got it out. I was relieved; I didn't want to come across as a wimp.

The tire didn't seem right, so I pressed hard on it. Sure enough, it was flat. It happens sometimes when a tire hasn't been used for a very long time. The next gas station was about three miles north.

"Tell you what," I said, as I inspected the rest of her tires. "Your spare tire is bald. I'll let you borrow mine for now, and I can get it back once your tire situation is resolved. You might need to buy a new set of four and use one of these old ones as a spare."

"I don't know if I should take your tire. You might need it! You know?"

"It's okay. My tires are in great condition, and besides I live just down the street, so I think it is safe to say I won't need a spare anytime soon," I replied.

Before she could protest further, I walked over to my car and got the spare out. I took my dress shirt off to avoid getting it dirty. With only a tank top on, I got to working. She glanced at my body and looked away as if she didn't notice how sculptured I was. I smiled and continued working.

Ten minutes later, I was done, and I motioned to her indicating so. She walked over to inspect my work.

215

"Thank you, Phil. You're a lifesaver! I guess now I have to get your number so I can return your tire."

"You sure do!"

We exchanged numbers, and she thanked me again.

"No problem. Take your time, no rush. Return it whenever you're ready." I smiled at her as she hopped into her car.

For the second time that day, I watched her drive off. "There is a god!" I exclaimed.

Sarah called me the next day to return my tire. We met at the same grocery store parking lot where we had first met. She said she didn't like holding on to people's belongings. She had replaced all four tires and used one of the old ones as a spare as I had suggested. We kept the encounter brief, and when she was about to leave, I asked, "You wouldn't mind if I call you just to say hello sometime, would you?"

"You probably shouldn't. I don't think my boyfriend would like that, and besides, I don't like talking to other guys on the phone when I'm with someone."

"I can respect that. I will call once in a blue moon. I promise," I said.

"Suit yourself. Just understand—if I don't return your call, it's nothing personal."

"No problem."

"Have a good day, Phil, and thank you again."

"My pleasure . . . You have a good day as well," I responded, smiling.

A couple of months later, I gave her a call and left a message. I was surprised when she did call me back. We talked for a while, and she mentioned going to a concert with her girls. It was around Valentine's Day, and I asked her why she wasn't going with her man. She told me they had broken up a month earlier.

Patience is a virtue I thought.

About the Author

Bolaji Tijani-Qudus lives in the San Francisco Bay area, California.

He doubled as a portfolio accountant during the day and as a bar/lounge owner at night before exploring his passion for storytelling. When he's not at home spending time with his two sons, he indulges in writing and movies. WTF Moment is his first novel.